THE BLUE BEAD

D1528827

THE BLUE BEAD

Annette Israel

iUniverse, Inc.
Bloomington

The Blue Bead

iUniverse books may be ordered through booksellers or by contacting:

iUniverse
1663 Liberty Drive
Bloomington, IN 47403
www.iuniverse.com
1-800-Authors (1-800-288-4677)

Because of the dynamic nature of the Internet, any web addresses or links contained in this book may have changed since publication and may no longer be valid. The views expressed in this work are solely those of the author and do not necessarily reflect the views of the publisher, and the publisher hereby disclaims any responsibility for them.

Any people depicted in stock imagery provided by Thinkstock are models, and such images are being used for illustrative purposes only.
Certain stock imagery © Thinkstock.

ISBN: 978-1-4759-2604-0 (sc)
ISBN: 978-1-4759-2605-7 (ebk)

Library of Congress Control Number: 2012908755

Printed in the United States of America

iUniverse rev. date: 05/11/2012

The Blue Bead is dedicated to everyone who holds this book in his or her hands; past, present, and those to come. Thank you. I love you all.

May you find something on these pages that touches you or inspires. Perhaps you will find the symbolic, a message or two. Perhaps the story will just entertain you on a rainy afternoon.

I encourage you to research names, words, and dates. In so doing, may you find additional two-tracks to explore.

ACKNOWLEDGMENTS

Thank you, Lord. For all that you are and all that you do.

My special thanks to Grace, Nancy Z, and my first readers.

I have been blessed with an abundance of wonderful friends who have always been with me throughout my many escapades and dreams.

Thank you, Nancy, Kathy, and so many others.

Thanks to the entire team at iUniverse.

AUTHOR'S NOTE

Although this novel refers to actual historical persons, events, and social issues, the setting of Lake Luffit and all of the characters are entirely fictional. Any similarities to real persons or places are purely coincidental

Chapter One

He hovered so low that she could almost reach up high enough to touch him. She watched, instead, as the wind held him poised in the air, next to her and just above.

How does he do it?

With his wings outstretched, the seagull faced into the wind. Although in flight, he remained unmoving, as if he'd been painted into the scene by an artist. Suspended. Close to his soul. The seagull cried out, then banked to the right, heading home to the shore. She watched him until he vanished into the gray sky.

Her eyes then drifted down to her feet. Each foot shoveled into the fallen leaves on the road: left, right, left, right. A reassuring rhythm as they rustled through.

Hanna Tauber enjoyed these peaceful walks, alone with thoughts that seldom amounted to much of anything. Other times, she found things to ponder. The lack of pressure to concentrate, or have to do anything, pleased her. Today, she contemplated the seagull.

She'd found the seldom-traveled dirt road a few months ago when she and her husband, George, moved into their new house. Prior to moving, they'd lived in the city all of their lives. George developed a thriving law practice over the years and he'd done well as an attorney. But as he'd grown older, his fire for wrangling corporate law waned. Rather than retire, he asked her one day what she thought of moving to the country. He would still practice law but wanted to turn his attention to contracts, wills, and trusts. In their later years they'd grown weary of mere existence in the city. The traffic and the noise pummeled against aging eardrums. The faceless people you passed on the street with which you never shared a cracked smile, bored even the busiest souls, though they didn't know it. All of this gnawed away at your youth. The opportunity to move sallied into their lives within days of the discussion.

"Let's go for it," she said.

"Lake Luffit is just a spot on the map," he told her as he presented the brochure that had been delivered to his office by mistake. It described a new, secluded subdivision being built in the woods on the outskirts of the small town. The town itself had been shelled from a natural beach that sloped its way down to a large puzzle piece-shaped lake. The first family that settled on that beach, the Crenshaws, named the lake in 1890. As more people arrived, and stayed, the name of the lake also became the name of the town.

Most activities in the obscure burg revolved around the lake. Everyone, except George and Hanna, had a boat. And everyone, except George and Hanna, spent ninety percent of their free time on their boats on the lake fishing. George once suggested that they also buy a boat.

"Wouldn't you like to learn how to fish?"

"Yuck," she said about the fishing. But the boat part wasn't such a bad idea. She'd think about it.

The road elbowed off to the right of the street Hanna lived on and then formed a long, swallowing curve. Sage-old pines stood like ancient sentries along the way. Ash, oak, and poplar mingled with the spruce and cedar. An occasional birch found a place to squeeze in among them. Wild blueberry bushes grew on the lower level along with an assortment of bramble and weeds. The blueberry bush leaves changed from green to red in the fall. Red and wild—she thought this a superb combination.

2

In the winter, the evergreens caught most of the snow and weighed the boughs down so that the bottom branches anchored to the ground. Then they froze like that, like snow tents.

A stiff breeze sideswiped her. She clutched her zippered sweatshirt tight up to her throat. She threw her braid over her shoulder and felt the familiar thump against her back. Not quite brown and not quite blonde, the braid was the color and weight of a sea-beaten nautical rope. As it went zinging out of her sight, new unwelcome hairs subtly sparkled in the overcast light. *One day it will all be gray*, she thought. *Then what: cut it? Dye it? Dying it'll be a lot of work. And George'll shoot me if I cut it.*

She looked up to check her progress. She walked two and a half miles from her house to the end of this road, turned around and came back; five miles, seven days a week. She chuckled as she did every day at this same spot. In the distance she could see the yellow sign in front of the forest where the road stopped. It read: ROAD ENDS. *Don't they know that people can see that the road ends at that point?* By the time you reached the sign you knew the road dead ended because you were right *at* the end. No sign planted at the corner where the road began alerted you. It brought a smile to Hanna's face each time she saw it.

Everyone who lived in Lake Luffit knew everyone and knew where everything was already. Directions, if needed at all, were offered not by street names and signs, but by places and people. "Turn left at the bank" and "It's next door to Joe's farm" were common ways of telling people where to go. The lake gauged most everything and served as a common reference point: "Just around the curve from Cappy's" (one of six bait shops). "Upside of the inlet." "Just past the north shore."

She'd reach the sign and the end of the road in minutes.

She hummed a Vivaldi concerto, mulling over ideas for supper, as visions of chicken or fish; potatoes or pasta, passed through her mind. Just as she remembered that she didn't have onions or tomatoes for salad, the bushes and branches to her right crunched and snapped as something ventured toward her. It came from deep within the woods, coming straight at her. She stopped. Stopped walking, stopped breathing. The ominous racket awkwardly hustled closer as an unknown creature crashed its way through the thicket.

"Stop! I'll squirt you with mace!" (She had no such thing with her).

Her pulse ticked off machine gun rounds as the noises grew louder and nearer. She tried to run but her feet stuck at the ends of her spastic legs and refused to budge. She focused on her would be attacker.

"Leave me alone!"

Silence.

Then another sound purled in her direction. She could hear the thing breathing. A twig snapped again. Leaves crackled. It took another breath.

It sounds wounded.

Terror grounded Hanna as the tangle of blueberry bushes began to part. She gulped so hard it hurt, as if she'd wolfed a boiled egg down her throat whole. She braced for the evil assailant, man or beast, to pounce upon her. She'd never known that type of fear. Fear that leaves you crippled and useless yet wired and charged.

The final blockade of brambles split. The thing snorted and out into the open it came.

Her shoulders plummeted under the weight they'd supported and her body shuddered as fear gushed out of her. She released her breath in a long whoosh.

"It's just a horse," she said.

One lone white horse.

The horse's dark eyes penetrated Hanna, as if hands, instead of eyes, reached out to her. They sought and grasped an area of her core that she'd never been aware of until that moment. She frowned, shook her head, and shook it once more, trying to get free of it.

She'd never been around horses in her life. Like so many, the closest she'd ever come was that chance meeting at a county fair. In fact, she'd never once devoted even a scrap of thought to horses.

And now she stood face to face with this one. Moments ago, she'd been shackled with fear. But in a flash the fear had dissolved, as if it had never been.

"Hello, horse," she said.

The horse remained motionless and gazed straight into her. A strand of barbed wire that she'd never seen before ran beside the road just beyond the ditch. An overlay of weeds and brier disguised most of it. She noticed a driveway for the first time as well, a two-track that cut a passage through rows of pines.

She shrugged. She exhaled. She shook once more, hoping to dislodge from the emotion-packed experience. She made four strides past the horse, toward the sign at the end of the road. Then the horse nickered. Hanna stopped again. She felt a chill. Her attention remained riveted to the sign in front of her, her destination. *Horses don't talk.* Yet the animal called out as if it had spoken one word. Jumbled thoughts shimmied through her brain all at the same time, each vying for that coveted place; the chance to surface first. If she pressed onward, the horse would turn and go back to its home, somewhere behind the forest from where it came and Hanna would never see it again. But when the horse whinnied, the accent of desperation resounded, one last, final chance. Tears welled in Hanna's eyes. But why? She didn't know the answer, wouldn't have been able to explain *why*, had she been asked. She turned around for a second glance at the horse, one more chance to look back.

"My God."

The horse's mane formed a mass of knots woven with leaves and dried mud. The scene became more gruesome the longer Hanna viewed it. The animal's neck, so thin, didn't appear capable of supporting mere hair let alone the weight of the spine it contained. Corrugated hide clung to bones sharp enough it seemed they should have cut through its skin.

Hanna stumbled backward, as if pushed, and almost fell when the horse dropped to the ground with a moan.

"Oh my! What's happening to you?"

The horse's body fell in a heap of desolation. But it kept its head up. Its eyes remained focused into Hanna and not once strayed off target.

"I'll get your owners!"

She bolted down the two-track to find help. But the urgency, and sense of obligation, ebbed. She slowed to a jog, and then to a walk, as she thought about the horse's condition. *These people don't deserve to have a horse. What am I going to say to them?*

A cabin topped with a sagged roof sat at the end of the driveway. Stained curtains hung limp out of a broken window. The half-attached screen door rested against chipped siding.

She knew that there wasn't anyone around, but she sidled up to the home anyway. The two bowed steps to the deck grumbled "leave me alone" as she crept up them. She knocked on the blemished door and waited a few minutes. She peered over the right edge of the railing. An abandoned dog house sat lopsided over holes the dog had dug. Weeds had grown partway into the house. A chain raced from inside about fifteen feet straight to its end. *Where's the dog?*

To the left of the home and about one hundred feet away, a barn, she assessed as haunted, towered above the loneliness. Hanna knocked once more on the door and peeked in a window. She saw no evidence of life, human or animal. She sailed from the deck onto the ground, skipping the steps altogether, and went to the barn.

The wooden barn door, blanched from the sun, and kindling dry, denied her entrance though she rattled the handle several times. "Locked," she said, needing to hear some form of human babble. She traipsed through weeds to the rear of the barn and squeezed through broken fence rails. Once near the barn, she found an open half door, from where the horse had come. No activity. No sign of life. A putrid stench stabbed at her. The glands in her throat rose. The source of the stench lurked next her and she almost vomited when she saw the tub of green sludge in a rusted metal tank. *That's all it has to drink.*

Inside the horse's stall, her track shoes sunk in urine soaked manure. She extracted her feet and sidestepped on the aged cement-like manure along the edge of the walls to the other door. She opened the door to the main part of the barn and stepped into the aisle. A lost, bare wind filled five otherwise empty stalls. The stall across from the rank one seemed more suitable for the horse. Except for dust it was clean and the dirt floor was dry.

She winced. Cobwebs hung in opaque curtains from the highest corners and draped to mere inches above the earthen floor. She wouldn't look up at them. If she didn't *see* them, they might cease to exist. Spiders and June bugs sat together at the top of her phobia list, and at the moment, spiders ranked number one.

She plucked a bucket from a stack, tapped it against a wall to knock the dust out, and went looking for water. A city girl, she searched for a sink, unaware that barns seldom have them. Frustrated, she came close to abandoning her mission when she discovered a spigot outside next to the tank of swill. She filled the bucket and hauled it back to the stall and placed it on the floor. The word 'hurry' tugged at her to get the task completed, and the new stall for the horse prepared as best she could, and soon.

"I don't know anything about horses, but this'll have to do."

She went through the stall and out the back door to go to the woods to get the horse and almost smacked into it. The horse leaned its full weight against the barn, staring at her.

"Good Lord, you scared me! You're kind of creepy . . . the way you just . . . appear."

The horse stared at her, ears forward.

"At least you got up and came back to your barn. But you sure scared the snot out of me."

The horse jutted its muzzle forward, acknowledging human chatter. Its nostrils fluttered.

"Come on in. I have a new room for you. You won't have to be in that filthy one."

The horse didn't move, just stared at her.

"Rope. I need a rope. I've got to find a leash for it." She faced the horse. "I'll be right back."

Every time Hanna needed something to help her with the horse, she scrunched her lashes together in the somber light, roamed a bit and found a useful item, convenient enough. It had been a working horse barn at one time. Lead ropes of assorted lengths and colors hung on a spike in the aisle. She took one, shook off the dust, and then looped it around the horse's withered neck.

She used her most assertive tone. "Let's go."

The horse stretched its neck out as far forward as it could without moving its feet. That was the most it agreed to do. Hanna stepped back to better assess the situation and contemplate her next move. *This is the thinnest, sorriest looking creature I've ever seen. It's nothing more than a breathing skeleton.* As she scanned the horse, wondering what to do, she noticed the horse's feet for the first time. She didn't know anything about horses, but *anyone* could see that its feet were grossly disfigured. The toes of both front hooves curled up, like Aladdin's slippers, about a foot in length, years overgrown. The sides of the hooves twisted under, as if it stood on gnarled pine roots. The horse *couldn't* walk.

"You poor little thing. I think you need to come inside. I'll help you. I'll be right here. Just take a small step." When the horse moved a foot, Hanna said, "Good horse," and patted the fleshless neck. The horse plodded into the stall, warm to the touch and sweating from the pain of the effort expended to travel the short distance.

"Okay, horsey girl," she said, noticing the gender of the animal. "There is fresh water for you."

The mare's head plunged into the bucket of clear water. At first, Hanna thought it amusing as she watched the guzzling and slurping. But sorrow soon replaced gaiety because the mare drank with her eyes closed. Water had become that foreign to her—and that spectacular to reach. Hanna had never known, never witnessed, thirst that claimed dominion over life itself. She filled the bucket again. The mare emptied it. Hanna filled it a third time, a fourth time, a fifth time. The sixth bucket remained full. The mare swung her head toward it every few seconds, not to drink, but as if to assure its presence.

Hanna leaned against the stall wall. She shook her head at the pathetic sight in front of her. "I may not know anything, but you seem pretty small to me as far as horses go. You're way littler than those big Budweiser horses. You're not so scary. What happened to you? How'd you get left here?"

Once again, the mare crumpled to the ground. Her breaths came unsynchronized and inaudible, as if she might be too weak to continue on with the work of filling her lungs. Even though the horse had water to drink, Hanna doubted that any animal in such condition could survive. *And what am I supposed to do about it?*

She left the stall and walked around the barn. "There has to be something to feed her." Climbing the cobweb-laced stairs in the far corner seemed the most logical thing to do in the search for food. She swallowed hard and took a deep breath to prepare for the journey.

Spider webs twitched in the drafty stairwell as she began her ascent. She remembered not to look overhead. "Who knows what I'll find up there," she said, still needing to hear conversation. But she pressed on and up the crotchety stairs. She used the broom she'd found to push the cobwebs away from her face. She didn't want to disturb the spiders so much that they'd jump or fall down onto her hair. The mere thought of that made her skin crinkle.

The sun shone in slanted streaks through cracks in the loft walls, illuminating a stack of hay bales. "Horses do eat hay. That much I know." Speaking it provided validation. She'd have to walk across the loft floor to get to the bales. "My luck, I'll fall through and no one will ever find me. No one knows where I am." So, she tapped the floor in front of her with the broom to test its security before taking each solid step toward the hay.

She had no idea how much hay to give a horse. "I'll just push one bale down the steps and make a good guess." Two hemp strings cinched around the bale made it easy to pull and slide the bale across the worn-shiny plank floor. Once she had the bale poised at the top of the steps, she gave it a shove with her foot and sent it careening end over end all the way to the bottom. A whinny rose straight up to the rafters—she remembered the sound.

Hanna ambled sideways down the odd-sized steps. The strings on the bale had snapped and the hay exploded into square sections all over the floor. She carried three of the squares to the mare and placed them in front of her. The mare bit into them and tore the sections apart. She crammed the hay into her mouth at first but then settled down to less frantic munching. It filled Hanna with polar emotions: cold and pity for the horse's circumstances, warmth and pride for having done a kind deed for another living thing.

George would be home from work soon and he'd wonder where his wife was. She was always home from her walks by dusk.

"You have water and food," she said, wondering if the horse had a name. "I have to go, horsey, but I'll come back to check on you tomorrow."

Cumbersome thoughts hindered her as she walked down the driveway and back to her world. She plowed through the leaves on the side of the road, kicking them asunder. *What am I supposed to do now, call the police? Call animal control? Tell George?* She kept her face down, ducking the biting wind, hands balled in her pockets. She had told the horse that she'd see her tomorrow, but she didn't believe that would happen. She knew in her heart of hearts that the horse couldn't and wouldn't survive another night.

On that walk home, she made a decision that would change the course of her future. She would not tell anyone, not even George.

CHAPTER TWO

"WHERE HAVE YOU been?" he asked, when she bounded up the steps at the back of the house. He held the door open for her. "It's dark. You're not usually out this late. I was getting worried."

"I think I might have dillydallied to pick wildflowers on the way home."

"Flowers, this time of year?"

"Okay, weeds then."

"Where are they?"

"Where are what?"

"The *flowers*."

Hanna, looking straight ahead and thinking fast said, "Good question. I must have dropped them when I put my hands in my sweatshirt. It's getting chilly out there."

Later in the evening, George asked, "What happened to your shoes?"

She breezed into the mudroom for a quick look. The white, and previously unblemished, shoes had returned home entombed in crusted crud.

"I stepped in a puddle," she said, thinking, *that will do*.

"Looks like you about drowned in it. Why didn't you step around it?"

"Because I didn't. I just didn't. Okay?"

End of conversation. After twenty-three years of marriage to the longhaired vixen, George Tauber had come to accept his wife's unique quirks. He loved her, though mystery hovered around her. He watched her heave the braid, like she did at least fifty times each day, as she bent over her defiled shoes.

"I'm going to toss them," she said. Once again, the braid wandered forward to dangle in front of her, dusting the floor. He joked that if she cut it he'd divorce her. She intrigued him and excited him and it happened most when her hair fussed with her and got in the way of a task. He longed to see her hair loose again and draped around her, hiding her naked body. Even now, as she inspected her stinky shoes, he wanted her.

That head of hair caused George to smash the brakes to the pavement the first time she crossed in front of him with a group of her friends. Once he got past the tornado of hair, swirling all around her on that windy day, the rest of her kept him interested, too. All doled out in pleasing proportions, it suited her. Like a thoughtfully wrapped present, everything matched. She smiled at him on that day; a cute, not beautiful face. She flashed her gemstone-green eyes, doused with too much makeup, and flirted with him. But it was the hair that hooked George.

They seldom fought. They enjoyed the same movies and foods and they shared a much more than stable lifestyle. There was just one area that needed bolstering. Hanna wasn't enthralled with sex. George brought her flowers, he lit candles, he held her, and he took his time. He knew he was good to her. Although they shared a decent sex life, there were times it seemed awkward. In part, he blamed himself for this. Hanna had told him that she'd never had sex with any other man, not even with Leonard Levine, whom she dated for a year in college.

On their wedding night, George knew that Hanna wasn't a virgin. She'd lied to him and this angered him. He demanded to know who he was, someone she wanted to protect. She cried and she begged him to believe her. He finally said that he believed her, but he couldn't, and never did. Though George had done his best to bury it, it had glommed onto their relationship like fungus on a tree. Pretend it doesn't exist. It's not that serious. Besides, fungus might not kill the whole tree. It wasn't that she'd slept with another man that bothered him. It was the lie that ate away at George. He wished that she'd never said that he was her first. He'd been honest with her. He told her that she wasn't the first woman he'd had sex with. George surmised that his obsession with the lie had made things difficult for Hanna right from the beginning. But he could think of no way to undo the damage.

He loved Hanna and they were comfortable with each other. It wasn't that they never had sex; they did, just not often enough as far as George was concerned. And Hanna never wanted to discuss it. George assumed that there were things in Hanna's past that she preferred to keep to herself.

He thought about cheating just once. It had been six years ago, when Trisha, the twenty-two year old secretary hired in at his previous law firm. She simmered in sex appeal. She purred conversation and her figure begged to be explored. Soon after Trisha started at the firm she made her interest in George known. When she brought him coffee one morning, she touched him on the collar of his shirt and drew her index finger halfway around his neck. Her interest made him feel desired as a man. That afternoon, after everyone else had gone home he held her in his arms and kissed her. He kissed her deep with passion, treading onto forbidden turf. She kissed him back with matched fervor. She backed out of his arms, waiting. He could lower her down onto the pullout sofa two feet away; so close, so easy. But George also backed away. They faced each other not speaking. Trisha's slim arms crossed in front of her, perhaps to ease embarrassment, perhaps to temper the rejection. Her bedroom eyes remained soft, inviting.

He yelled at her. "Trisha, go home!" He yelled again, "Go!"

He couldn't make himself look at her. He knew that he'd hurt her. He didn't watch her close his office door. He didn't love her, didn't know anything about her, and had no interest in knowing anything about her. But he wanted her.

George went home that night tormented by hatred. He hated himself because he'd almost crossed over the line and he hated himself because he hadn't.

"You seem different tonight," she'd said. George remembered how Hanna paused for just a second when she tossed out that observation.

Does she know? Does it show?

One month later, Trisha accepted a job at another law firm and she was gone. George learned two days after she left that Trisha was Judge Harrington's niece. The worry over where that might lead devoured his thoughts for two solid weeks. He couldn't eat. He couldn't sleep. And he still worried about the consequences if his actions ever became known. But in the last few years, and especially since they'd moved to Lake Luffit, George had given himself a measure of forgiveness. He hadn't crossed over that line. Close, but it had been just a kiss. He'd remained faithful to his vows.

"I threw them in the garbage," Hanna said. "Want a beer?"

"*What* did you throw in the garbage?"

"Earth to George: my shoes. What do you think I threw in the garbage? You asked me what happened to my shoes. I told you what happened to them and I tossed them in the garbage. Do you want a beer?"

"Sure."

George felt secure in what he considered a safe and uncomplicated world. The only son of immigrant parents, he'd been encouraged to go to law school and craft a successful career. He just so happened to have a neurotic wife whom he loved in spite of herself.

George put his arms around Hanna from behind and cupped her breasts. She pivoted into him and kissed him on the cheek.

"Have you been crying?" he asked. "It looks like tears have been running down your face."

Hanna hadn't seen her face since morning and she had no idea what it looked like. *Music. Blame it on music.* "I was listening to a sonata . . . you know how I get." She wriggled out of his embrace. *Not tonight. You have no idea what's on my mind.*

Dear sweet George. She considered him handsome, not according to Hollywood standards, but handsome in his own intellectual sort of way. She told him that with his moustache and matching goatee he appeared scholarly, especially when wearing his reading glasses. His head of thick hair had more gray than black now. He had never been thin and he'd never been a pound overweight.

George could be fanatical about certain things, such as his shoes. He polished his shoes every night. He preached that she wouldn't go through so many pairs of shoes if she started polishing hers, too. But when Hanna's shoes got a scratch or a smudge she bought new ones. "It's that simple," she told him, "you just get new ones." And she had many to prove it.

She loved him and she loved being married. But the great hoopla concerning sex didn't register with her. She enjoyed it, some of the time, but it wasn't at the top of her list of favorite things to do. Sometimes strange things happened when they had sex. As soon as George fell asleep afterward she would crawl out of the covers and go into the bathroom. She promised herself that it would never happen again. But every now and then, when she least expected it, she would find herself curled up in the dry bathtub with the curtain pulled shut, a bath towel wrapped around her body. She never remembered climbing into the bathtub, never remembered clutching the towel. She never remembered closing the curtain. She would just find herself there. Those moments where she lost track of everything, scared her. She wondered if sex was awkward for her because it created those times at the end when she lost herself. If she could not let that happen again, maybe their sex life would be more enjoyable. She couldn't understand why her own husband refused to believe that she'd never had sex before she married him. And years ago, her family doctor didn't believe her either.

When she was sixteen, her mom took her to the doctor after the neighbors' terrier, Sam, leaped up and bit her on the thigh. She had the dog's stuffed penguin toy and he didn't like it. The bite broke the skin near her crotch. Hanna's mom dropped her off at Dr. Kirkland's office, said she had errands to run, and told Hanna it would be okay for her to walk home.

Dr. Kirkland said that, other than leaving a bruise, the small puncture was nothing to worry about. But he kept her sitting on the table. He asked her to lie back. Hanna trembled so much that the exam table bounced when Dr. Kirkland said that he would do a pelvic exam, her first one ever.

Why is this necessary? Please don't make me do this! Stop!

She had never felt so vulnerable. There was nothing she could do. He was the doctor—she, just a kid. You didn't question or refuse.

Dr. Kirkland leaned sideways from the sheet covering Hanna's bent knees to ask, "How long have you been sexually active?"

Hanna, her face flaming hot, felt as if steam pumped from her whole body. "I've . . . never had sex."

"Now, young lady . . ."

"I'm telling you the truth . . . *never*. How can you say that?"

Trapped and feeling violated, she nearly gagged over the accusation. And then the tears came. She couldn't stop them. She couldn't hide them. And the tears scared her all the more because she didn't know where they came from.

"Hanna, it's not horrible. I won't tell your mother. But we do need to talk about some things," Dr. Kirkland said. "I asked, because your hymen is no longer intact and . . ."

"Why don't you believe me?" Hanna didn't wait for an answer. She scooted off the table. Ashamed and on display, she scrabbled for her panties, dropping them several times. She jerked her clothes on and fled from the exam room. She ran from the clinic. She ran for blocks. Eventually, she slowed to a fast paced, cadenced walk. She watched her feet: left, right, left, right. They carried her away, carried her back to the truth; carried her to the safety of her bedroom.

She stayed in her room the whole night. She wept. Again, the tears came from so deep within her that she almost didn't recognize them as her own. She told her mom that she was tired and skipped supper. She wanted to tell her what had happened. But besides being a respected physician, Dr. Kirkland had been a close family friend for years. Hanna's mom and dad kept close watch over her. They would not allow her to go on a date until she turned eighteen. They only permitted her to go on group outings with several friends. Now, Dr. Kirkland would tell them that she'd broken the rules.

She told the truth. Dr. Kirkland didn't believe her. She told George the truth. He didn't believe her. The frustration, the confusion, and the jabbing anxiety, threatened to infect her entire mind. Sometimes she wanted to soar far away from the craziness it caused inside her. She felt caged because she couldn't.

And tonight, as Hanna gazed at George, she knew that he still didn't believe her. But they'd managed to lock it away in a secret place.

CHAPTER THREE

HANNA OVER COOKED waffles for breakfast the next morning just like her mom did, with black lace edging that crumbled in a circle on the plate. She ate a few bites. She drank one cup of coffee, not her usual two.

"You seem antsy this morning," he said as he dug out the middle of his waffle.

"I just need to go for my walk."

"You don't have shoes."

"Oh. That's right. I'll wear boots then."

George didn't say anything. He returned to reading the Lake Luffit Laureate. He didn't think Hanna owned a pair of boots.

She ushered George on his way and watched the Lexus swing onto the road. She gathered the dishes and packed them into the sink. "I'll do them later."

She smirked when she found the low-heeled boots in the closet. "I knew I had these old granny boots in here." She'd bought them years ago to wear to a Halloween party at George's office. She'd been a witch that year. She'd never forget Trisha: Sleeping Beauty in a micro-mini skirt. Though stiff, the leather boots still fit.

She put her head phones on and headed out the door. She seldom listened to music on her walks, but she did that morning, to spare her the one thing she dreaded. She didn't want to walk down the two-track to the barn and not hear the horse whinny.

It would be easier to deal with if she opened the door and found her dead, rather than walk the length of the driveway with hope in her heart.

She didn't notice the flock of seagulls soaring overhead. She didn't pay any attention to her feet or to the leaves that morning. She never gave a thought to the sign at the end of the road. She never even looked at it. When she reached the driveway to the farm, she hesitated. Though she had never seen a car on that road, she looked both ways, just to make sure that no one was coming, and then began the trek down the sandy path to the barn.

What was that she heard? She pulled her headset off and waited. Once again, a soprano whinny sang out over the trees, aimed square at her.

She ran the rest of the way to the barn. "I hear you! I'm coming!"

She spun through the door to find the mare's face over the stall door with her ears locked forward and her expression bright. Hanna sought to touch her then paused, wondering if she should be so bold. The mare bumped her muzzle, warm and covered with downy white whiskers, against Hanna's palm, giving her permission. This time, she would remember to wash away the tear marks before George got home, even these tears of joy the horse had lived through the night.

"You made it . . . you're alive," she whispered excitedly. Then she laughed. "I'm crying over a horse; a skinny, lonely horse."

The bucket of water was still half full. Hanna beamed with pride over her own effort and for the horse. The animal had drunk what she wanted through the night and had water left.

Hanna climbed the stairs to the loft to push down another bale of hay. But once up in the loft, her skin bristled when it hit her: *the cobwebs are gone.* Alone, and in danger, she tiptoed back to the loft opening to make sure. All of the cobwebs had been swept clean from the stairwell. Downstairs, the horse nickered.

Her heart pounded. She snuck down the stairs with an armload of hay. A chill weaved its way over her body when she remembered that she'd left almost a full bale of hay on the ground the day before. When the strings broke, the hay had made quite a mess. Someone had raked it all away.

As soon as both feet landed, Hanna swooped into the open. "Stop right there or I'll throw this at you!"

A black woman held a pitchfork with the tines pointed straight ahead. "What are you going to do with a handful of grass? I've got a pitchfork!"

Hanna dropped the hay to the floor. Hay was no match for an angry pitchfork.

"Who are you and what are you doing here?" Hanna said. In her mind she sounded strong and sure. But as soon as she spoke the sentence came out limp as cooked pasta. "Do you live here? Is this your barn?"

"I do not live here. Do you?"

"No," Hanna said.

"Is that your horse?"

"No."

"Then what are you doing here?" the black woman asked.

"I was on a walk and I found her out by the road. I got her to come back in here and I made a clean place for her and I gave her water and hay. What are *you* doing here?"

"I was riding my bike and found the trail that leads back here. I didn't realize it was a driveway. I heard her neigh so I came in to see. I gave her hay, too, and filled her bucket up with fresh water."

The black woman propped the pitchfork up against the wall. The silence between the two women overflowed with, *now what?*

Do old barns laugh? Do they cry? Do they delight in company when someone finds them once again? Only they know the answers. But they groan with what some would call emotion, with what some would call verse. These emotions filled the quiet, until the black woman spoke again.

"Pretty pitiful isn't it?"

With the worry and the danger expired, Hanna said, "I don't think I've ever seen an animal in such bad shape. I didn't think she'd make it through the night"

Hanna picked up the hay and tossed it into the stall. Both women leaned over the door and watched the horse limp over to it. They cringed at seeing an animal in such discomfort. The horse's knees bent and quivered and the mare sighed from pain.

"She's hurting," Hanna said. "I wish I could do something for her."

"Yeah," Rochelle said. "Those feet have to hurt her."

"By the way, I'm Hanna Tauber."

"Rochelle," the woman said. They shook hands. "Rochelle Harris."

Rochelle Harris. You would first notice her red lipstick. But the color, so striking in the early morning, won acceptance because of its elegance against her flawless skin. Her black hair fell to about chin level and flipped under. She wore black spandex pants and a gray oversized sweatshirt, a husband's sweatshirt.

"What do you suppose happened here?" Hanna said.

"I have no idea. I walked all around the farm yesterday. Obviously, there used to be a lot of horses here at one time. Why she's the only one left, I couldn't even begin to imagine."

"What should we do?"

"I don't know," Rochelle said. "I think she was left and nobody knows she's here. Or they abandoned her on purpose."

"They don't deserve to have her back," Hanna said.

"I agree."

Hanna felt more at ease with this woman. They at least thought alike.

"I believe she needs a lot of care," Rochelle said. "Do you know anything about horses? I sure don't."

"Nothing. Never been around horses in my life."

"I suppose we could call the police. We could call animal control."

"I don't like that idea. I don't know why but it doesn't feel right," Hanna said.

The sound of the mare's jaws grinding and an occasional creak of the seasoned barn walls interrupted awkward gaps in conversation. The horse swatted a fly off her hip with her tail.

She raked her teeth across her knee to scratch it. When she flexed her knees they trembled again and remained bent as she tried to balance on her impossible feet.

How could anyone have done this to a horse? Rochelle thought.

Think of something to do, Hanna thought. *Think of something to say to get the conversation going again.* "Do you live around here?"

"My husband and I just moved into the house on Feather Lane."

"You're on the next street from me," Hanna said. "I live on Stony Drive. We've lived here a few months. It's okay. The town is tiny. It seems the people are nice enough, although I don't know many of them."

Hanna wondered why a black couple had moved into the upscale neighborhood. Sections of trees had been cleared away to erect the trendy, high-priced homes. Five houses, each spaced about an eighth of a mile apart, had been built on Feather Lane and five more on Stony Drive. But . . . the woman seemed friendly enough.

"So what are we going to do about this horse?" Rochelle said. "I'm guessing that she needs more to eat than hay. I'm guessing that she needs special attention that neither of us knows how to give her."

They returned to staring at the mare again. The horse left her hay and tottered over to her bucket for a few sips of water. Rochelle went into the stall and moved the pail next to the hay so the horse could just turn her head for a drink.

She's sensitive to the needs of this horse, Hanna thought. *I like that.*

"What about if we went to the library and got books on horse care? There's a dinky library on Main Street," Hanna said.

"That's a good idea. But don't you think we have to tell someone, like the authorities about her?"

"No. Look at her. If we tell anyone, and her owners are found, do you think they should have her back? Look at her."

Hanna flicked her hand into the stall toward the horse. "I say we don't tell anyone."

"I shouldn't tell Marc?"

"Who's Marc?"

"My husband, Marcus. Marc for short."

"I say that we shouldn't. I didn't even tell my husband, George. I want you to promise me that this is a secret. I want you to make a pact with me that we don't tell anyone."

"Just how long do you think we can continue doing that? She belongs to someone. This isn't even our property."

"I don't know the answer to that," Hanna said, becoming irritated. "I just know this is the way we have to do it. We don't tell anyone. Agreed?"

Rochelle pursed her lips and hesitated. But it was a lot easier to agree to the terms than she thought it would be. "Okay," she said limply.

Hanna topped off the water bucket again. Rochelle stacked more hay near the horse and scanned the stall. The horse had enough hay and water to last for hours.

The day shone brighter when they stepped out of the dark barn and away from the reality they'd just experienced with the neglected horse; like when an elevator door opens and you aren't sure it's your floor. You just want to get off and be reassured it's still your world.

Rochelle's mountain bike looked brand new. Pastel green. It was the same pastel green as the mints shaped like bitsy pillows that some restaurants have in a bamboo basket by the cashier that go stale because no one eats them. Hanna ate them. And she had a few in the pockets of most of her jackets.

Hanna had never seen a mint-green bike. She fell in love with Rochelle's bike and wanted one like it, even though she hadn't ridden a bicycle since she her teenage years. She didn't necessarily want to *ride* the bike. She just wanted one exactly like Rochelle's. But she wasn't about to let on that she envied it that much.

Rochelle jabbed at the kickstand twice with her foot. "It sticks," she said. She gave it the third and final blow and walked with her bike, holding the handlebars. The pedals made pinwheel sounds as they spun aimlessly. "I'll go home and get my car," she said when they stood in the road. "I'll pick you up in an hour."

Hanna pointed down. "You left tire tracks."

Several sets of bicycle tire tracks from that day and yesterday engraved the spongy turf, all leading back to the horse.

"Whatever should we do?" Rochelle whispered, with sarcasm. She believed Hanna to be joking. "Should we cover them up with leaves . . . or dirt?"

"No. But from now on, walk over here."

She's serious, Rochelle thought.

"Are you coming?" Hanna said. She turned back to view Rochelle, who, still stunned, hadn't moved.

Rochelle jogged a few paces to take up her position again and continued to escort her bike beside Hanna, thinking, *Lord, this sure is an odd one. What have I gotten myself into?*

Hanna scurried around the house. She washed up and changed into clean jeans and a fresh sweatshirt. She took a package out of the freezer to thaw for dinner. She flipped through the mail. An hour later she waited at the picture window in her living room. She watched as the vehicle slowed and turned into her driveway. *Hmm . . . Jaguar. Someone's got a good job.*

Lake Luffit's narrow seams bulged with a department store, two grocery stores, one cinema, a small hospital, a few churches, a golf course, a courthouse, and two parks. But Hanna most enjoyed the downtown section. Everything you needed you'd find within walking distance. The pharmacy, with a black and white checkerboard floor, served ice cream while you sat on round chrome stools with vinyl seats. A book store, two clothing stores, a bank, the post office, George's office, and the library completed downtown Lake Luffit.

"Where can we find books on horses?" Hanna asked the woman seated behind the desk at the library. A gold plastic name tag on the woman's cotton blouse read: "Mildred."

Mildred smiled at Hanna, but she glanced away briefly to peer at the woman standing next to her. "They are all in J-2." She smiled again.

Rochelle followed Hanna deeper into the library. The librarian scuttled from her chair over to another woman seated at a metal desk stamping papers. The stamping stopped as Mildred approached the woman. Rochelle surmised that *she* was reason enough for Mildred to leave her chair to go chat with the other woman.

"I had no idea there could possibly be so many horse books, did you?" Hanna said.

"Here's one on horse breeds," Rochelle said. "We don't even know what kind of horse she is."

"And this one is all about caring for horses, in simple terms," Hanna said. "Just what we need . . . simple terms." She opened the book wide and pushed it up close to her face. "Smells good, too."

Rochelle's laugh broke open. She lidded it with her palm. "I've never met anyone else who smells books like I do!" She breathed into the book she held. "I've been smelling books since I was two!"

"Are you finding everything you need?" Mildred asked, with her polished whisper. She'd snuck up on them, as all good librarians do, when the hoots and snorts disturbed her. Her mission: find the culprits and shush them.

"Yes, thank you," Hanna said.

When she no longer heard Mildred's pantyhose rasping against her thighs, Hanna peeked around the shelves: she's back at her desk now. The coast is clear. They opened their books and smelled them all. They tried not to laugh out loud again, but a few squeaks leaked out anyway.

They carried six books each up to the desk. Mildred scanned them. "We don't use cards inside the covers anymore," she said, as if no one knew. "It's all done by computer now. I hope you found everything you were searching for. Come back if you need more books. You may check out more books here even if you have others out at the same time."

"This will be enough to get us started," Rochelle said. "Thank you."

"Do you want to come in for a pop, tea, coffee?" Hanna asked as the Jaguar made the curve into her driveway and idled in front of the two story brick house with white trim and green shutters.

"Another time."

"What're we going to do with the books? George'll know something's up if he sees me reading horse books," Hanna said.

"I'll keep them in my car. Marc never drives it. I'll put them in a bag and bring them to the barn tomorrow. We can read through them there. Nine o'clock okay for you?"

CHAPTER FOUR

NINE O'CLOCK THE next morning couldn't come fast enough for Hanna. As soon as she had George fed and shooed out the door, headed to his office, she walked to the barn. She'd packed two cans of Diet Pepsi in her back pack and two apples.

It thrilled Hanna to find no bicycle parked in front of the barn. This meant that she might have time alone with the horse. But she opened the barn door to find Rochelle busy swatting at cobwebs and whistling. Hanna sauntered in, both pleased and ticked. She was pleased that Rochelle had left the bike home, and ticked, because she wouldn't get the alone time with the horse. The combination made her cranky.

"Good morning," Rochelle said, as Hanna slunk in to join her. "I fed her and watered her. I'm trying to get more of these natty old cobwebs down . . ."

"How's she doing this morning?" Hanna interrupted her, fuming that she hadn't been the first one to the barn, and still perturbed that she didn't have a mint-green bicycle.

"She ate up all the hay and she drank her water. I think it's so cute how she talks when she hears us coming. She let me know you were here. She whinnied for me, too."

"Hi, sweetie," Hanna said. She stroked the mare's face. As soon as she touched the wide, flat cheek, Hanna filled with warmth and the doldrums fled. "We have to come up with a name for her," she said. "Have you been calling her anything?"

"No."

"I think she needs a classy name."

"Let's not get too crazy. Nothing like Cleopatra or Citation. We don't need to be that dramatic. It might help if we knew something about her . . . if we even knew what kind of horse she is."

"Citation was a boy. I think," Hanna said, thinking, *but Cleopatra does have a nice ring to it.* "Did you bring the books?"

"I did," Rochelle said. "Where're we going to sit?"

Hanna dumped her backpack onto the dirt floor and clambered up the stairs to the loft. Bits and pieces of hay and dust fell through the cracks in the loft and onto Rochelle's head. It didn't matter where she stood, the chaff still rained down upon her.

The mare whinnied when a bale of hay, and then another, rambled down the steps and landed at the bottom of the stairs with respective plunks. Hanna pulled each bale into the stall and lined them up against the wall. She dusted her hands off and with a theatrical sweep of her arms said, "How about this? We can sit on the bales facing her and read."

"Cool," Rochelle said. "But she's probably going to eat the sofa when we're not here."

"So . . . then . . . we'll get two more bales. It's not that difficult to figure out . . . is it?"

Bitch.

They sat down on their hay bales to give them a try. Rochelle dug into the bag that she'd brought and pulled out one of the books. "Her care is crucial. We know there is something horribly wrong with her feet."

She flipped to the index and then turned the pages to a section on hooves. Hanna leaned in to see the photographs.

Rochelle gasped. "Those feet look just like hers."

They read that a terrible hoof malady called, "laminitis" could lead to the worsened state of "founder." The unbearably painful condition had caused the mare's hooves to grow to such grotesque length and deformity. Lack of proper hoof care made it much worse.

"There are a number of causes but the most important thing to try to correct it is proper trimming of her hooves," Rochelle said. "It says that a lot of horses have to be put down when they founder this bad."

"So we have to find someone who knows how to trim her feet," Hanna said.

"And right away. We need supplies too . . . it says we need brushes, a hoof pick, a halter. Most of all we need grain for her. She won't do well on just hay, thin as she is."

"There's a feed store on M-30 as you're going out of town. I've passed it." Hanna said. "We should go."

They left the books on the two bales, gave the horse a pat on the neck, and walked the two miles to Hanna's house. This time, they took Hanna's Jeep.

Lake Luffit, unpredictable and aloof, spit its waves against the rocks on the shore near the road that brought you into town. The town, Lake Luffit, though a bit groggy, greeted you with pleasant consistency. They passed through town, west to M-30.

Rochelle sniffed the air in the store. "Smells like cereal in here."

"This is a feed store, Rochelle. They sell oats here. Of course it smells like cereal."

Rochelle made a sarcastic face behind Ms. Know-it-all.

Hanna got sidetracked by the rack of halters in front of her. Halters of every color filled the display. There were red ones, pink ones, green ones, both navy and royal blue, and even zebra print. Some had rhinestones sewn or glued onto them. Horse toys and so many different kinds and flavors of horse treats filled the shelf next to the halters. You would not try to count them all.

"They make all this stuff for horses?" They said this at the same time.

Rochelle left her partner ogling the halters and browsed up and down the aisles. She filled a bucket with the items she thought they'd need and went to the counter with her pail of goodies. No Hanna. So Rochelle went back to the halter rack in search of her. As best as Rochelle could count, Hanna had fifteen halters hanging from her arms. She grinned as she held them out. Rochelle started to point to a halter she liked, but two men talking on the other side of the rack caught her attention.

"Whatever happened to those horses out on the dead end?"

"You're talking about old Durfee's place. When Durfee kicked the bucket, animal control came and took 'em. They put some down. Some of 'em; the stud, two mares, and two youngsters went for slaughter."

"A few of them horses was dead-broke. That stud of his was a champion. Too bad."

Rochelle grabbed Hanna by the wrist. "We're leaving," she mouthed.

They sat in the Jeep. They stared at the gravel parking lot. They hadn't purchased a thing. All fifteen halters had been hung on one hook and abandoned. They left the bucket of supplies on the floor next to the halter rack.

"Now what do we do?" Hanna said. "Everyone knows everyone here. Someone's sure to find us out."

"We find another store. Let's go."

"We needed to hear what those men were talking about," Hanna said. "It's proof that we shouldn't tell anyone about her. They'll just take her away."

She kicked the Jeep out onto the street and headed west again. "We'll just drive until we find another feed store. There has to be another one, someplace."

"Are you speeding? It feels like you're speeding," Rochelle said.

"What do you suppose they slaughter horses for?" Hanna asked, ignoring Rochelle. But with Lake Luffit behind them, Hanna slowed to sixty.

"So . . . what do you suppose they slaughter horses for?" she asked again.

"Dog food, I guess," Rochelle said. But we won't let that happen to . . ."

"We've got to find a name for her," Hanna said.

"She was forgotten," Rochelle said. "She was a throwaway. Unwanted. You know what they say about one person's junk being someone else's treasure."

"We could call her Treasure," Hanna said.

"We'd end up calling her Tresh. That sounds too much like trash."

"And it sounds too much like Trish," Hanna mumbled.

"Angels had to be watching over her. I don't know how she survived otherwise," Rochelle said.

"I think it was a miracle."

"I agree. Lord only knows what she's been through."

"We could call her Angel," Hanna said.

"That's so obvious. We found her. *We* remembered. What about Remembrance?"

"Remembrance," Hanna said. She stepped on the gas. "I like it! That's what we'll call her!"

Rochelle's sight shot to the speedometer. She said nothing.

"Paw through my backpack. I brought us pop," Hanna said. "And I changed my mind on the name. Remembrance is too hard to say. It's too big a name for such a little horse, don't you think?"

"Funny, I was thinking the same thing," Rochelle said as she unzipped the flap of the backpack. "We'll have to come up with something else."

"What's wrong?" Hanna asked.

Rochelle wrinkled her nose. "I don't drink Diet Pepsi. How can you drink that sludge? Tastes like something that dribbled out of a car."

"No it doesn't."

"Yes it does."

"No it doesn't."

"I drink Diet Coke," Rochelle said.

"Now that's disgusting. Way too sweet for me."

"It's not too sweet. Diet Pepsi is."

"No it's not."

"Yes it is."

Rochelle pointed and tapped the air toward a gas station. Hanna pulled into the parking lot of the New Adventure gas station-combination-convenience store. The Jeep barely came to a stop. Rochelle hopped out. She returned moments later holding a can of Diet Coke. She held it high and rocked it back and forth to make sure that Hanna saw that *this* red and silver can is soda perfection. She popped the top and tipped the can toward Hanna.

"The attendant told me that there's a feed store on the left up the road a ways, about eight miles ahead."

"Look, kids on . . . bikes." Hanna said, leaning almost in Rochelle's lap. "I wonder where they got those . . . bikes."

"Probably at a store." Rochelle gave her seatbelt an extra tug. *What a weirdo.*

Fifteen miles later, not eight, they cruised into Ashton Township, and sure enough, they found the feed store on the left. A clerk helped them get all of the supplies they needed. The many different kinds and brands of horse feed interrupted their flowing shopping spree. An endless variety of feed mixes confounded them. Some had pellets. Some came with oats, some without oats, some with corn, and some without corn. There were mixes with molasses and without molasses, mixes for young horses, for old horses, for breeding horses, and for race horses. They had no clue what the horse had ever been used for and didn't know her age.

"How about a basic horse food that's good for any type of horse?" Rochelle said.

The clerk, a teenaged boy with freckles and wayward red curls pointed to a stack of burlap bags on the floor. "That's like a maintenance mix," he said. "It sounds like what you need, a general feed for a horse that don't do nothin'. My dad feeds it to his horses and they do good on it. Got pellets, got oats, little of everything."

"Sounds perfect," Rochelle said.

Then she whispered to Hanna, "How much does a horse eat anyway?"

"I don't know. Why would you think I would know that? Let's just buy a bunch."

Next, they went to the halter rack.

"What color should we get?" Rochelle asked.

"Blue," Hanna said. "We said that angels were watching over her. Angels come from heaven and heaven is blue. We have to get her a blue halter . . . with rhinestones."

Hanna selected a royal blue halter with a lead rope attached, then paused. Rochelle held the new *green* water bucket. Hanna grabbed the lip of the bucket and pulled it closer to her, towing Rochelle with it, and inspected its contents.

She scowled. "This won't do. It all has to match." She bugged her eyes and stuck her chin out. "Blue. Do you hear me? *Ba-loo.*"

"You mean I have to put all this stuff back?"

"Absolutely," Hanna said. She flounced off with the blue halter on her way to the cash register.

Rochelle grimaced. She'd picked out six different brushes, all for different purposes, two mane combs, two hoof picks, two scrubbers, a shedding comb, and an assortment of other things that horse owners use, none of which happened to be blue. *Darn her. But she's right. It should all match.*

"They make special shampoo and conditioner for horses," Rochelle said. She pushed two bottles at Hanna. "This one is made for white horses. And this one smells like aloe."

"Get a couple different ones," Hanna said. "I still can't get over how much stuff they make for horses."

"I don't think the horses care too much. They make all this cute stuff for horse *owners*. A dog doesn't care if he gets to dress up like Santa. But his owner does. I don't think that little horse cares if she has a blue halter or a red one. And I don't think she's going to care if she has rhinestones or not," Rochelle said.

Hanna's face washed over with devastation.

"Get the rhinestones," Rochelle added swiftly. "She'll look adorable." Rochelle hadn't meant to burst any bubbles, certainly not for the strange one.

They assembled all of their selections on the counter. Hanna approached another clerk, a woman picking at a salad that smelled of bleu cheese. Four dime-sized pieces of lettuce (Hanna counted them) gathered on the woman's ample bust, adept at catching those missed bites.

"Where can we find a furrier?" Hanna asked.

The woman dipped her head down and then swung it up. She rode out her bewilderment with furrows on her face. "I don't know anybody in this area who does that type of work."

"But there has to be someone who can help us."

The woman blared out in the direction of the dog food. "Hey, Hank! These ladies need a furrier, know anybody who does that kind of work round here?" She waited, her head cocked in that direction as she burst a cherry tomato in her mouth. Then she shook her head. "No. If he don't answer right away, that means no. Don't know what to tell you. I think that's one of them dyin' arts."

"I thought everyone who had horses used a furrier. Her feet are in such bad shape . . . *we* can't fix them," Hanna said. She pouted, dismayed.

"Her feet? Do you mean a *farrier*, a horse shoer?"

"Yes, yes!" Hanna said. "That's it! That's what we need, a farrier."

The clerk immediately scanned the ceiling. *Boy, have I got a couple a doozies here. Haven't heard 'furrier' in years.* She didn't mean to let it happen, but a walloping guffaw skipped free. She quickly reined it in. "There's a bulletin board in back." She pointed to the rear of the store with another tomato pinned to a plastic fork. "Lotsa guys have their business cards posted there."

Hanna tossed out her credit card and paid for their stuff. Rochelle wrote a check for the feed. The clerks huddled together snickering, not maliciously, but snickering nonetheless.

Rochelle plucked a business card from the wall. "Let's get out of here. You know they're laughing at us."

"It was just a simple mistake. Furrier, farrier, what's the big deal? What's the dif?"

"A *lot.*"

They jabbered all the way back to the barn, eager to share all of the new stuff with the horse.

"She's going to look so pretty in her new halter," Hanna said.

"She needs a bath. She's filthy," Rochelle said.

Back at the barn, Hanna clutched Rochelle's arm just before she got out of the Jeep. "We drove here. We weren't going to do that, remember?"

"What is the matter with you, girl? There is no way on God's green Earth that I am going to walk two miles from home carrying hundreds of pounds of horse feed on my shoulders. You can. Not me."

"I didn't think about that."

Rochelle rolled her eyes and shook her head.

They'd purchased six hundred pounds of grain. They lugged the twelve bags, each weighing fifty pounds, one at a time, from the Jeep to the barn in waist high weeds. Hanna gripped the top end of the bag, and Rochelle took up the bottom end. They walked out of step, tugging and twisting the bags. The first one ended up on the ground.

"At least the bag didn't break," Rochelle said. "I think we're out of shape."

"That kid just tossed the bag up on his shoulder and carried it. It didn't take two people," Hanna said. "Maybe there's a trick to it."

"There's no trick. We're out of shape. Maybe we'll be able to do that one day," Rochelle said. The sweat beaded her forehead.

They dumped all twelve bags into metal garbage cans, three bags in each. The day before, they'd tripped over the cans next to a brush pile near the barn, rinsed them, and brought them in. Two cans didn't have lids. Rochelle found pieces of plywood to use as lids and rocks to hold each secure.

Throughout all of this, the mare hadn't nickered once. She lay on the dirt floor and didn't get up when they came in.

"That's not like her not to say anything," Rochelle said. She scooped out a few pounds of the sweet smelling feed and dropped it into one of the new blue buckets and took it in to the mare. "She didn't eat any of her hay," she said. The acrid taste of worry stung her mouth as she spoke. "She didn't drink any water, either. I don't think she feels good."

"For one thing, we've gotta call that farrier right away. I don't think we should leave her," Hanna said. "I think we should stay with her. We can sit right here and keep watch over her and read our books."

"We're not horse people, remember," Rochelle said. "The last thing we need is a sick horse." She cracked open a book and scanned for relevant paragraphs to read. "This part is about rescued horses that have been abused or neglected. And here's a scale, with photographs, that rates their body condition."

They began at the top of the list and searched for the degree that most fit. They ended at the bottom.

"That's her," Hanna said. "She's emaciated. She's so thin she's actually not on the list."

Rochelle continued reading: "Sometimes, horses that are emaciated . . ."

"What? Finish the sentence."

". . . don't survive." She let the book rest on her thighs. "I don't think we're out of the woods with her. It says that they should eat all of the hay they want and drink all the water they want, but only give small servings of grain. They can die if they overload on grain too soon."

Hanna took the bucket of feed away. She poured all but a cup back into the storage can and brought the bucket back to the horse. "I don't think this handful will hurt her."

"Good heavens!" Rochelle said. "It just occurred to me that we have enough grain to feed a herd of horses."

"At least we won't have to go back there anytime soon," Hanna said. "That will help keep our secret under the wrapping."

"Under wraps."

"Whatever."

Rochelle opened the book again. "Here's more stuff about feet. Look at this horse. Its feet are just like hers. The book says it's one of the most painful things a horse can have. I'm going to call that farrier and see if we can get him here today. I didn't realize it's so serious."

Hanna listened as Rochelle explained the situation to the man on the other end of the cell phone. Rochelle wisely omitted the fact that the horse didn't belong to her. She gave him directions and snapped the phone shut.

"That's his cell phone number. He's in his truck and is actually headed to Lake Luffit. He said he'll switch another appointment around and he'll be here in an hour. He said that it sounded like he needed to make this a priority."

They could have gone home to wait. They could have taken the broom to the cobweb metropolis. They could have continued reading. But they didn't do any of those things. They sat side by side on the hay sofa, feeling queasy and useless. Rochelle wiped her palms on her jeans, once, twice, four times.

Hanna wanted to put her arms around the mare's twiggy neck. She wanted to touch her muzzle and ruffle through her knotted mane. But she didn't. *I won't touch her. I'm not going to love her anymore than I do right now if she's just going to die.* She twiddled her thumbs. She unbraided her hair and braided it again, tighter.

"Girl, you got some long hair," Rochelle said.

"It used to be even longer. In high school it hung to my knees."

"Have you ever cut it, I mean, really cut it?"

"No. I just trim it," Hanna said, thinking, *blah, blah, blah. People talk about stupid stuff when they're nervous. Next it'll be the weather.*

"I hear something out there," Rochelle said.

"What, rain?" Hanna knew she sounded sarcastic, meant it that way.

"No. It's a vehicle. He's here."

Hanna rose to her feet beside Rochelle. They remained still and conjoined. They couldn't make themselves walk to the door to greet him.

CHAPTER FIVE

"HELLO . . . ANYBODY HERE?"

He angled his body over the stall door and saw the twosome for the first time. Still standing next to each other like mismatched bookends with no books between them, they hadn't moved.

A northwestern drawl tumbled from his lips. "Afternoon, ladies." He brushed his cowboy hat with two fingers. "Josh Stevens."

He'd spent most of his life outdoors. To linger in buildings, beyond minimal necessity, was a waste of good daylight. He carried the sun and the wind with him. He wore storms on his face, etched and bronzed, like canyon crevice. With only mild erosion, no significant age owned him. He wore a cowboy hat, with sweat marks around the band, glued to his head.

Josh Stevens lived and breathed horses. He smelled like a horse most of the time and he communicated with them so well that he joked it had been a mistake that he'd been born human. Horses were Josh Stevens' first love. Women came in at a close second. He enjoyed watching women, studying women, talking to women, and hearing them laugh. He noticed things about women that most men failed to see. More than anything, he delighted in the special bond that women had with horses. He also loved the bond that women share with each other. Men seemed reluctant, or unable, to form those same heartfelt friendships—or maybe it just isn't manly enough to express it. Women ranked among Josh's best friends. These delights had gotten Mr. Stevens into trouble more times than ground squirrels have burrows.

Throughout four rounds of marriage he'd intended to remain faithful each time, but it never worked out that way. After his marriage to Liz failed two years ago, Josh thought it a good idea to stay single. He hung up his spurs, quit riding the rodeo circuit, and headed east.

Yet he was a good man. He knew that. His friends described him as one of those men who 'would give you the shirt off his back.' And Josh would. He once gave his favorite pair of buffalo hide boots to a man who had no boots at all. Josh had to drive home from the rodeo that night in holey socks, one green and one brown.

He couldn't drive by a kids' lemonade stand without buying at least two paper cups of the too sweet or too watery drink that had been sitting out too long. He gave money to the Red Cross and to almost every charity that corralled him. If veterans sat in front of a store, Josh tossed dollars, not change, into their cans when he went into the store and when he came out. He had such a collection of paper roses that he lined them up above the visor in his truck. He kept them until they turned pale pink from months of sun. Only then would he discard them. He even fed the stray dogs and cats that wandered onto his property looking for a handout.

Yes, a good man indeed. But Josh Stevens clung fast to one intolerant idea. He could not and would not try to understand gay people.

"Deviant disruptions to a civilized democracy," he said.

A number of his rodeo buddies agreed with him. Others, like Mutton Mouth Mike, the rodeo clown who whittled his own working dentures out of a chunk of Douglas fir stump, took a different stance. "T'ain't right ta hate. Ain't like Jesus," Mutton Mouth Mike said. "Makes'm sad. Wanna pick on somebody, go after'm tel-ee-vanglists flyin' round in a billion dollar air-o-plane an stoppin' off'n some country a zillion miles away where'm folks is droppin' like flies from hunger. Wha's wrong a ridin' coach an feedin'm folks an skippin' a gawd-awful 'spensive ride like at? Don't make no sense ta me. Maybe'm preachers got a low self-of-steam."

Josh wouldn't be swayed. He knew he was right.

Josh dropped the bag of clinking tools near the horse. Rage tore at his chest when he saw her. "Holy shit!" He whirled around to face the women. "How long have you had her?"

"Almost a month," one said at the exact same moment the other said, "A week."

They caved to embarrassment. "Just a few days," Rochelle said.

Josh's anger drained away when he realized that the women weren't responsible for the horse's condition. His mood softened. "She's in real bad shape. Only weighs 'bout half what she should. Even so . . ." he said, taking a closer look. He stepped like a dancer around the horse. "This is the finest Arabian I've seen. Even lying down . . . you can see she's got powerful good breeding in her. Where'd you get her? Where'd she come from?"

Hanna chose not to answer. She pushed beyond and changed the subject, her voice wavering as she spoke. "Do you think she'll live?"

Pangs pierced Josh. It happened every time a woman got 'loose eyed' as he called it. He couldn't stand to see a woman cry. His insides turned to a pail of water without the pail every time. Her little girl voice and tears brimming, flattened him.

"I reckon she might. Got a ways to go before I'd say for sure"

He lifted one of the front hooves, examined it, and pulled a wood saw from his bag.

Hanna blurted, "A saw! What are you doing with a saw?"

Josh had knelt next to the mare. "I have to cut her legs off . . ." He waited just long enough for a gasp, or two, and then said, "No, just messin' with ya. I only saw off the overgrown hoof. It's the only way to get rid of it and free this mare. She can't feel it. It's just like sawing through a log. Don't worry. She'll be just fine. Done this before. Many times. Okay?"

Hanna sat back and nodded, still wide-eyed.

"This'll take awhile," Josh said. "Not in any hurry to be anywhere's are ya?"

They shook their heads. No.

"And I can't correct it in one, two, even four trims. Her feet are in *bad* shape. The worst I seen. In all my years in horses this is the worst case a neglect I seen."

Rochelle grasped Hanna's hand in a tight squeeze that said, "She'll be okay." Hanna nodded, more to herself than to Rochelle, in response.

"What should we be doing? Can we help?" Rochelle asked.

"Usually the owner stands with the horse, holds the shank while I work. But I can do her while she's down. You can just sit there. How old is she?"

Once again, Josh read the silence. *They don't know nothin'.* He opened the horse's mouth and peered inside. He wiped his hand on his leather chaps.

Hanna piped like the first scream of a tea kettle when it hits the boiling point. "Well?"

"Well what?" Josh steamed back. "Don't you know how old your own horse is?"

"The previous owners never told us how old she is. They didn't know either," Hanna said. *And that's not a lie. The previous owners didn't tell us anything.*

"Thirty," Josh said, "give or take. Couple years older, let's say." He couldn't see their faces but he knew their thoughts. He continued. "Pretty old for a horse. Sometimes they make it to their twenties. Sometimes they hit this age and older. Oldest horse back home hit thirty-eight. I'm not gonna try to play God. Can't even guess how long you'll have her. She's in rough shape. Not good for a horse this old. We don't know what else has happened to her, what other damage was done. She foundered bad at one point. Those things take a toll on a horse." Then he downshifted, to that chesty baritone that only some men possess, never know it, and that women crave. "Looks like she's getting good care now. Makes a difference."

Hanna and Rochelle sat on the sofa, watching and listening. Josh told them all about growing up on a cattle ranch in Idaho and about his days on the rodeo circuit riding bulls.

"Why would anyone climb up on one ton of angry animal, get jostled around, broken, and then do it again?" Hanna asked.

"All 'bout the adrenaline. Eight seconds of the biggest rush known in the universe. Nothin' like it."

"But you said you got hurt," Rochelle said.

"Yes ma'am. Four ribs broken, broken collar bone, broken femur, skull fracture. In the hospital unconscious eleven days once. Stayed in the hospital another two months after that when a bull fell on me. Terrible Terrence. He's still buckin' 'em off. Next year I got hung up on a bull and ripped my elbow out of the socket," he said. He never stopped his work on the distorted hooves. "Rode broncs, too. But the bulls are where it's at for me. I was good at it, won good money."

Josh stretched his lean six foot two frame upright. "And this buckle." Both hands grasped the belt buckle, big as a saucer, strapped to the front of his jeans. He winked. "Solid silver."

Warmth bubbled in Rochelle. Her eyes wandered over to Hanna's crimson face. The polished-every day hunk of silver sat heavy on his belt. Impressive. So were the tight jeans.

Hanna cleared her throat. "Did you stop riding bulls because you got hurt?" she asked.

"Yes and no. Getting old for it, but mostly because I got tired of being on the road. So I quit, moved east. Got a small farm with my horses 'bout ten miles from here."

"How many horses do you have?" Rochelle asked.

"Nine."

"Do you have Arabians?" Hanna asked.

"Nope."

Josh wiped his face with the towel he pulled out of his tool bag. "Done."

"Why won't she get up?" Hanna asked, alarmed that the mare hadn't jumped to her feet.

"Listen ladies, she's been in a lot of pain. Still in a lot of pain, pain that I wouldn't wish on anyone, except maybe her previous owner. Don't stick your expectations for her up in the tree tops. Gonna take time. Soles are bruised bad from the ingrown hoof. Gotta heal. She's got bad arthritis to deal with on top of everything else."

"What can we do for her?" Rochelle asked.

"Make her comfortable. You're doing everything right. Easy on the grain, just a couple handfuls twice a day. Increase it gradually. Giv'er all the hay she wants. Is there still straw in the loft?" He read through the blank stares, reminded that they knew nothing about horses or farm life. "Hay's green. Straw's also in bales, but it's yellow. Use the straw to make a nice bed for her. Clean the stall everyday."

It had taken over two hours for Josh to saw, chop, nip, and rasp the overgrown and misshapen hooves. The mare had lain without making a fuss. She seemed to know that he would help her feel better.

Josh swung the leather bag up and onto his back. Rochelle and Hanna followed him, ducklings tagging along after a drake, through the stall door, down the barn aisle, and out to his truck. *He knows everything.*

"I'm not a veterinarian," he said. "She should be seen by a vet. There are two good ones in town. I use Huffstead."

"We'll think about it," Rochelle said. "What do we owe you?"

Josh climbed into his pickup. Rusted in sharp creases, dents embellished the full length of the Ford. Even the hood sported craters.

The bulls must have done all that, Hanna thought.

The engine wheezed in protest when Josh turned the key then settled down to mere putters of objection. Josh tapped the steering wheel. "It's okay, Regina. You're doing just fine old gal," he said. "Not charging you nothing today, ladies. But I need to come back and trim her in three weeks. Restoring a horse like this takes time, a year of regular trimming."

Josh gave Rochelle a plastic bottle partially filled with white pills. "For pain. You can have what's left. Date says it's expired but it still works. Used these for one of my own horses last week."

Josh took a swig of water from the jug beside him and made a face. It had sat in the warm truck all day. "Giv'er one pill in the morning and one at night. Crush 'em up and dump it in her grain. Use a hammer to smash 'em on a hard surface." He poured a long swallow of water down his throat. *Least it's wet.*

Regina, sputtering and jouncing her driver, turned left out of the driveway onto the road. He was gone.

"I like him," Hanna said. "He really knows his stuff. He's a *real* cowboy. I didn't know they them made them anymore. I've never met a real cowboy, have you?"

"No. And for all his tough talking, I think he's a big softy, too," Rochelle said. "By the way, we've got a bunch of pill crushers at home. Marc brings them home from the hospital. The pharmaceutical sales reps pass them out."

Hanna, tired and preoccupied with concern for the horse, didn't pay any attention to what Rochelle said. She worried that the horse hadn't gotten to her feet when Josh finished with her. She went into the stall and sat on the hard dirt beside her. Frustrated. She put her arms around the mare's neck and burst into tears, though that wasn't her intent. It just happened that way. Seconds later, Rochelle joined them. She touched the mare's face, all it took, and she sobbed.

Sometimes a good cry feels right; a healing cry of release, one that's shared, and for which no words are needed. Hanna cried. She cried for the little mare. She cried for herself, she cried for her, she cried for him, and she cried for all things locked inside. And she cried because she didn't want to lose again.

"We can only try our best," Rochelle said, tenderly. "The rest is up to God. Let's go sit on the hay." She tugged on Hanna's sleeve. "Let's go read about Arabian horses. At least we know what kind of horse she is now." Rochelle hoped that she sounded cheerful once again. "Josh said that she's an Arabian."

They didn't open any books right then. They sat on the hay and stared at the barn walls and at the horse lying in front of them. Every now and then the horse moved an ear. Her eyelids closed to slits. Her rib cage rose and fell as she slumbered.

"What's happened to me?" Rochelle said. "I keep asking myself how I ended up loving a horse, of all things, this much and so quickly."

"It's because she's innocent. She didn't deserve this and she needs us. Somewhere beyond those awful bones there was once a gorgeous horse. You heard Josh. A week ago, I didn't care whether or not horses existed. Now look at me. She sure wriggled her way in, didn't she?"

"We have to keep reminding ourselves that she doesn't belong to us . . . and I'm not sure what we're supposed to do with her," Rochelle said.

"But for now we have her. Or, she has us. Who knows? Maybe it will always be like this," Hanna said.

"I don't think we can keep her a secret forever," Rochelle said. "Let's read."

The book on horse breeds opened up the world of the Arabian. They read that the blood of the desert horse went back thousands of years; that historians believed it to be the oldest and purest breed. They read that the blood of the Arabian flowed through the veins of most all other breeds. Throughout the centuries, Arabian mares lived in tents with the Bedouins as family members.

Rochelle read out loud the physical traits and they compared the photographs in the book to the horse lying on the straw in front of them. It was all there: the dished profile of her face, the wide forehead, the delicate muzzle, the huge dark eyes, and ears so dainty they spanned just the length of Hanna's palm when she curled it around each. Although the thin neck didn't match the robust horses pictured in the books, starvation hadn't stolen the graceful arch.

"Listen to this," Rochelle said, "it says that Arabian horses have one less set of ribs than other horses do and their spine is shorter.

Says it makes them super strong. How about that? Marc would love to study this." Hanna's silent reprimand bored into her.

"Don't worry. I'm not going to tell Marc," Rochelle said, sing-song. She turned the page in the book. "They probably originated near the Arabian Peninsula some five thousand years ago. They carry their tails like a banner. Can you imagine that?"

No, Hanna couldn't. The mare lay crumpled like a discarded dish rag. If mystical secrets and a noble heritage existed, they had long ago shriveled away, leaving the debacle before them. Hanna couldn't envision the horse ever walking again, let alone carrying her tail in such a lofty manner.

"I wish she could talk," Hanna said. "I wish she could tell us everything that has happened to her and tell us how we can help her."

"Look at this," Rochelle said. She pointed to the book on horse breeds. "The author's name is Safiyyah. Isn't that beautiful?"

They smiled at each other and nodded. They smiled again. They smiled at the mare.

Through the cracks in the side of the barn, the west sun filled the stall with an irregular pattern of bright strips. Dusk would soon follow. Hanna went up to the loft and kicked down two straw bales. She broke open the strings and fluffed the straw all around Safiyyah. The mare wiggled her muzzle in the yellow wheat stalks, as you do, cozying into fresh sheets and taking in that comfy, clean scent.

Rochelle filled the water bucket. She smashed one of the pills down onto the plywood with a rock, all she had, and mixed it in with a handful of feed. They placed all of the things that Safiyyah might need in the night near her; water, hay, and feed. She'd only have to move her head to reach whichever one she wanted. She snuggled in her straw bed, like a white chocolate confection nestled in Easter basket grass. They hugged her, tousled her forelock, and wished her a good night.

"It's been quite a day," Rochelle said, as she opened the passenger door of the Jeep and settled in.

"Don't you think there are things that come along in your life that you just know you're supposed to do? I don't know why, but this all happened for a reason. We're supposed to be doing this," Hanna said. She turned the Jeep out onto the road. "If anyone had told me a year ago that I'd be spending my days in a barn caring for a sad horse, I'd have said they were crazy. Do you think she's going to pull through?"

Rochelle looked out the window. She watched the trees chucking their leaves into the wind. She poked a vent shut with her thumb. "I'm going to believe that she will. We need to be positive."

"I think that's a good attitude."

"Nine o'clock tomorrow morning?" Rochelle said, as she dropped her tired feet on the driveway to her house. The lights were on. Marc was home.

"Walk." Hanna commanded. "No bike. No car."

"Yes ma'am."

On the short jaunt to the house, Rochelle's eyes became misty. This seemed to happen more now than it ever had before, since Safiyyah had come into her life. She'd never had a pet of her own. She smiled as she thought of her daughter, Marquitta. It had always puzzled Rochelle where the girl's love of animals had come from. She loved all creatures and had a special way of speaking their languages and working with them. Rochelle used to think that the apple had fallen, not just from a different tree . . . but from a different *orchard*. "Maybe the apple didn't fall too far from the tree after all," she said, laughing.

As a child, Marquitta had never asked for a pony, as most little girls do. Instead, she asked daily, "Mommy, can I please have a dolphin?"

Words began to descend onto Rochelle. Words, poems, had come to her since her childhood. They seemed to flutter down to her. She felt them, listened to them, and picked each word up in her mind and composed. But she kept them all to herself. She never wrote her poems down on paper and she never told anyone about them.

Annette Israel

Little one, little one
Alone in the dirt
Alone in this world
Alone with your hurt
Did you cry out too
Did anyone hear
Knowing, they left you
With your broken heart
Little one, little one
No knowledge of hate
No grudge do you hold
Bring me through the gate
To lessons of old
Free up my heart
To see and to know
Give joy to my soul
Little one, little one
No longer alone

CHAPTER SIX

HANNA HAD JUST enough time to wash up, change her clothes, and sauté a type of made up, never-to-be-repeated chicken creation for George. *He'll be happy with it. If it's got chicken in it, he'll be happy.*

With her mind back at the barn, she felt distracted. "Maybe he won't notice," she muttered.

"What's up with you tonight?" he asked. He watched her chase a piece of chicken all over her plate with her fork. "You seem distracted."

She continued to chase the chicken. *Dang him.* He nailed that one, just as he always did.

"And what's with all the Diet Coke in the fridge?"

She speared the piece of chicken and drove it around her plate, faster and faster it went until it skidded off the plate and onto the table. She pushed the chunk under the rim of the plate so he wouldn't see it.

"I'm not distracted. No, I don't think so. I just met this lady and I think we'll be hanging out, you know going for walks and doing stuff together. I bought the Coke for her. She and her husband moved here a little while ago. She's black . . . but she's really friendly."

"What's her name?"

"Rochelle Harris," Hanna said, glad that the focus had shifted away from her.

"That must be Dr. Harris' wife. He's the new oncologist that just opened an office down the street from me. I met him at the coffee shop at the golf course the other day. Nice guy, really personable, super intelligent."

Hanna remembered fragments of Rochelle's offer to bring pill crushers. *Her husband is a doctor. Not bad. Not bad at all.*

The rest of the evening went by without incident and with no further conversations about Hanna's daily activities. They watched television for an hour and then went to bed early.

The next morning Hanna beat Rochelle to the barn. Safiyyah hadn't moved throughout the night, but she did drink water and she cleaned up all of the hay. Hanna patted her on the forehead and gave her a hug. She filled the bucket and carried in two large arm loads of hay. She used the rock on the plywood to crunch up a pain pill. She mixed it in with the grain and put the pail in front of the horse.

"I have some work to do, angel girl."

She'd brought a larger backpack with her. As she hummed a hodgepodge of Mozart parts, she unpacked it. She shook out the turquoise, coral, and purple blanket that she bought years ago when she'd gone to Cancun with several girlfriends from college. She draped this around the two hay bales that they used as their makeshift sofa. She propped two blue and white striped throw pillows up against the wall for them to lean back on. She snapped out a second blanket, the pink, green, and orange Mexican spare from the linen closet, which she folded again, and placed on the bales. "In case we get cold." She lifted a small Styrofoam cooler containing two Diet Pepsis and two cans of Diet Coke out of the backpack. She'd stashed four apples and two bananas in there, too. Her camera, strung around her neck with a piece of baling twine, bounced against her chest. She had four light bulbs stuffed in the pockets of her hooded sweatshirt. She'd counted four empty sockets in the barn.

"I was planning on doing the same thing," Rochelle said, when she appeared in the doorway to the stall. "I rummaged through the closet last night looking for spare blankets and then I forgot them.

Getting old I guess. I brought us munchies. Doritos. I hope you like taco flavor. And I brought M&M's."

"Great! We can fix this up all cozy. We got some pretty wild colors going on here, but it'll be comfy," Hanna said.

"I brought this, too," Rochelle said. "My lap top. We can look up more about horses. And you're not going to believe this. I researched names last night . . . Safiyyah means 'best friend' in Arabic."

Hanna's hands dropped to her sides. "Wow," she said softly.

"Kind of feels like her name was handed to us doesn't it?" Rochelle said.

"I think she's a very, very special horse. The name is beautiful and it fits her," Hanna said. "I brought my camera. I think we need to capture all of this. Don't know how long . . ."

"Now don't go getting sad. Let's just have fun with this and not make any assumptions."

Rochelle put the computer on the sofa and changed the subject. "Did she eat and drink in the night?"

"I think she's drinking enough. She ate up the medicine from last night and all of the hay. And she ate the grain with the medicine this morning, too. I cleaned the soiled straw from behind her."

"That's good. I brought this pill crusher. You unscrew the cap, drop the pill in and screw the cap down onto the pill, crushing it as you go. It'll make it a lot easier and we won't waste so much medicine."

"I wonder if she's ever going to stand up," Hanna said. "I don't think it's healthy for a horse to lie down for such a long time."

"Maybe we should call a vet . . ."

"No! He will report us and they will take her away. I don't think good things happen to old horses that can no longer stand." Effectively changing the subject, Hanna said, "Here, I have a job for you." She rushed her collection of light bulbs at Rochelle, who appropriately, opened her hands. "Put these in. I can't," Hanna said.

"Why can't you?"

"Because I'm afraid of electricity."

"*What?*"

"I'm serious. I don't touch anything electrical. I'm not going to get electrocuted." Hanna fussed with and fluffed the pillows on the hay bales for the fifth time.

"But these are . . . light bulbs. People usually don't get electrocuted by changing ordinary every day light bulbs."

"Stranger things have happened."

"It's not like you're changing fuses in a jet."

The final words: "Not doing it."

Rochelle tucked three light bulbs into her jacket pockets, held the fourth, and went in search of the first socket. "She's crazy. This woman is absolutely crazy," Rochelle said, almost loud enough so that Hanna could have heard her. Maybe, just maybe, she wanted her to hear.

"Two sockets work," Rochelle reported after she'd finished the job. "This one right over the stall door and the one by the outside door both work. I think this gives us enough light. If it's lit up too much someone might see it from the road."

"Now you're thinking," Hanna said. She nodded, as a teacher when a student solves a math equation.

"And notice how I didn't get killed," Rochelle said.

Of course Hanna ignored that last comment.

Then they sat on their hay bales, cracked open their correct cans of pop, and broke open the Doritos bag. "It may not be the healthiest breakfast," Hanna said, "but I don't care."

"Kind of fun, isn't it?"

Safiyyah quit munching hay. Her ears sprung in the direction of the cooler and she listened. She moved her jaws two more times. She appeared focused, intent. Then she screamed.

Rochelle jumped to her feet, spilling pop all over her sweatshirt. "Good Lord, what's wrong with her!"

Hanna chomped up the taco chip remnants in her mouth before speaking. "I'm thinking that maybe she wants something. What do you want, Safiyyah?" Hanna asked when she stood up, accidentally kicking the cooler. The horse screamed again with joyful anticipation and with demand.

"Apples!" Hanna said. "She heard the apples rolling around in the cooler. I think we need to give her one."

Rochelle dove into the cooler and brought out a firm Gala. She offered the whole apple but the mare's small muzzle couldn't get a good grip on it to bite off a piece. So, Rochelle bit off a bite and gave it to her. She fed Safiyyah the entire apple that way, bite by bite.

Rochelle's beaming face added more light to the dim stall. "She's absolutely delightful. She fills my soul with such joy." She smiled again. "An apple. Just an apple," she said. "I love how something so simple gives her so much happiness."

"Kind of like us and chocolate," Hanna said. She gave Rochelle the second apple and watched as the pieces were gently fed to the mare. When Hanna offered a third apple, Rochelle shook her head. "I think two is enough. She can have that one tomorrow. It's probably been years since she's had apples."

"I hope you like, or at least, don't mind, classical music," Hanna said. She turned up the volume on the CD player she'd brought with her. "This is Mozart. Safiyyah likes music."

"Fine with me. I love music. It relaxes patients and I know music helps animals in distress, too."

With the Mexican blankets tucked around them and the pillows in back, the bales became an almost believable sofa. They sipped pop and ate chips and candy while the rest of the world went on about its business without them.

"You mentioned patients," Hanna said. "Why?"

"I'm a registered nurse."

"That's awesome. Maybe you'll know what to do about me getting ill on all of this crap," Hanna said, laughing, not expecting an answer. She got up, stretched, and turned back to Rochelle. "Smile," she said. She clicked her camera just as Rochelle's mouth hung open, a chip stuck to her lower lip. Hanna snapped in quick sequence; Rochelle frowning, Rochelle standing up, Rochelle coming at her, saying, "Give me that thing!"

"You got hay in your hair, too!" Hanna said.

Rochelle wrenched the camera from her. "I can't believe you took those pictures of me with my mouth hanging open!"

"You looked like you were drunk *and* your mouth was hanging open. You were goofy looking. We need to capture all of these moments," Hanna said. "Now take my picture. I want one of me sitting on the straw right next to her with my arm around her neck."

They took photographs of everything: the mare eating hay, the mare drinking water, the mare dozing. They took pictures of each other, beside Safiyyah, carrying hay, and carrying buckets of water. They took pictures of the sofa and the library station that they had fashioned in the stall.

Every day they came to the barn armed with treats and fun things to eat and apples for Safiyyah. Every day they found things to laugh about and things to chat about. But they held back, their conversations stodgy and reserved, their laughter tainted with nervousness, because Safiyyah never got to her feet. Though they didn't speak the actual words, they knew that Safiyyah would never stand again. They clung to the bittersweet moments. They combed her mane and tail and picked out all of the mud balls. They rubbed her body with their hands when they realized that the brushes hurt her. The hard brushes pinched against her bones and caused her to flinch. They talked with her, to her, and they told her they loved her. Special days, just the three of them.

CHAPTER SEVEN

"GEORGE SAID THAT he met your husband at the golf course. Is your husband an oncologist?" Of course Hanna already knew the answer. Of course she wanted to know more.

"Yes he is."

"Do you have kids?"

"We have one daughter, Marquitta. She's twenty-four. She lives in Australia."

"Australia! What for?"

"She's a marine biologist, works with dolphins. She's my baby. She's great. She's pretty, smart, always been a good kid, and so animal crazy . . . she'd be right in here with us if she was home."

"When do you get to see her?"

"Just twice a year. She usually comes home for Christmas and once in the summer. But this year she has special work she's doing and we won't see her for a long time. That's hard." Rochelle wiggled loose a piece of straw pinned under her watch. "Do you have kids?"

Hanna popped to her feet. "No," she said. She checked Safiyyah's water. Full. She changed the subject. "How did you and Marc meet?"

"I worked in the emergency room where he did his internship. We started dating, hit it off real good, couldn't shake each other, though we tried once, fell in love, and here we are."

"But you're not a nurse now, how come?"

"It's one of those things that came to an end when it was supposed to. When Marquitta was born I quit my job and stayed home with her until she started school. Then I went back part time, then on call, then back to fulltime in a hospital way across town. It took an hour to get there in the morning and an hour to come home at the end of the day. It got to be too much. When Marc took the position here it was the right time for me to retire permanently. With his career, I don't *have* to work. I want to get involved in community things; do volunteer work, maybe with kids."

"Or . . . take care of starved horses?"

"Yeah. Something like that," Rochelle said.

A sparrow flew into the barn. It spotted them, and without pause, zoomed back out the door into the sunlight.

"You must not work either," Rochelle said, "since we're both spending all this time in a barn."

"I teach flute," Hanna said. "I played for years as a soloist and then when George and I got married I wanted to be home for him, so I started teaching."

"Who takes flute lessons in Lake Luffit?"

"No one."

Rochelle waited for the next sentence, expecting Hanna to continue. She listened politely and then waited more. After another long minute she realized that no explanation would follow. Rochelle, convinced at that point, thought Hanna Tauber to be the most bizarre person she'd ever met in her life. She didn't ask any more questions about the flute.

"Did you have pets as a kid?" Hanna asked.

"No I didn't. But we did when Marquitta was home. She had hamsters and lizards and every kind of fish you can think of. How about you?"

"Not me. My sister got to have goldfish. I wanted a dog *so* bad when I was a kid. But my father refused to let me have one. He said it would interfere with my music. I still think about having a dog someday . . . looks like I got a horse instead."

Hanna relished every minute she spent in the old horse barn. She'd developed a need to be there every day. She loved Safiyyah and she was drawn also to the conversations and the time she spent with Rochelle.

A few days later, on one of their usual quiet afternoons, Hanna sat stirring the dirt with her shoe. She tossed her braid for the tenth time, sighed, and continued looking at her feet. She took a deep breath. She wrung her hands and cleared her throat.

"I do want to tell you something. I'm not sure why I'm telling you. I just want to." Void of all emotion and with jarring candor, she said, "I did have a child. But I lost her as a baby. She was four months old."

Rochelle's thoughts and breaths jammed to a halt. She never expected Hanna to drop something like that.

"Cherise Claire. That's what we named her. She was so perfect. She was my dream. My perfect dream sent from God. I got to hold her in my arms right after she was born. I got to feed her, felt her tiny hand on my breast . . . and then they took her away for tests. They'd bring her back to me and take her again. Each time it got longer and longer before they'd bring her back."

"What happened?"

"The doctors said some of her blood tests weren't normal. They had to put her in intensive care right away." Hanna leaned back against her pillow. "I'm sure you would know the name of the disease, big long name I choose not to say. I don't want to give it any credit. They said she had a chance. And she did improve . . . enough that we were able to take her home, though she had to have all these tubes and wires. At that point, we all thought she would make it, because, you know, she got to come home. But then one night we had to take CeeCee back to the hospital because she was having trouble breathing. We never left her. They let us stay right there with her. In the middle of the night the machines beeped and everyone came rushing into the room and they took her away. When morning came . . . as soon as the nurse and my doctor . . . I knew they were coming to tell me that she had died."

Hanna's lips clamped so that the muscles in her cheeks bulged. "We had her four months. Four months wasn't long enough, but in some ways it was *too* long, because I got to know her. In those four months she became my daughter. I knew her personality. I knew her likes and dislikes, what would make her smile, what would make this little frown she had. She knew I was her mom. It was supposed to be for decades and decades." Hanna rubbed her nose, though it wasn't itchy. "We had a service for her. Our parents came and just two or three friends. She hadn't lived long enough to make any friends of her own."

Rochelle almost said, "I'm sorry," those proper, safe words that stumble out, lame words, yet sincere words, words people spill because they feel they have to say something, anything, to ease the pain. But Rochelle had learned: not yet. She listened.

"I pretended that if I had taken her away, sneaked out of the hospital, and just gone . . . gone away some place . . . and if she could have had just seven months . . . that was the magic number in my mind . . . if she could have made it seven months, God's perfect number, she would have lived to grow up and one day I would be fluffing her dress and helping her with her makeup and shoes on her wedding day." Hanna looked into Rochelle's face. "You know?"

The agony in Hanna's face; Rochelle had seen it so many times before, in others, pleading, searching for answers. In the hospital setting Rochelle had always managed to conjure up the appropriate and effective stoicism with a patient. This was different. Quirky as Hanna could be, they'd become friends. Rochelle also knew the loss of a child to be the single greatest trauma a person could ever face.

"It changed everything. Everything," Hanna said. She flipped a piece of hay off to the side. The same sparrow flittered back in, checking to see if the intruders had come back into her barn, and then soared in an unbroken straight line back out the door.

"Today is . . . would be . . . her birthday."

Rochelle's lip quivered. Her vision blurred. She waited until the sentence had formed in her mind before she spoke. "How old is she?"

At that moment, for Hanna, Rochelle arose high above anything mortal, above anything earthly; higher than the clouds. All because of that one word: is. And Hanna loved her for it.

"Twenty-one," Hanna said.

Rochelle wanted to hug Hanna, though Hanna hadn't cried. She wanted to take it all away, though she knew she couldn't. "It must be . . . so hard for both of you," she said.

Hanna shrugged. "We just seem to coast. We're sailing on through now, towards what, I don't really know. It wasn't that big a deal for George. Don't get me wrong, I know he was sad . . . but he has his law practice . . . I think it was easier for him to go on than it was for me."

Hanna pushed the persistent braid once more. She blew her nose.

"Enough of this sad stuff," she said. She smiled stiffly. "I don't know why I told you. I guess I just needed to tell someone about today. You're the only person I've told this much. But look at *you!* You have a healthy daughter and a good marriage."

"Yes. I do." Rochelle wanted to reach Hanna, to connect in some manner. She knew that if she rushed, she'd struggle ahead with an assortment of words that lacked empathy. She didn't want to do that. She wanted to tell her, but she didn't want to step on Hanna's moment. Yet, she wanted to share.

"Marc is my *second* husband, Hanna. First there was Alonzo, my high school sweetheart. We got married right out of school. Everybody said it was too soon but we didn't care. We were in love. It baffles me how adults look down on kids who are in love, like love is something you can only earn as you get older, that it can't possibly be real if you haven't lived a specific number of years. But our love was real. We were married four years. He dropped dead from a heart attack. Can you imagine dying of a heart attack at twenty-one?"

Twenty-one. What a coincidence.

"He was a fine young man. Marc's wonderful. He is. I'm thankful that I've been blessed with two good men . . . you just don't expect that your first love is going to be torn away from you so soon, so abruptly."

They sat mute, looking straight ahead, as they frequently did. Their upper arms pressed against each other. Safiyyah lay before them cuddled up in her straw. The mare's tranquil midnight eyes blinked and then her white eyelashes covered them. Each breath came long and deep as the mare slumbered.

Old barns and old horses, like old wooden rocking chairs filled with history and pushed by memories, churn out sounds that are ignored by most. But Rochelle gave heed to those creaks and groans in the wood, in the horse, in the old hay, and in the chaff falling down through the cracks in the loft floor.

> *All aboard, all aboard*
> *That man barked*
> *Ain't you got some, can't you see?*
> *Got some with me*
> *Old and new*
> *Got some dings and*
> *Got some dents*
> *Got some scrapes and*
> *Got some scars*
> *Bring it on, bring it on*
> *Bring it on down that train*
> *Hold it, hold it*
> *Ain't no room*
> *Hold them, hide them*
> *No one sees*
> *Stop them, stop them*
> *Can't be seen*
> *All aboard, all aboard*
> *That man barked*
> *Ain't no seats*
> *No room above*

CHAPTER EIGHT

THE NEXT MORNING, as Rochelle measured out Safiyyah's grain, she heard a summons loud enough to send bats on the wing.

"Rochelle! Rochelle! Come quick!"

Rochelle dropped the can of grain, scattering the contents everywhere on the floor, and darted to the stall door expecting the worst. She braced her arms on the stall door in preparation for the catastrophe.

Hanna waved and pointed to the floor. "Come here! Hurry! There's poop over *here*! That means she got up! Rochelle, she was up in the night!"

They collided, laughing, crying in gibberish, and hugging and jumping up and down all at the same time. They hugged a bewildered Safiyyah, who had no clue she'd done anything so phenomenal, so deserving of such celebration.

"I'm so proud of you Safiyyah!"

"This calls for treats!"

Rochelle went to the corner at the front of the barn where they stored the feed tubs and where they now kept a bucket of apples. She chose the most perfect red and pale green Gala. An apple's coolness and firm weight gave Rochelle a pleasant sensation every time she brought the special gift to her special friend. Just as Safiyyah found joy in the simplicity of receiving an apple, so too, had Rochelle in giving.

The next morning Hanna hurried to get there first. But when she came into the barn, Rochelle met her at the stall door grinning. "She's up. She's standing on all four feet."

Hanna rushed in to see for herself. Safiyyah chewed on a mouthful of hay, standing solidly.

"I never thought I'd see this," Hanna whispered, all quivery.

"It looks like she's been up all night, too," Rochelle said. "She peeled our blanket off the hay and sampled a bit of the sofa. But she didn't mess with our stuff. By the way, I called Josh. He's going to be here to do her feet again at ten."

Josh whistled when he saw the horse. "You done a awesome job with her. I wasn't so sure she was gonna pull through." Now, he could tell them how iffy the mare's chances had been. "She looks great." Did he try to hide that tear in his eye by ducking his brow deeper into his hat? Probably so.

He trimmed the mare's hooves, a much simpler and much quicker job than it had been the first time. "Hooves're doing good," he said. "Still a ways to go. Takes a year for a whole new hoof to grow. You need to let her outside. Keeps blood moving in her feet for her to go around as she chooses. Open up that other stall door to the paddock and let her come and go. Horses are happier outside."

Hanna didn't like that idea. She paid Josh and walked with him out of the barn. She watched him drive the length of the driveway.

Josh's suggestion to let Safiyyah outside sounded good. But Rochelle and Hanna had plans of their own, and those plans did not include opening up the door to the rest of the world any time soon. Maybe they didn't want their secret revealed. Maybe they fretted that Safiyyah would choose her paddock and freedom over them. Maybe this, maybe that, but Safiyyah remained in her stall.

They settled onto their comfortable blanket and leaned back against the pillows daring to feel a good old healthy dose of triumph. Josh had whistled. They'd done a good job. They stuck their feet out in front of them and locked their hands behind their heads, salty sailors. *We did it.* The horse lived. The horse stood.

"Have a load of M&Ms," Rochelle said. She gave Hanna the bag of candy. They passed it back and forth.

"Here, take these brown ones. And the orange ones. I don't eat these," Hanna said. She dropped the unwanted morsels into Rochelle's hand. "I only eat the pretty ones."

"Of course," Rochelle said.

Another day with Safiyyah came to a close. They basked in their success with the horse and each day bloomed into the next as the relationship between the three of them deepened.

That night, George scrutinized his wife. She seemed slimmer. Her arms had become toned and the muscles defined. "You've been walking a lot more. What gives?"

"Rochelle and I walk everyday and I've been carrying some weights, too."

It wasn't a lie. She and Rochelle did walk every single day—to the barn. And Hanna carried weights when she lifted buckets and hay bales. She had promised herself all along that if George asked her, 'are you caring for a horse?' she would tell him the truth. But he never asked the correct question.

"Whatever it is you're doing, keep it up. You look great, sweetie."

"There," Hanna said, as she squished out toothpaste, "he's okay with it."

She wasn't sleepy when she crawled under the covers, just deep in thought. Everything that had happened over the past weeks had been so different from her expected life experiences. She felt a delicious mix of joy and excitement with the thrill of risk folded in. She was drawn to the little white horse, couldn't get enough of her. What was it that drew her in? She couldn't put it to words . . . release? Freedom? Healing?

She thought about Rochelle and what an unusual relationship they had. It made no sense, yet made perfect sense. They had nothing in common but Safiyyah. Yet, Hanna was drawn to Rochelle as much as she was drawn to the horse.

CHAPTER NINE

THE RAIN CAME down in slices. George raised an eyebrow as he watched Hanna, who didn't "do rain" zip up a slicker. This struck him as peculiar. She left to go for a walk in a downpour.

Whenever Hanna beat Rochelle to the barn she might have as much as an hour to spend alone with the horse. That morning, as she combed the mare's mane and tail, she studied her. She studied Safiyyah's sculpted features, her dished face, the chiseled bone structure, her magical dark eyes, and how the hair traveled in different directions on her chest.

"Where did you come from? Did anyone in the past ever love you? How can you still trust and enjoy the company of humans? Someday you might meet my little girl. Would you like that? I think she would love to meet you."

She asked these questions, sometimes out loud, sometimes just in her mind. She would never remember the day that she started talking with Safiyyah, confiding in her. She would only remember, collectively, the sweet days of those special sessions. There was no need for Safiyyah to speak, even if she'd had that ability. This was time spent with a friend. Time Hanna would remember . . . when age holds you to a standstill and permits only memories.

They seldom found Safiyyah lying down. She stayed on her feet the entire time that the women spent with her. When they sat with her, Safiyyah kept an eye on them and an ear cocked in their direction. Sometimes, she'd leave her hay and stand square in front of them, over them and dozing, yet attentive. She seemed to be guarding them. This prompted Rochelle to search online. Rochelle tapped Hanna on the shoulder and pointed to the screen at the images of mares standing over their foals as the babies slept just in front of and beneath them.

Adept at balancing her computer on her lap, Rochelle rapped on the keys later in the morning as they sipped chocolate almond coffee and dined on powdered donut holes. "All Arabians have black skin no matter what color their hair is. They come in chestnut, bay, black, and gray," she said.

"But she's white," Hanna said.

"There is no white in the Arabian breed. The color is called gray. Even though the horse might end up white, they all start out at some shade of gray and lighten as they age."

"What do people do with them?"

"It says that they are the most versatile horse. They are show and pleasure horses. They jump, cut cattle, race, pull carts, all sorts of stuff. They excel at something that looks like mountain climbing; endurance. And they wear these fancy costumes with tassels and jewels."

"Have you ever ridden a horse?"

"No."

"I think we should learn."

Rochelle cast one of *those* looks at her. "Maybe in another life." She jabbed at the keyboard again. "I want to check out something else. Horse slaughter.

Rochelle frowned. "Thousands upon thousands of American horses have been slaughtered yearly so that people overseas can eat them. Dogs don't eat them, girl, *people* do," she said. "This is awful." She clicked to the next page and to the next.

"If they want to eat horses they need to grow their own," Hanna said.

"Horses don't stun the same way cattle do, with this bolt gun that they use to shoot them in the head," Rochelle said.

Horrific scenes of actual slaughter appeared without warning. A pinto mare swung from a chain, her throat slit to bleed out, a brown horse kicking and kicking after being hit ineffectively with the bolt.

"Oh my God," Hanna said. "She's still alive . . . and that one lying on the floor, she's giving birth . . . I'm going to be sick."

Rochelle's vision blurred. She could no longer make out the images in front of her. She heard Hanna retching outside. Safiyyah chewed her hay. Oblivious.

Rochelle called out, "Are you okay?"

"I'll be back in a minute. I need air. The rain feels good."

Rochelle pressed the IBM lid down. She'd seen enough for one day.

Hanna sank onto the sofa when she returned. Her stomach and her brain sloshed as watered down oatmeal. "That pretty much wrecked the day," she said.

"I know too much now. I've lost some of my innocence and I don't like that," Rochelle said.

Hanna clasped her arms around the front of her, as if doing so might keep the contents of her stomach in place. The rain railed on the roof now with more force. It sounded angry. Too troubled to remain seated, Hanna paced. She stopped at the back of the stall and rested her forearms on the paddock door. She watched the rain hit the ground. Tiny explosions erupted as each drop fell onto the powdery dirt of the paddock until the clay became soaked and glistened.

Hanna scanned the entire paddock. Safiyyah had found every blade of grass out there, and its root. She'd eaten every leaf and she'd peeled the bark off the trees that she could reach in order to sustain herself. She'd eaten the pine boughs as high up on the tree as her neck would permit her. She'd chewed through the fence rails until they broke in two, and freed her on that day she headed for the road. (They'd tied the fence back together with baling twine). She'd survived on rain water when it gave the sludge tub an inch of water or filled a small crevice in the dirt. *All this was going on while I was in my nice, well-stocked home . . .*

"Do you hear something?" Rochelle said, interrupting Hanna's thoughts. "Don't you hear that?" Rochelle stood. She craned her neck in the direction of the sound and crept closer. She peeked over the door to the barn aisle. And then her tone went babyish. "What have we here?"

Rochelle opened the warped plywood half door and bent down to pick up something low to the ground. She faced Hanna with a ball of gray fluff. "A kitten!"

"Let me see it!"

Rochelle placed the trembling creature into Hanna's open hands. Hanna clutched him to her. "He's a rack of bones. How do you think he got in here?"

"I'll bet that someone dumped him at the driveway and he found his way to the barn. He's too small to have walked much more than that."

Rochelle rummaged around in the dusty shelves and crannies looking for something that would do as a water dish for the kitty. She found the lid to a missing Miracle Whip jar, rinsed it, filled it, and brought that to their new charge. The kitten curled up tighter on Hanna's lap when presented with the water.

"I guess he's not thirsty," Rochelle said.

"He needs food. Let's walk home and go to town."

Hanna positioned the kitten so that he sat on his haunches on the hay sofa. Then she and Rochelle backed away. He leaped off the bale and pitched head first into the straw, completely immersed. He surfaced moments later with his white front paws on Hanna's shoe.

"Now what're we going to do? He wants to come with us," Hanna said. "It might not be safe for him to be in here. What if she steps on him?"

"There's a cardboard box at the top of the stairs. I'll get it and we can make him a bed in that," Rochelle said. She put the box in the aisle, lined it with straw, and put a frayed rug remnant she'd found on top of that. She put the water in the box and the kitten next to it. He glowered at them. How dare they?

CHAPTER TEN

WITHIN AN HOUR they'd made it into town. They bought a dozen cans of cat food and another kind of food in a bag. "Something crunchy," Rochelle suggested.

On the way home they caught the red of the solitary traffic light in Lake Luffit. The traffic light, just like a sign at the end of a dirt road, didn't make sense. You sat there and waited for a long time, thinking about what you would do when you got home, what to fix for supper, checking your makeup in the mirror, or inspecting six different kinds of cat food, hoping that at least one of them would be tasty. Not once did another car approach from any direction. Waiting for the light to change, Rochelle noticed the brick building to the right.

"There's the animal control department," she said. She zipped the Jaguar into the lot. "I want to know more."

The building smelled of dogs and cats, infused with the sharp odor of bleach. Busy kittens in cages in the lobby scrambled after feather-laden toys, pounced on each other, flipped each other over, and kicked with their back feet. Every one of them stopped playing the instant Hanna and Rochelle walked through the door. They had found something to gawk at and of greater importance than feathers.

"Excuse me," Rochelle said. An older woman sat on a roller chair behind a chest-high counter. She tilted her head to listen. "I have a few questions about those horses that Mr. Durfee owned," Rochelle said.

Hanna punched Rochelle in the back.

Rochelle ignored her.

"Did you know Roger Durfee?"

"No I didn't. We're just curious about what happened to the horses," Rochelle said.

Another punch to Rochelle's back: *we* aren't curious about anything.

"I'll get the officer who handled that. She just came in off the road. I don't know enough about it to answer your questions. I just take care of the phones and clean." She left the counter and went through a metal door. The scent of bleach and disinfectant trolled along behind her.

Hanna hissed. "What *are* you doing?"

"Calm down. I have to know . . ."

The door opened and a young woman wearing a brown uniform walked up to the counter. "I'm Erin Roderick," she said. "I understand you have some questions about the Durfee horses. Are you relatives, friends of his?"

"No," Rochelle said, "neither. We're just curious. What happened?"

"Roger Durfee was a source of consternation for us and for the police. We knew he didn't take the best care of his horses. We'd get a call once a year or so from someone complaining. We'd go out there but by the time we arrived they all had food and water. It was hard to keep up with because his place is so far back in the woods. It's not like we can drive by to check on things. Then one day a horse got loose . . ."

"What did it look like?" Hanna asked.

"Big rangy Quarter Horse stallion. Red sorrel, nice color. He was actually the best Quarter Horse I've ever seen. Durfee was no where to be found. So we called the deputies. They went out and found him dead in the house. Drank himself to death. That's what they said. Odd man."

"What happened to the horses?" Rochelle asked. "We heard they were seized."

Erin sensed them staring at her. She was accustomed to this. Everyone became lost in her face; the perfect cheek bones, the uncommonly long lashes, her full lips, and clear skin. Her hypnotic beauty interrupted everything. She wore her shoulder length auburn hair pulled back while in uniform so that it didn't touch her collar. She'd grown up swimming in compliments, though she believed her physical attributes more a curse than a blessing. She had more to offer than just looks.

"We took them," Erin said.

"How many?"

"Eight. They were all outside in small corrals huddled together with no water and no food. A few had injuries and had to be put down right then. They couldn't get up, too far gone. Durfee was as odd as they come. He didn't associate with anyone. He'd been arrested a few times in years past for larceny of farm equipment. He had quite an assortment of horses out there; couple of Quarter Horses, Paints, a Morgan, and a few Thoroughbreds. He did put food out for them, infrequently, and some of the more timid horses had to just stand by and watch while others had food."

Hanna stared into Rochelle. *Have we been imagining things or is that loft filled with hay?*

They wanted to tell Erin about the mountain of hay in Roger Durfee's barn, enough to last all of those horses for a year. They wanted to ask someone who could make sense out of this, someone like Erin Roderick, why a man would have hay on his property and *not* give it to all of his horses. Any explanation would be acceptable other than having to come to grips with this level of cruelty.

Rochelle kept her face down so that Erin couldn't read it. *Don't let the secret out.*

"We found homes for a few, but it's so hard now. Lots of people don't have the money to care for the horses they have and they don't want to take on any more. The really thin Durfee horses we found homes for. People always feel sorry for the skinny ones, but they aren't the ones at most risk. We didn't find any takers for the healthy ones and for the Quarter Horse stud. We had no choice but to take them to an auction. A kill buyer bought them all. The sad thing is they were all good riding horses. That stud had been a top reining horse."

"So, they're gone now?" Rochelle asked.

"Yes."

"It sickens me," Hanna said.

"I struggle with it constantly," Erin said. "It's not that simple though. There are thousands of unwanted horses in America and there's no place for them to go."

Rochelle bent across the counter. "Why would you get a horse . . . I mean, doesn't common sense tell you that a horse is an expensive pet . . . if you can't care for it? They're pets for crying out loud! They make horse toys and clothes . . . we don't do that for cattle."

"We read an article that the horses no longer useful; the old ones, the lame, are the ones that go," Hanna said.

"That's the pro-slaughter propaganda. The ideal meat horse is fat and healthy, about eight to nine hundred pounds. A nice round Quarter Horse is ideal. It's not always the sick, aged, nasty looking horses. The slaughter market wants, and gets, the healthy ones in their prime. I've seen countless horses go through auctions, ridden into the sale ring, kid-safe, show quality, and they peel the saddle off a nice horse and it ends up shipped to the plant for processing."

"So, what's the answer?" Rochelle said.

"People need to stop breeding," Erin said. "There's just too many and people keep right on breeding more of them. There are reputable breeders, but there are just as many who jump on whatever fad they think might make them a few bucks and they mass produce them. A breeder might end up with twenty foals a year that have no place to go, except to slaughter. Erin said. "Horses don't roam the alleys and fields at large like stray dogs and cats. They're kept in barns and fences. It takes a deliberate choice and effort to transport a mare to a stallion to breed her.

Many breed associations are notorious for encouraging excessive breeding. And why wouldn't they? They can mass produce them, keep their numbers up, and have a continual dumping place for the unwanted. Many of the breed associations are pro-slaughter. There's no accountability for the mass production and as long as there is a slaughter market, they are free to do it."

Erin continued. "Lots of people agree with slaughter. There are so many horses and not enough homes for them. They have to go someplace. Slaughter is an option. It's just like most animal shelters that have oodles of dogs and cats. So very few of them get a home. What are the shelters supposed to do? And with a horse you have a one thousand pound animal to decide what to do with. Putting them down is expensive, disposing of them is expensive, and there are people who want that last bit of money out of a horse. Shipping them can be the solution to the problem. It's sad when a horse has worked hard all his life, raced all his life, but is no longer wanted. It gets hauled to an auction and goes from the home its known, sometimes its entire life, onto a trailer filled with other uprooted horses, and he finishes out his life of service at a slaughterhouse . . . all for a hundred bucks. Sadder yet, is when a mare and foal go through an auction. The foal is sometimes lucky enough to be taken from her that day and sold to an actual home, but the mare is loaded onto that kill truck terrified and screaming for the foal she'll never see again. What a way to wean a foal from its mother. What a reward for having served humans."

Erin looked away. In her mind, she saw the track in front of her. She visualized Ferdinand crossing the Kentucky Derby finish line in slow-motion. She could see him. She watched as he galloped on and on and disappeared into a dense fog.

Erin quickly shifted her attention to the two women in front of her again. "The racing industry inadvertently supplies a lot of horses . . . and there's no lack of money in that world," she said. "I find it so ironic that people will flock to the races to watch them run, or go to a movie about a dashing black stallion, and they leave, moved to tears, and in the next breath say that slaughter is humane and necessary."

"It seems the easy way out," Rochelle said. "I don't know much about horses but I would think part of horse ownership is taking responsibility and planning for the animal's ill health or loss of use. I don't think you have to be a brain surgeon to know that owning a horse is expensive."

"I agree," Erin said. "But that's the way things are. It's a very heated subject among horsemen. The majority of Americans are against horse slaughter. But horse *owners* are split and the emotions run high and deep on both sides. Slaughter would make some sense to me if the meat got sent overseas to feed starving children. But that's not what happens. In all the countries where horsemeat is eaten, it's a delicacy. And why anyone would want to eat American horses is beyond me. We feed them medicines and supplements that clearly state on the labels that they aren't intended for horses for human consumption. I've seen horses go to slaughter with horrible stinking infections, wounds, and tumors . . . still they want to eat them. And the meat companies brag about the quality of the meat they sell."

"Do you see more cases of neglect if people don't send them to slaughter?" Hanna asked.

"Horse neglect has always been. There have always been neglected horses in pastures and abandoned in barns. Slaughter's always been an option and neglect's always existed. The same number of American horses is slaughtered every year, whether it occurs in this country, or in Canada or Mexico. The rise and fall of the economy is what causes neglect . . . and just plain cruelty. Cruel people have always existed. Those in favor of slaughter claim that people who can't afford to feed their horses should have a place to get rid of them. But I've seen it over and over; those same folks that say they can't afford to feed the horse take it to an auction . . . and buy another one the same day." Erin shook her head and chuckled. "Roger Durfee had a ton of money."

Erin tightened up her barrette. The clock hit five o'clock, almost time to feed the animals, and she had the responsibility that shift.

"You seem like such a compassionate young woman," Rochelle said, "how can you do this work . . . and stay sane?"

"I wanted to go to veterinary school, but my parents didn't have the money to send me. Then my dad died and what money I saved for school had to go to help my mom. I worked as the manager of a racing stable for a year. Then I set up my own business selling horse tack. I didn't make much money at it so I had to find a job with benefits. I didn't plan on becoming an animal control officer but when you need work, you take what comes along. I've been here six years and I love it now. I get to do a lot of public speaking. Teachers in all of the schools in six counties ask me to speak to the kids. Gives me a chance to educate young people about proper care of pets and livestock."

"It's got to be difficult seeing these pets here put to sleep," Hanna said.

"Ours is a no-kill shelter," Erin said, thinking, *it is now*. She had devoted her first two years at the shelter lobbying the county officials to make the change.

"Are you horse people?" Erin asked. "Looking to buy a horse?"

"We've been thinking about it," Rochelle said. "Rescuing one that is headed for slaughter or has no place to go seems the right way to do it."

"Here." Erin passed a notepad and pen to Rochelle. "Write down your names and phone numbers. The next time we do a seizure I'll call you."

For some reason, Safiyyah had been spared. Erin and the deputies must not have gone into the barn. If they had, Safiyyah would have whinnied to tell them not to forget her. She'd been left behind and no one knew she existed. The curious thing about the whole story; had Safiyyah been found, she'd have been put down or sent to slaughter. Yet, *not* being found had sealed the fate of starvation. Almost.

Erin watched the two women walk out of the building. She thought of her mom. Erin had been preparing all day to call her that night and tell her the truth. She knew it would devastate her, but keeping it from her any longer wasn't fair. Erin's mother lived for the day that her only daughter would get married. Just last night when they talked on the phone, Mom said, "Erin, you're twenty-eight years old. Don't you think it's time?"

Erin was born in Boston. Her mom still lived in Boston, in the same two-story Victorian house that Erin had grown up in. And this whole thing would be a lot easier there, rather than in Lake Luffit. It would be a lot easier being gay in Boston. Erin didn't know one other gay person in Lake Luffit, or, . . . no one said.

The dating scene frustrated Erin. She'd had inklings about her sexual orientation since her teens. But she'd heard it over and over: that the lifestyle is perverse. So she kept to herself. She enjoyed palling around with boys in school but dated only occasionally, and because she had to, in order to fit in. A few years ago, she confided in her buddy, Nelson. Though they never shared a romantic interest, they hung out together, going to movies and concerts and serving as the other's date for weddings. One night after a movie, she told him. At first, Nelson retreated. The next day, it became Nelson's personal crusade to help his friend. He would help her change. Erin told him that his quest offended her. "Why am I not good enough the way that I am?"

Nelson, however, didn't have the stuffing to remain her friend and the rift was permanent. She missed his friendship. Most of all, she longed for a loving relationship and a partner for life. That might prove to be difficult in Lake Luffit.

It would not be easy to have this conversation with her mother. *She'll cry. She'll ask me about grandkids.* It would be rugged, but in the end, Erin knew that her mom would still love her. And she would say so.

Church presented a more delicate, more frustrating piece for Erin to place. She loved going to church. She'd been raised Baptist but she'd visited churches of other denominations, too. She wrestled with Christianity and the church in her mind because Jesus taught that Christians should not judge. They should love each other and encourage people to come to him. Yet, these same Christians despised those who loved someone of the same gender.

75

Jesus never told Christians to despise *anyone*. She could not find one word in the Bible that said God despised any of his creation.

Erin once sat in church beside a man who beat his kids. Everyone knew it. Behind her sat a woman who had slept with most of the married men in the congregation, including the pastor. A priest at the Catholic Church next door had been asked to leave because he had sodomized two boys. No criminal charges were filed. The Church transferred him to another parish. That same week, a nationally known preacher had been exposed for bilking millions of dollars from his devoted followers.

Erin hadn't done any of those things. She hadn't so much as lifted a pencil from an employer. She hadn't ever gone out of her way to hurt another person. They'd call her vile, only because one day she might fall in love. She wondered how many religious leaders, employers, politicians, and ordinary people merely say they do not judge people because of their sexual orientation, just because you won more points being politically correct. Did they believe it? Erin guessed that, more than likely, they did not. She hoped that they blushed when confronted with their duplicity.

She'd been at war mentally with it so much over the years. *Is it a sin? Perhaps it is. Perhaps it isn't. Is love a sin? Perhaps it is. Perhaps it isn't.*

She saw a blurb on television that very morning about obesity in America. *Isn't gluttony a sin, too?* What about her neighbor, Shawna Tompkins? She'd faked a slip and fall accident in front of a shop so she'd never have to work again. She won her lawsuit. *Isn't sloth a sin? What about deceit? What about the rampant sex outside of marriage among heterosexuals? Which sins carry the greatest weight?* What about Erin's friend, Bonita, who got married two years ago? From high school on, Bonita had kept track of all of the boys and men she had slept with. She kept the list hidden under the carpet in her bedroom. The last Erin knew the tally hit forty-one. Then Bonita met Howard Rathbun. On her wedding day, Bonita wore the standard proclamation of her status—a huge white dress. Everyone put their hands to their faces to wipe away tears at the beauty of it all as the dress sashayed its way down the aisle at St.

Anne's. Erin also put her hands to her face, but to smother her laughter.

As the days and the years had gone by, Erin clung to a few shreds of belief in which she found solace. *God alone has the answers. Probably every single thing we do is sin motivated. God loves us in spite of those sins. He never said that loving someone is a sin.*

Erin hadn't awakened one morning, took a sip of tea, and declared, "Today, I think I will be gay." *That's not how it happens.*

If people hated her for it, they'd have to take it up with God. *They will have to tell him that he is the one who has made a mistake.*

God reminded Erin of his existence and his compassion. He had answered so many prayers throughout her life. She welcomed his presence in the early morning dew that blanketed the field behind her house. She knew that he'd answered prayers the night when she cried out to him after the county vehicle slid off the road and got stuck in the snow. It missed an oak tree by mere inches. She knew his embrace when Nelson would no longer be her friend and she cried herself to sleep. She knew the Lord's presence all around her. She knew his touch and she knew his voice. She noticed these things and she remembered them all.

Tonight, she would share these truths with her mom.

"I don't get it," Rochelle said. The Jag skimmed along so quietly you never heard the motor. "There is a ton of hay in that barn. Why wouldn't he give it to them?"

"And there's water," Hanna said. "Water's free. And everything we heard convinces me this is why we can't tell anyone about her. Not yet anyway. Think about it. She has no known owner. She's old and she's skinny. Where do you think she'd end up? I think we should at least wait until Josh tells us that she looks the best she'll ever look before we tell anyone we have her. Maybe she'll have a chance then. This whole idea of eating horses makes me sick."

"My dad has been the pastor of our church his whole life," Rochelle said. "I remember him quoting from Revelation so many times, that Jesus returns on a white horse . . . there is something really wrong with this . . . It doesn't say he returns on a Hereford."

"And for us Jews, horses aren't kosher. We can only eat animals that have a cloven hoof and chew a cud. Horses are neither," Hanna said.

"The Lone Ranger and Silver, his trusty wonder chicken," Rochelle said. And they both laughed, as people do, to soften the collision with reality.

They rode the rest of the way in silence. Words came to Rochelle again. They were coming to her more often since Safiyyah had come into her life. Sometimes, Rochelle thought about jotting a poem down on paper. But the notion, along with the words, always evaporated.

I was a good horse
You wanted me then
And you brought me home
To live with you then
I carried that young child
Your little girl
So many years
It filled her with joy
She was, oh so safe
Upon my strong back
And you walked beside me
Holding her fast
Year after year
I carried her safe
And then that day came
Just she and I
When we shared my wings
And we shared my speed
Not once did you worry
So safe was your child
I came when you called
Did all that you asked

And now it's my turn
Now I ask why?
I was a good horse
You wanted me then

"He's not in here," Rochelle said, as she sifted through the straw in the kitten box.

Hanna breezed through the barn in search of the crafty feline. "Here kitty, kitty," she sang. Rochelle was just about to yell at her to be quiet when the sing-song stopped.

"Rochelle I found him. You gotta see this."

The pint-sized creature had crawled onto Safiyyah's back while the mare relaxed in her bedding, curled up, and fallen asleep. He sprung back to life and went airborne off the horse when she rose to her feet. Hanna picked him up and rubbed his nose against her own. "We brought you something to eat."

Rochelle pried open a can and dug out the stinky contents with the plastic spoon she'd taken from the coffee setup at the store. She mashed the flaked tuna into a lumpy paste.

Hanna nuzzled him. "You da coodest widdo ting," she cooed. Seconds later, the word "tang" got attached to "ting" and his official name became, Ting Tang.

And so it was. An Arabian horse, a kitten, a Jewish woman, and an African American woman, all found each other and spent their days in someone else's dilapidated barn.

CHAPTER ELEVEN

"Let's give her a bath today," Rochelle said on the phone one morning. "It's sunny and unusually warm for a fall day. We should make use of it. I think she'd enjoy it. We've got to get her clean before bad weather gets here."

"It would also be a nice day for a . . . bike ride wouldn't it?" Hanna said when they met at noon.

Rochelle had almost grown used to Hanna's bike-obsessed interruptions. She held two bottles up. She'd planned to ask Hanna, "Which shampoo?" But the bottles hovered in space as Rochelle considered asking, "What's a bike got to do with all of this?" *No, don't even ask.* She stared at Hanna for no more than two seconds and asked, as planned, "Which shampoo should we use?"

"That purply one, the one that says it makes white horses super white," the boss lady said.

Rochelle wore a lightweight baby blue T-shirt and track shorts. "It's supposed to get hot today," she said. Hanna wore a red and white striped swimsuit top and ragged jeans chopped off at the knees.

Rochelle gathered the supplies they'd need: buckets, the shampoo, two sponges, and a few brushes. She carried the items in the buckets out into the paddock, leading the horse with the lead rope held in her teeth. She placed everything in a neat configuration next to the fence. She tied Safiyyah to a post. Safiyyah warily eyed the proceedings.

In the meantime, Hanna hooked up the stiff green hose they'd found in the loft and sent catapulting in a spiraled mass down the stairs. She pulled it out and stomped on the hoops and coils to mash the whole thing down flat without snapping the brittle thing into pieces.

"I'll turn the water on," Rochelle said. "I think it will smooth out once water is running through it."

The collision of emotions came out of nowhere. Nuts and bolts joggled around in Hanna's stomach. At first, the slivers of sudden memory thrilled her. But apprehension and alarm slashed that joy away from her. In place of the red and white stripes, she saw the pink top of her first two piece swimsuit. She remembered, but how was that possible? *I was . . . three . . .* She could actually see the frilly pink ruffles that crossed her pudgy baby chest. She could *see* it on her body. She sensed something sinister and then the swimsuit top appeared to take on an eerie glow.

He spoke clearly, as if he was right there. But he wasn't. And she couldn't envision him. She just heard his voice. A stinging, searing shiver burned her body.

"Twirl for me," she heard him say. "Shake your little butt for Uncle Larry. Then come see me."

Hanna trembled. Her chest heaved. The salty taste of sweat dampened her lips.

It had flashed in front of her so fast and so vividly that she thought she'd pass out. But why? Everything in her mind spun. Pink ruffles, Uncle Larry's voice, twirl again, pink ruffles.

No, no, no!

Her mind rumbled, ready to explode. *Run! Run to the bathroom, close the curtain. Cover, cover. Don't look.* In and out, dizzy, Uncle Larry talking. *Get the towel, get the towel! Hide away!*

"I hope she won't be afraid of the hose and the water," Rochelle said.

No response.

"I hope she won't be afraid of the hose and the water," she said again, with crescendo. Rochelle eyed Hanna, who stood, rigid and sweating, the hose kinked in her hand, water drizzling out anyway, forming a puddle at her feet.

Rochelle put the second bucket of supplies down on the ground and touched Hanna's arm. "Are you okay? Your face is ashen. You look like you've seen a ghost. You don't look well."

Jolted back, Hanna lied. "I'm okay. I'm okay," she said. But she wasn't okay.

What just happened? It was just a swimsuit . . . just a swimsuit and . . . Uncle Larry.

It came so sudden, so fractured, and so real. And then nothing.

Something just happened to me now. But what happened . . . then? The panic and the anxiety, like an overpowering shadow, rolled over her and threatened to trap her. Had she been alone she would have slumped into that puddle and stayed there for hours.

Uncle Larry wasn't Hanna's real uncle. She'd never had any memory of him until now. Hanna's mother had told her that Uncle Larry was the neighbor who used to bring his little girl, Chelsea, over to play with Hanna. He would watch both girls on the rare occasions that Hanna's mom and dad went away for the day by themselves. Hanna had no conscious memory of those days, but just moments ago she did remember. She heard his voice, heard him say his name and she remembered fear. She sensed that something very terrifying and very wrong had happened but she could only remember his voice.

Rochelle had been right beside her the whole time, waiting, watching, and worrying. She tapped Hanna's forearm again. "Come on . . . let's get started. Are you sure you're okay?"

Then Hanna noticed Safiyyah's ears pricked forward as she watched the bath preparations. Those little ears; comical in the moment, yet serene, safe, prompted a still jittered to-the-bone-and-feeling-dislodged Hanna to run the hose on the horse's back. The water flowed over the mare's body like brown sheets as the dirt washed away, revealing brighter shades of white.

Ting Tang thought that they did this all just for him. He sped back and forth, leaped in the air, and batted at the clumps of purple soap suds on the ground. He'd crouch low, like a lion in the bush, rocking from paw to paw, shoot forward and smash into the bubbles. A bowling ball made of fur.

Without warning, Hanna belted, "She's got four pink socks!"

Hanna never heard the first scream but those that followed clanged into her ears. Rochelle's T-shirt, all she wore on that hot day, clung to her skin, drenched clean through. Hanna, excited about finding the pink socks on the horse, had flung the hose up and out to the side, continually waving it and shooting Rochelle with the frigid water.

Rochelle screamed and she hopped and danced as she held the clinging Saran Wrap shirt away from her body. "It's cold! God, it's cold! What did you do that for? Are you nuts?" She howled while Hanna ignored her.

"Remember the books said that if they have white markings, the skin under those markings is always pink," Hanna said. "She's all white now but when she was younger she would have been much darker, with four white socks."

"That's it? That's all you've got to say? You just drenched me to the bone . . . and that's it? How do you do this to me?"

"I didn't mean to do it. Sorry."

Rochelle planned revenge.

"I'll scrub her mane," Hanna said, still ignoring her partner. "You do her tail."

Hanna tried to separate the mane hairs with a comb without ripping them but the many knots were packed in solid and a mound of loose white hair built up on the ground anyway. One persistent knot on the underside and tight up against the mare's neck wouldn't loosen. Determined to remove that one last knot, Hanna flipped that section of mane over so that the hair fell on the opposite side of the horse's neck. She picked at the hairs with her nimble flute fingers and tried to weave the hairs back through the knot from where they'd come, but she couldn't avoid breaking some of them. She whittled the knot down to a final hard object. She dipped a rag into the bucket of water and rubbed the lump, chipping encrusted dirt off of it with her thumbnail.

Rochelle ran the wide-toothed hair pick through the ground sweeping tail. The wet hairs squeaked and glimmered. They felt like skeins of silk as she held them up and across her arm so they wouldn't drag in the dirt.

"Come see this," Hanna said.

She'd said it with such potency that Rochelle dropped the comb. She let the tail slide off her forearm. "What did you find?"

The hard object attached to the mane was round and about a half inch in diameter. Royal blue. Deep inside the blue, glistening flecks of gold danced and sparkled in the sunlight. It held fast to the hairs no matter how Hanna toyed with it. Hairs had grown around it and through it, keeping it in place. They stared at the fascinating find.

"Wow," Rochelle said.

"What do you suppose it is?" Hanna said.

"I've never seen anything like it. It's not what you'd expect to find on a horse anyway. It's a jewel, or crystal bead of some kind. She didn't grow it, that's for sure. It must have meaning. I think we should leave it," Rochelle said.

Hanna pulled Safiyyah's mane back over to the left side where it fell naturally and covered the bead, thinking it one of the most beautiful and interesting things she'd ever seen.

They finished combing out Safiyyah's mane and tail without speaking. Someone in the horse's life had cared about her at some time. The bead didn't grow or find the horse on its own. Someone put it there. But who, why, and when? From that day forward, Hanna lifted Safiyyah's mane every single day to see the bead. But she never tried to remove it again.

When they were finished with the bath, Safiyyah pawed the ground. She fidgeted and twisted her body from side to side. Rochelle slipped her halter off. "I think we need to do what Josh said and let her loose. We can't keep her cooped up all the time."

Once free, Safiyyah broke into a canter. She tossed her head and she bucked as if she had never known lameness and didn't know age. The mare's clean bright coat shimmered like an opal as different hues teased the light. Her white tail and mane billowed and furled, forming a living frame around her body.

Safiyyah slowed from a canter to a trot. One slender front leg stretched out and appeared to levitate, to remain in mid air, as if held up by an invisible thread. Her hooves never appeared to touch the ground. She arched her neck and flared her nostrils as her aura and the wind and the clouds carried her over the turf.

"I have never seen anything like this in my life. She floats," Rochelle whispered. "She absolutely floats above the ground."

Hanna watched through the camera lens. "She gives me chills, wave after wave of chills."

The little mare seemed to be caught up in a private moment as she trotted and pranced, as if urged on by a cheering crowd. Her precise, fiery gait entertained and mesmerized the women.

Abruptly, it came to an end. Ten minutes. The damaged feet gave Safiyyah just ten minutes before they reminded her of her limitations. The mare limped to a walk and then stopped. She stood with her nostrils wide into the breeze, rejoicing, as she caught her breath.

Rochelle and Hanna stared at Safiyyah, in awe of what they'd seen, and wondering what kind of creature they'd found. They knew nothing about horses, but only something as dense as a stone wouldn't have been able to appreciate the gift that the little white horse had been given. Breathtaking.

After the show was over, Safiyyah's head dropped straight to the dirt. Her back hunched and the joints in all four legs buckled. She turned in small circles. She seemed unable to lift her head. She became crippled. She pawed with a front hoof. She flopped onto the ground, grunted, and began rolling and grinding her sides into the sand. She flipped over again, got to her feet, shook her body twice, and then walked straight to them, yawning. Done. Happy as could be. Leaves and sticks clung to her mane. She'd transformed herself from a clean horse into something that appeared coated in bread crumbs. Her dazzling white coat, her face, her ears, and every inch of her she'd covered with sand.

"Oh no! Look what she did to herself," Hanna said.

"We did read that horses will roll after they've been bathed. I guess we forgot about that. It said you can tie them up or walk them until they dry. They will still roll once they're dry but the dirt won't stick because they aren't wet," Rochelle said.

"All that work," Hanna said, "for nothing."

"We're going to have to do it again."

So they did.

"I'll hose her down," Rochelle said. "But first . . ." She turned the hose on Hanna and sprayed her in the face. "You deserve that!"

They squealed and rollicked in the slapstick afternoon. They squirted each other with the hose. They threw water from the bucket and flicked soap suds at each other all the while Beethoven's Fifth Symphony roared. Safiyyah kept her head down and her ears back. She was wet and covered in purple foam. *Two* back to back baths in one day defied all sense of reason.

When the bath party ended, Rochelle tied Safiyyah in the sun until she dried. Hanna opened a new bale of straw and fluffed it in the stall. They gave her hay and water, spooned out a few more dollops of chicken liver mush for Ting Tang, and they closed up the barn for the night.

"Eee!" Rochelle shrieked. She pulled her damp T-shirt away from her body. "How am I going to walk home like this?"

"You're right," Hanna said. "You can see . . . everything. Just cross your arms in front of you. You'll be okay. No one will see."

Their track shoes sloshed and squeaked with each homeward bound step. Rochelle kept her arms folded across her chest. But she continued to grin.

George's office assistant, Andy, greeted them at Hanna's driveway. He'd just pulled in to drop off a file. "Please, give it to George," he said. "He'll need it tomorrow." Andy stared at Hanna as if she had broccoli stuck to her teeth, as if she'd shaved her eyebrows off.

Rochelle snickered. "I'll see you tomorrow at nine," she said.

Hanna watched her slosh and squeak away. No arms visible and swinging at her sides; Rochelle was just a body in sloppy shoes.

Why did Andy stare? Hanna bent down to catch a view of her face in the side view mirror of the Jeep. She yelped like a puppy stung by a bee, yanked opened the car door, fumbled through the glove box, and tossed contents out until she found Kleenex. She scrubbed at the fountain of mascara that had liquefied and drizzled down her face from each eye and dried as it ran. Pillars of mascara, nearly the width of each of her cheeks, appeared to be supporting her face. Caked droplets splattered her chest.

"How could she!" Hanna wailed. "I look like a clown, a stupid, soggy clown." She stomped her squishy shoes to the house. She washed her face and hands and loosed and braided her hair. She would have pouted and peeved longer but she heard the water running in the shower upstairs. George would be down for supper soon.

She took a frozen block of meat in white wrapping from the stack in the freezer to thaw in the microwave. As the plumes of frosted air cleared, she turned the package over a few times. She'd forgotten to label it. *Fish, chicken, or beef?*

She shuddered. Ugly feelings cut through her, down to her feet, and surged back up. A white wrapping of frozen meat. But its hidden contents terrified her and pulled her into a panic attack. *Drop it! Pitch it out the window!*

She held it, even though numb from the cold, and tried to remember. *What's in this package?* She so forced her eyes shut that the tears, with no place else to go, seeped from under her lashes. She gritted her teeth.

She yelled. "Why can't I remember?" She yelled again, louder and louder. "I don't know! I don't know!"

When George tried to take it from her, she held the meat wrapper so tightly that it stuck to her hands. Her body shook.

He put the hard package in the kitchen sink. He rubbed her red hands and blew on them. Then he held her in his arms and rocked her until the whimpering ceased. "It's okay. We can put it in water and peel the paper off. Do you want me to fix supper?" Confusion enveloped him. He ached with dread. When she screamed, he'd fled straight from the shower wearing just a towel, so fast, he left the water running. He had no idea how to console her about a simple unmarked hunk of meat.

Hanna dragged her body to the living room and eased down onto her glider in the dark. No one had turned the lights on. She tried to force the sight out of her mind, but no matter where she turned, no matter what else she tried to picture in her mind, the vision appeared in front of her. Reality told her that if she thawed it and scratched away the paper on the package there would have been an ordinary block of chicken. But she *saw* something completely different. Every time she envisioned herself opening that package, she'd find a wadded up frozen ball, a toddler's pink swimsuit top.

"Why can't I shake this?" she said, her head in her still throbbing hands.

Why had that swimsuit shocked her and plagued her thoughts so persistently? It had taken on a wicked persona. Up until that afternoon, Hanna had no recollection of that garment. She'd seen one photograph of her wearing it, taken decades ago, as she sat in a kiddy wading pool. Of course she couldn't remember that day. She was only three on that day. She asked her mom several years ago about the photo. "Why do I look so sad in that one?"

Mom hesitated and scratched her nose as she did when flustered. "I think the water might have been cool," she said.

"Mom, whatever happened to that Uncle Larry you told me about?"

"He went away that year. We never saw him again."

And why, during Safiyyah's bath, had the sudden and buried memory of Uncle Larry caused her so much panic, urging her to flee?

Now, Hanna had many questions. The frustration that they'd never be answered burned inside her. Her parents were both gone. Father died three four years ago of a heart attack. Mom died two years later of cancer. Hanna's sister, Helen, wasn't born until Hanna was six. She wouldn't have known Uncle Larry.

As Hanna sat on the glider, shooting back and forth, she tried to conjure up his voice once again . . . just to be sure. But it, too, stayed bound inside the frozen package.

CHAPTER TWELVE

IN THE MORNING Hanna sat in front of the bedroom mirror over her dresser before she went down to make breakfast. She countered the urge to apply mascara. "Maybe horses and this stuff don't mix." She screwed the wand into the tube and tucked it back into the basket along with the other twenty pounds of makeup. "I guess this will save me a lot of time."

From bath day on, Safiyyah's door leading to the paddock remained open. At first, Hanna objected. She claimed that if out in the open, someone would see the horse and report it. But Rochelle defended the mare's freedom. "We're in the middle of the woods. No one knows the horse is here, remember? Besides, Josh hasn't steered us wrong once and we should listen to him. Horses belong outside in the sunshine.

Hanna gave in. But she said, "It's against my better judgment." Of course she said that to hide the real reason for objecting. She worried that Safiyyah would no longer want to be with her. If Safiyyah could be kept in the stall, she'd have no choice. She would always be there for Hanna to enjoy, as *Hanna* wanted. But once they opened the door and allowed her to come and go, Safiyyah chose to be with her women. She spent almost all of her time in the stall with them. Only when they left for the day did she show any interest in being outside by herself. Leaving the door open also gave them a nice and unexpected reward. They no longer had to clean the stall. Safiyyah went out into the paddock to relieve herself every time she had to go.

"She's housebroken," Rochelle said, laughing.

"I can imagine the look on George's face when I tell him I want to keep a horse in the house."

"Speaking of that, how long do you think we can keep this charade going with the guys? And don't look at me in horror like that. It *is* something we have to consider," Rochelle said.

"I try not to think about it."

"I know you don't think about it. Does George ever ask you what you are doing all day?"

"Not really. Every now and then he might ask if I had a good day, did I do anything interesting. He thinks I play my flute, score music, shop with you, walk with you, and maybe watch television. What about you? Does Marc ask?"

"Yeah. I tell him that we walk, a *lot*. I tell him that we go to the library, go shopping, and chat. I just leave out the part about the horse. I don't feel good about this. I've never lied to Marc."

"I don't think it's lying at all. It's just not telling. There's a difference," Hanna said.

"We spend a lot of time here. I hope it doesn't cost me my marriage when he finds out," Rochelle said, shaking the morning newspaper out in front of her.

"Why should it? We're not doing anything wrong. We saved her life. That's a good thing. I'm not ashamed of that."

"I'm just saying that if Marc did this, and I had been left out, I would feel hurt."

"It'll be okay," Hanna said. "What are you reading? Something's got you. You look really serious all of a sudden. Give me that." She snatched the paper. "Which one are you reading?" She pointed to an article about the Moon now being off kilter since scientists decided to shoot a hole in it a while back, though she knew that wasn't it.

It was the article about the woman who reported that her car had been stolen at gunpoint by a black man. Two weeks later, they found the car hidden in the woods. The woman admitted that she'd lied. She'd hid the car and made up the story to collect insurance money. She accused a fictitious stranger of the crime.

The distance between Hanna and Rochelle waxed wide, as if each had been exiled to opposite sides of a troubled river. It had started out as one of their sweet days with Safiyyah. Now, Hanna sensed Rochelle's anger, not just with that woman but with her and with all of the other people on the planet who happened to be white. And that made Hanna angry.

"But the woman changed her story," Hanna said. "So now you're not going to talk to me? That's foolish. I didn't have anything to do with it." Her skin prickled.

"I'm not blaming you," Rochelle said. "It's just the big picture. She picked a black man because that would make it all the more believable. She'd be a victim deserving of sympathy and belief if a black man had done it."

"But she recanted her story."

"That's not good enough. Where's the apology? Why didn't she do the right thing, the fair thing, and apologize for making such an unfair accusation? Why did she say it to begin with?"

Let's not go there. Let's drop it and enjoy our day with Safiyyah. Those words lodged between Hanna's brain and her mouth but she blundered forward. "I think you are making too big a deal out of this. I'm tired of the race card. We never get a break from it. No matter what happens, everything is because of race."

"That's because it exists."

"Don't tell me that things aren't better for you people. Look at all of the athletes and movie stars who make millions. You can't tell me that things haven't improved. When are we ever going to be able to go on and leave things that happened a long time ago in the past?"

"For those celebrities who make millions, it doesn't mean so much when you look at the distance between them, way up here, and the majority of blacks, way down here." Rochelle demonstrated the chasm between the two with her hands far apart. "That's the problem," Rochelle said.

"But look at you. Your husband is a doctor. He makes more than my husband does. Surely his folks had money to send him to medical school. And you were a nurse. You have a lovely home and drive a Jaguar."

Rochelle noticed her heart beating. She noticed each blink, tasted the smoothness of her lips, things you seldom pay attention to.

Ting Tang scampered between them in pursuit of a moth with a broken wing that fluttered in futile spins too close to the ground. He would catch it and eat it. He ate lots of moths.

"Are you going to sit there and tell me that it never, not even just for a second, surprised you to learn those things about me?" Rochelle asked.

Hanna pushed a piece of straw away. The cat, fresh from a kill, clambered up onto her lap, flopped onto his back and exposed his cotton ball underside. She placed him on the ground. He pounced back onto her lap. She put him down by her feet. He jumped back up. She set him on the straw again.

"Wasn't there just a tiny fleeting thought that crossed your mind, even for just a second that you wondered why, or how, a black woman came to live in your neighborhood? If I were white that thought wouldn't have ever crossed your mind."

Hanna's face became warm. She squirmed. Uncomfortable. "I'm Jewish. I also know about discrimination and persecution," she said, unsticking the needle claws from her jeans.

"I know that. But if you choose not to tell anyone, no one would ever know. You will just fit in because your race is white and it's dominant. I cannot hide this." Rochelle made a cinematic swirl with her hand from her face brushing down and out to the side at her knees. "I can't hide who I am. But we're talking about race. Not religion. You are Jewish by faith. You are of the white *race.*"

Ting sprang onto Hanna's lap. Once again she pried him off and put him at her feet. The persistent kitten, his little cat brain engaged, intended to win the battle. Rochelle counted. Thirteen times he bounded onto Hanna's lap. Rochelle had no idea why she counted. She just did. Things you do to occupy your mind during awkward moments.

"Athletes and entertainers make lots of money but they aren't regular people," Rochelle said. "If you're determined to compare us, then answer this question. How many poor Jewish people do you know? How many Jews live in the inner cities . . . on welfare? How many regular black people do you know who live in affluent communities like this one? How many black kids are encouraged to become something other than an athlete or an entertainer?"

Hanna clutched Ting Tang close to her chest. He grinned as cats do when they win. And the turf beneath Hanna shifted as the river widened. "But isn't it better?"

"I'd love that to be true," Rochelle said. "But what you want, and what's reality, are two different things. People haven't changed all that much. I think they're better *at* being racist."

Ting Tang exploded off Hanna's lap. He charged the length of the barn in pursuit of another moth. A light sprinkle brought the fall smell of leaves, yellow grass, and earth into the barn.

"Crayola Crayons," Rochelle said. "Do you remember those big boxes of sixty-four crayons in school, in that big green and yellow box?"

Those were fond memories. All the pretty colors and all the fun when the teacher brought out the big boxes, one for each table, and told them that they'd have to share. Yes, Hanna remembered.

"Think about when you drew a picture of yourself . . . you just grabbed the crayon with the label that said 'flesh.' That wasn't two hundred years ago. It happened to me, Hanna. How do you deal with that when you are seven years old? And *I'm* the one playing the race card because I'm telling you how much that hurt; that I still remember that?" Rochelle tossed a pebble she'd found out into the paddock.

"I wanted to draw a picture of my daddy. I sat there and tried to come up with a crayon that would color him in. I think 'burnt sienna' was the best I could find. I was so envious. All the white kids could use that flesh-colored crayon. White people have . . . flesh. Wow. I must have something else. When you're seven years old that's how you think. It never went away. It's never once left me."

"But they changed that. They took that crayon out," Hanna said.

"My school had cases of them to use up. It took years."

Hanna thought back to that day in second grade when she spilled milk down the front of her blouse. It was only milk and an accident that didn't matter, but the embarrassment of being singled out as the one who had spilled milk on her blouse stayed with her for life. Her classmates had laughed at her, pointed at her, and avoided her. Even as an adult, whenever she poured milk it had become habit to check the bottom of every carton to make sure it didn't have a crack in it. Being the isolated one, for any reason, *is* a big deal when you are seven years old.

"Go to the store. Go right this minute Hanna Tauber and buy me a box of Band-Aids. Buy me Band-Aids that match me."

The foundation beneath Hanna shifted yet again. If she held still it might stabilize or it might pull her over and send her rumbling down the slope and into that river.

Rochelle continued. "Do you know how it feels to be stopped by the police, pulled over, just because you're black? Do you know about that? My husband, a good doctor, graduated at the top of his class in medical school, drives a new SUV, wears stylish shirts and ties to his office, has been stopped by the police for no reason other than he's a black man."

The sarcasm fired out with the words. "You don't know that for sure." A flashback caught Hanna off guard. She remembered the day when she and her sister, Helen, were traveling to see Mom and Dad in New York. Helen pulled into a gas station to fill the tank. Hanna saw the man again, in her mind. A lone black man bent over a gas can as he filled it. A grass covered lawnmower tied to the door handle with a bungee sat in the bed of his pickup. He never even noticed the car in the bay next to him. Helen clipped right on through, across the street and into another gas station lot. Hanna wanted to chase away that memory now. But she could not shake it. She knew. Had that man been white, she and Helen would have skipped out of the car and pumped the gas they needed. They never discussed it. It never occurred to Hanna, at the time, to ask her sister why she chose to drive away from a perfectly good gas pump to another one all the way across the street. It had been second nature. No thoughts and no questions necessary: avoid the black man.

"Go into any hospital cafeteria and you'll usually see the black staff eating with the black staff and the white staff sitting with the white staff," Rochelle said.

Hanna scowled. She hadn't noticed.

"And then the 'buts' come along," Rochelle said. "I remember once when I was in college, my dorm roommate said that she'd been cramming for a test in the library with a new girl. She said, "Kayleen is Chinese . . . but . . . she's cool.'"

Hanna's feet swirled around in the straw. Her cheeks became so hot she wouldn't dare reach up to touch them. They'd singe her fingers. Ouch. Did that one ever sting.

"I know people have said the same thing about me," Rochelle said. "Why do we have to put the word, 'but' in there?" Rochelle twisted her wedding band. "Yes, it stems from slavery, Hanna. And it has to do with today and tomorrow and the next day and the next."

"My husband said he's been called a dirty Jew before."

"I'm sure he has," Rochelle said. "But we've been talking about race. The worst thing we can do is start comparing notes. We'll end up hating each other trying to prove that our own people are the ones who have suffered the most. It doesn't work. There is nothing you can say to me to convince me that Jews have suffered more than we have and there is nothing I can say to you to convince you that we have suffered the most. I speak about what I know and what I live every day. I'm a black woman. Every one of us has racist tendencies, some type of bias that we carry around with us. Just nobody admits it. We're human, but there's no connection. It's like trying to compare apples to umbrellas. Are apples better or more useful than umbrellas?"

"Which one am I," Hanna asked, "an umbrella or an apple?"

"That's not the point. It doesn't matter. The point is, they are completely different, but they've all been thrown into the same basket. It's not about which one is best or more useful. It's about the differences being so great that there is no common thread that connects us. *That's* the point."

"Maybe you shouldn't dwell so much on the past and all of the negative stuff," Hanna said.

"The laws tell people that discrimination is a thing of the past. But just because there is a law, doesn't change people's hearts."

Safiyyah snuffled and snorted her nose at the chaff. She pushed her water pail over with her muzzle and dumped the water into the straw.

"Things can appear to be smooth until something happens, something that proves that race still divides us, like the differences in how we perceive the stolen car deal. It's still there, always there, under the surface at times, but right there." Rochelle whispered, her thumb and forefinger a hair apart to demonstrate, "right there, waiting. No one wants to admit it."

"I am *so* over slavery," Hanna said.

"I'm sure you are," Rochelle said. "That's because you don't have to live with what it did to you."

"The African chiefs had slaves, too."

"There really is no limit to how you're going to justify this, is there? We're not talking about what happened in foreign countries. We're talking about what happened in this great country of *ours*," Rochelle said. "Nobody wants to own it. Doesn't mean it didn't happen, doesn't mean it didn't destroy lives and someone did it."

Hanna thought about George's father. He said that when the Americans came and the war ended, "No Nazi found anywhere." He'd chuckle, but sorrow riddled the laughter. "Nazi not only one who hate us. School teacher all across Europe, not just German, told other children make fun of Jewish boy in class. Hundred of people, tousand of people, paint sign on park bench telling Jews not to sit. They tell us we can't go to store. Tousand boycott Jewish business and doctor. All people go to church on Sunday, killed

Jews during the week. When war ended, no longer so good to hate Jews . . . no Nazi to be found. Hid like bugs."

Hanna remembered the night that her girlfriends came over so they could all get ready together to go to an outdoor concert in one of the local parks. Hanna, Jill, Carrie, and Lana, all in their early twenties, started talking about their boobs and their butts, as girls do.

"Do I look okay in these jeans?" Lana asked. "How does my butt look?"

Jill pointed to Carrie and said, "*She's* the one who has a nigger butt! Look at that butt!" Everyone laughed. *Hanna* laughed. No one said anything to Jill. But they would be among those who proclaimed, "I'm not racist." *They* were just having fun.

The hot flushes continued to wave over Hanna's cheeks. Why did the blushing go on and on as Rochelle spoke? Why did those blasted scenes keep surfacing?

"It's all over the place. It pops up in so many ways," Rochelle said. She tossed a fist of straw up in the air and then caught it. "White people snicker that we straighten our hair and accuse us of longing to be white. Nobody says nothing if you get a perm or if you bleach your blonde hair whiter still. Don't nobody say nothing if you lay out in the sun to make yourself brown or pay to lie in a chamber that will cook you brown. It's not even for health reasons that you do it. We all know those ultra violet rays are *un*healthy. White people lay out in the sun to make yourselves dark. You want the darkest tan possible. That's what those bottles of suntan lotion promise, right? But that's not enough. You paint or spray yourselves so that you're orange. It's not even a human color. Everyone walking around orange but nobody says nothing. That's okay. Heaven forbid if we do anything like that. So which is it?" she asked, with a sweetly arrogant tone, "Do you want to be brown, like me . . . or do you want to be orange?" She didn't wait for an answer. "Cuz you sure not happy being white."

Hanna sat still. Her face, turned to porcelain, would crack into pieces if she dared flinch. She couldn't move and didn't think she should try.

"Being of the dominant race, you don't have to explain nothing to no one. No one questions the things you do, the choices you make," Rochelle said. She propped her right foot on her left knee, pulled the shoe strings loose and tied them again. She repeated the process with the other foot.

"Remember seeing that old vaudeville act where a guy spins a row of plates mounted on sticks? That's how I think of people. We're all right there next to each other. We can look to the left and look to the right and see the one next to us spinning, just like we are, spinning and spinning, completely independent even though we've all been set to spinning by that same man. Each plate has no connection to the plate next to it. It just knows it's there. We're all just spinning and spinning, whirling all by ourselves, on our own stick that's not connected to the one beside it."

She's good. She's damn good at this. But Hanna wasn't about to tell Rochelle that. She wanted to tell her about the gas station and about the conversation with her girlfriends before the concert, but that would be the admission, and she would be speaking for her entire race. Yet, Hanna knew that by not telling Rochelle, she'd be sweeping it away and not coming clean. She chose the broom.

"I'm not racist," she said.

Rochelle pursed her lips. "No one is."

Hanna and Helen had avoided the man at the gas station, not because he threatened them with a gun, not because they were two women alone. The man hadn't even noticed them. They had driven past him solely because of his color. Where had she learned this? Who had told her to do that? At what point in her life had she learned that it's best to avoid a black man? And for what reason, because he might harm them? It disturbed and confounded Hanna that she couldn't name who had forewarned her. She couldn't remember the day she'd learned that lesson. It irked her. And it proved all the more what Rochelle tried to make her understand.

"You call white people honkies and crackers," Hanna said. The blush spread from her chest to her scalp.

"Some do. Pay back. It feels good to some because for so many years no one could say a name or feeling like that. My dad remembers segregated hotels. He remembers the buses. In *our* lifetime, a black band could play for a white audience but they couldn't stay in a white hotel. My dad remembers the drinking fountains, one marked for whites and one marked for coloreds. Not two centuries ago. It's my dad who lived it."

Hanna fired six red M&Ms into the meat grinder one at a time and chewed them up. "Those same hotels denied Jews, too." She dusted her hands off and clamped them to her hips. "So what is the answer, Rochelle?"

"I don't know. I'm just telling you that it's still here." Rochelle rubbed the dust off her watch. "Let's pretend that there is no racism at all, that it's just in our heads. The mere fact that so many millions of people *believe* it exists, means we have to deal with it." Rochelle shook her head. "Not an easy fix by any means."

"How come it's okay then for rappers to use 'nigger' in their music?"

"Do you have a brother?"

"No," Hanna said, "a sister."

"If I say that your sister is stupid, we're probably going to have some words. You're going to be angry. But *you* can call her anything you want because she's family to you," Rochelle said. "Besides, I don't listen to music that makes me angry."

"What does that mean?"

"Turn the radio off. If what you're listening to angers you . . . don't listen. Nobody making you listen to rap music."

Hanna puttered around in Safiyyah's bucket of brushes, not searching for anything, just for something busy to do. She tapped two brushes together to loosen the dust and ran her fingers through one of them to pull the mane and tail hairs out. "Do you think that those who are racist can become not racist?"

"I don't think a child is born racist," Rochelle said. "We learn it. We learn it first from our parents then from teachers and peers. So if you're not born with it I guess you can unlearn it, discover that you don't have to be that way. But I think it will always be here. Blacks have a long, long way to go to catch up with you. I don't believe for a minute that we'll ever catch up to the point that we are equal because you keep making progress, too, and the gap is too wide. We both make progress. But the gap remains."

Ting Tang returned with a dead moth. He dropped it in front of Hanna. He waited a few seconds. When she didn't spring for it, he ate it. He flipped back and forth in the straw then raced against pretend cats up the loft steps.

Rochelle picked away at a hangnail she thought was there, but didn't exist. She adjusted her engagement ring so that the stone sat on top and tight against the band where it belonged.

Hanna coughed twice; fake, find-something-to-do kind of coughs. She noticed a few new cobwebs above the door. They had all kinds of spiders in the barn; shiny black spiders, furry gray spiders, daddy long legs, and tiny brown spiders. Almost every day Hanna found a new kind of spider.

"It always makes me laugh," Hanna said, trying again, "that people bash Jews and call us Christ Killers, yet around Christmas time, they all have hoards of Jewish people in their yards."

"What do you mean?"

"Nativity scenes."

"That's a good one," Rochelle said, chuckling. "I get it. I get it. But I'm black. I have the right to say that I don't like what goes on. And this is what matters to me." Rochelle said, thinking, *we're not talking about religion, we're talking about race.* She chipped a stalk of straw into quarter inch pieces with her thumbs and forefingers. "It's like when you go into the emergency room with flu symptoms. It doesn't matter that the person next to you is in cardiac arrest, that the doctor's wife just left him, another patient just tried to kill herself, or that two thousand people don't have power. All that matters to you is that they care for *you.*"

Rochelle shrugged. She crunched up more straw into bits.

"What about when white kids beat up a black kid? It's called racism. But if black kids beat up on a white kid it's called nothing," Hanna said. "That's playing the race card."

Rochelle had maintained her composure, but it had worn thin. "And all anyone hears is you poor Jews. You poor little rich

Jew girl. Don't matter if we're talking about race, you gotta throw the religion card into it. Same thing. Gets old."

"Damn you! You make me sick! Why did you move here anyway?" Hanna blinked several times. She seldom swore and she never yelled like that.

The words and the witchy tone burned Rochelle. They both crunched up straw. They didn't look at each other. Safiyyah pushed her empty water bucket toward them with her muzzle. Ting Tang sauntered back into the stall and hopped on the bucket, balancing on the round side like a logroller.

"I'm sorry. I didn't mean to yell at you," Hanna said.

Yes you did, Rochelle thought.

Ting gave up on the bucket and sat next to Rochelle cleaning his face with his paw.

"I don't have all the answers," Rochelle said. "I'm not the encyclopedia on racism. I'm one black woman. That's it. I don't have all the answers for you. Don't expect that of me. Don't expect me to be your answer. Don't expect me to take you on as my responsibility. You will never understand what it means to be black." Rochelle peeled a cobweb off one of the kitten's ears. "Don't you see when we go into town how clerks stare?"

"Maybe they're staring because we're new in town."

"You don't get it," Rochelle said. "You never will. You can't."

"Because I can't change places with you, because I'm not black, doesn't make me slime."

"I didn't say that! Don't stretch it to something I didn't say. I said that it's impossible for *any* white person to understand what it means to be black. It's like, as much as we love Safiyyah, there is no way for us to understand what it means to *be* her, how it feels, how she perceives things. It's not possible to do. *That's* how different things are for whites and blacks," Rochelle said. "We have absolutely nothing in common with this horse other than we share the same air and walk on the same ground."

Hanna picked up the newspaper. "Here's another article about the same woman and it's written by a black man. He sees it differently. He says that blacks are making too much of this, that since the woman recanted her story people shouldn't think of her as being racist." She put the paper down. "What do you think of that? Maybe it's not so bad. If a black man can see that it's not an issue about race, maybe he's right."

Rochelle said nothing. She said nothing to the extent that it made Hanna fidget. Hanna pulled a stem of hay out of the end of her braid. She slapped sand off her jeans, skimmed dirt out from under a fingernail, and started to whistle, though she never whistled. Finally, she sat down next to Rochelle on the sofa. What else was there to do? No bridge spanned across that widening river. She shrugged her shoulders and they brushed against Rochelle's shoulders.

"When I was in third grade," Hanna said, "there was a girl in class, Denise. A few times a week she would pee her pants right at her desk. All of the other kids called her names, like, 'peebody', and they all ran from her like she was a demon. The janitor would have to come in and clean up the mess and Denise would run into the cloak room in tears. I never poked fun at her. I never called her a name. I even told the other kids to stop teasing her."

"But did you sit with her at lunch?"

The tip of the sword pierced Hanna. "No. No, I didn't."

Rochelle sighed and leaned back.

Hanna sighed and leaned back.

Safiyyah walked out of her stall. She rolled in her sandy paddock, shook herself off, yawned, and came back in.

"When I was in fifth grade," Rochelle said, "there was a boy named Frank. White boy. His face and body were disfigured by a fire. His family lost everything when their home burned to the ground. Wherever Frank went, he ran full tilt. He'd be going so fast he couldn't stop and he'd smash into a wall or a door, like an alien had hold of him. Everyone, black and white, snickered at him and mocked him when he smacked into things. They called him a monster. I always wanted to go up to him and ask him why he ran."

"Did you?"

"No. But he is one of the main reasons I went into nursing. If he only knew . . ."

It had been a noble career choice for Rochelle, but whatever success she'd achieved over the years grew weightless at the moment. Frank needed to know that she had noticed him *then*.

The two women occupied a horse's stall and shared in its busy, fragile life. The boards creaked. The horse snorted. Her tail swished. Leaves scraped across the paddock in front of the door. A mouse twitched its nose. A spider bit into a dead fly trapped in dust-powdered wrapping. The sparrow flew in and out again. She carried a twig in her beak.

"We moved here for the same reasons you did," Rochelle said. "We wanted to try another place than the city . . . a quiet place. Marc wants to fish. He never got to do things like that as a kid in the city, never had time as an adult with his city practice. They say there are lots of huge fish in Lake Luffit. But it's not easy. We're kind of alone."

Hanna thought about that. She had seen only a few black people in town and it struck her as unusual, unusual enough that she'd noticed.

"There are two other black doctors at the hospital, some nurses, and a few orderlies. That's it," Rochelle said. "There are a few elderly people who live on the shore. They own the bait shops. Not many others."

Safiyyah came up to them. Bored, she pushed into Rochelle's hands and forced them open. The mare's muzzle rooted around as she searched for the apple she believed should be there.

"What determines whether a person is racist or not, is what you laugh about, how you talk, in the privacy of your own home, in the company of your own race," Rochelle said. "If I tell Jewish jokes with my other friends, but I don't tell them to you, what does that make me? If I don't tell you the same jokes, then I know better. I know what I'm doing."

Rochelle continued. "Consider this. Some white people have that one black friend. They're quick to tell everyone that they can't be racist because, 'I have a black friend.' And they take that black friend to all of the fun things they can think of . . . one solitary black person at an all white party. But would they go with that black friend into their world; to the inner city of Chicago, Detroit, or New York and be the lone white person at an all black gathering?"

Safiyyah pawed the stall floor right in front of them. Once she had their attention, she waited politely. They managed a stilted and choppy laugh. This prompted Rochelle to fish the apple out from behind the sofa where she'd hidden it and begin cutting it up with her knife for their impatient buddy. She fed Safiyyah small pieces, sneaking a slice for herself now and then.

"Rochelle, where are the books?" Hanna said, bug-eyed. "Where is the book bag?"

"They were right beside us," Rochelle said. She stood up and kicked through the straw. "Oh, no," she said, and held up the straw-filled book bag. "Safiyyah took it." Rochelle clawed the straw out of the bag. "There's eleven in here. We're missing one."

Hanna shuffled around in the bedding. Her foot tunked against an object. She pulled the book on horse breeds from deep within the straw. Its cover had been broken and all of the pages from one to fifty-eight fashioned into a solid clump, one giant spitball.

"What are we going to do?" Hanna said. "I'm taking the books back tonight."

"Just tell Mildred the truth and offer to pay for it. That's all we can do."

They trudged home. They made clumsy attempts at bites of conversation. Neither would have returned to the barn the following morning had it not been for the horse. But just like employees forced to work together, they would return and make the best of it.

CHAPTER THIRTEEN

AFTER SUPPER THAT evening, Hanna hopped into her Jeep and drove to the library. It stayed open until nine on Wednesdays.

"Good evening," Mildred said. "Did you enjoy the books?"

"Yes. But I have to show you this one. I'll gladly pay for it."

She'd put the book, or what was left of it, in a garbage bag. With its sprung cover, the book no longer fit into the book bag. To make it fit she would have had to break the cover into pieces. She offered the book to Mildred. "My horse ate it," Hanna said.

Mildred examined the object that had once been a fine book. The cover, open and cracked down the middle, stuck straight up, like the mast and sails on a ship.

Ghastly, Mildred thought of the now hardened wad of pages. She shook her head at the sadness of it all. *They always say, 'my dog ate it.'* Once, it had been a goat, but never a horse. "Oh dear," she said.

"I'll pay for it. I know it's an expensive book. Just tell me what I owe you. I'm sorry. She didn't mean to do it."

"I shall have to let the director see it. He will have to decide if we should bill you for it or if it's one we can just write off. I will call you and let you know."

"I really am sorry," Hanna said. "It won't ever happen again."

"Don't worry about it. Things like this happen." Mildred quickly recovered. She patted Hanna's wrist. "Where is your friend, that nice colored lady?"

Tossed into the spotlight and expected to perform, Hanna's thoughts ricocheted throughout her skull for the right response. She moved in close enough to see that Mildred had one brown eye and one hazel eye. "What color might you suppose she is; green, blue maybe?"

Mildred jerked back. Her face flooded near burgundy.

Hanna turned and walked out of the library. When she got to the safety of the Jeep, her nerves churned like a washing machine idling between rinse and spin. She'd asserted herself, yet gloom closed in around her, all because she'd opened her mouth.

"I don't think I'll be going back there any time soon," she said. *Is Mildred racist? Maybe no one told her that we don't use that word anymore.* Hanna felt bad—for Mildred. Then she felt angry because of those feelings. Mildred was wrong.

Later, Hanna sat at the kitchen table with George. She watched him spoon up butter pecan ice cream from a bowl.

"Do you think it's difficult for Marc to be a doctor in Lake Luffit because he's black?" she asked.

"It's probably been difficult for him in any town. People say he's a great doctor. I'm surprised you haven't already invited them over for dinner. Why don't you?"

"Do you think that most people are racist?"

"Two ways of looking at it: some people are racist and some people are just underexposed to people of different cultures and backgrounds."

"If someone used the word 'colored' would you think they are racist or underexposed?"

"That depends. Some people are ignorant. It's like when you hear people say they jewed the price down. Once you tell them that it's offensive, they aren't anti-Semitic if they refrain from using it. They just didn't know, because they've heard the phrase used and didn't think anything of it. If they persist, then there's probably more to it."

"That's what I figured."

"I suppose if a person said the word colored they might not know any different," George said. He spooned up the last pecan in his bowl. "What's with you tonight? You're really into this."

"Rochelle told me that people don't make the effort, everybody just kind of sticks to their own kind. That they don't even sit together at lunch."

"When I was in law school," George said, "whites sat together in the university cafeteria and the blacks sat together. Then along came Gordon Dunnings. Gordie always had a mission. He adopted one cause after the next. One day he went over to the lunch table where a certain group of black students always sat. There was plenty of room for Gordie. He took his lunch tray over there and sat at their table." George licked his spoon. "All of the black students got up and moved to another table."

Hanna didn't want to hear that story. She wanted the black students to embrace Gordie, proving that racial tension wasn't that bad, and proving Rochelle incorrect.

"Did you see the article in the paper today about the woman who blamed a black guy for taking her car and then changed her story?" Hanna asked.

"Yeah, I did. What about it?"

"Did you see the article just below it by that black writer? He said that blacks were making too much of it and overreacting to call it racism."

"He's a new columnist," George said. "That's his first column. He's a black columnist working at an all white newspaper. I would imagine he wants to keep his job. He's going to write what they want to see. It takes a strong person to be assertive and it takes a doubly stronger minority to be assertive. Nobody wants to make waves. People stay on the surface where it's safe. We don't dive in. None of us. If I asked you if I was getting a paunch, you wouldn't come out and totally agree with me. You'd say things to lighten the truth. If you ask black friends if they encounter racism, most are going to tell you that they don't, because they don't want to rock the boat. Lots of white people find consolation in saying that they've asked all of their black friends if racism is an issue for them, and the black friends assure them that it's not. That's all it is. Consolation. Doesn't change a damn thing."

George opened the freezer. "Do we have any more ice cream?"

CHAPTER FOURTEEN

MARC WAS IN bed but awoke to mutter a few words and kiss Rochelle on the lips when she came into the bedroom. In the darkness he became one with the night, such was the intensity of his coloring. The night existed as with a matte finish. Marc's darkness pulsed with hues that changed in depth and vibrancy with every breath he took and with every move he made. She loved to see him lying like that; shirtless, in the dark. He slept again.

The old scar bubbled up to reach her as she traced its outline, just as she'd done so many times before. The jagged knife wound from Marc's youth hadn't been sutured when the injury occurred.

Raised in foster homes since infancy, Marc made it to adulthood never having called the same woman, Mom. His last foster mother treated him with indifference, though she never abused him. Her friend, Edgar, came in and out of the apartment, like the mouse that snuck under the door at night, at will, and always searching for something. Marc watched Edgar steal from his foster mom. He'd take half the money from the Maxwell House can in the kitchen and lift a few bills from her purse. Marc knew that Edgar used the money to buy drugs.

Marc missed a lot of school. If he found something more interesting to do, he'd skip. Some days, he played down by the stinky river that lounged beside the railroad tracks. The desire to do well in school, and knowledge of a world beyond a stinky river, had no way to flow into Marc's thoughts no more than a stinky river is able to contemplate the Sun.

Marc's school took pride in being an equal opportunity school. Yet, the white boys joined the math and science clubs, the debate teams, and the music groups. The black boys played basketball. One day, one of those white boys, John Matthew Hanley III, (Marc and his friends called him Handjob) taunted Marc. "That's all you can do, isn't it?"

Marc answered. He made a basket. He sent that ball right through the gymnasium window, shattering it. The principal suspended Marc from school for a week and he got kicked off the basketball team for good. He would never again pick up a basketball. The night after it happened, Marc snuck into a game anyway, just to watch. Handjob sat on the top rung of the bleachers with Ava, the most popular girl in school, cheering for his school's team. Every single player on that team was black.

They found shards of glass for weeks.

By the time Marc turned sixteen he'd been lifting Edgar's drugs and selling them out on the streets for two years. He got real good at selling them right back to the same dealer. He didn't care. He made money and he made a name for himself.

Marc never joined a gang. He preferred to walk the streets alone. His world changed one night as he prowled through a back alley on the way home. Older boys snarled in hushed tones and scuffled. There was a scream, whispers, and then the gang ran straight at him, like bulls scrambling on the streets of Spain, desperate to make a getaway. They pushed into him and knocked him flat on his back to the dank pavement.

One of them, Derrick Norton, crouched over the top of Marc. Marc knew him from grade school. Derrick was two years older than Marc and had dropped out of school in the eighth grade. But Derrick, too stoned, didn't recognize Marc. The knife flashed in the moonlight and Marc flipped onto his side, just in time. The blade missed his chest and slashed through the skin on his left arm.

Derrick hissed, rose up to strike, like an asp. He stunk of old sweat, old beer, and old cigarettes; a rank smell, one you never forget. His body, too wired, jigged in spasms from whatever drugs he'd popped that evening. A dangerous combination of crud and nerves coursed in his blood and possessed his body and mind. Derrick would have stuck Marc again, and finished the job, but one of the others barked orders to him to flee.

Marc lay on his back, bleeding and dazed. He listened to the racing footsteps fade. All sound, the stars above, and his pain, blurred in and out. He got to his feet and staggered to the overturned trashcans where the boys had been. He knew he would find the body of a rival gang member or some other wretched soul who'd been in the wrong place at the wrong time. He held onto his arm and felt the warm stickiness seep through his jacket. He kicked the man lying in the garbage. The man didn't move. Marc bent over to get a closer look at the face. Joey Pete, a homeless wino. His pockets had been pulled inside out and the exposed white lining swayed like miniature ghosts.

Marc ran. He ran as fast as he could out of the alley, thinking over and over, *one used cigarette butt, all for one used cigarette butt.* He ran in the dark, in the cold, alone and scared, as light snow flakes fell. He ran to his girlfriend's apartment. Neva bandaged the wound as best she could, chattering nonstop, "You need to go to the hospital." Marc stayed with Neva, at her mom's, for a week. Then he went back to the streets. He never went home.

Two weeks later, his buddy, Reggie, introduced him to a new guy, Tyree. Marc handed Tyree the Percodan tablets and collected forty bucks as they'd agreed upon. Tyree turned out to be Officer Louis Wilkins. Marc got arrested for selling drugs. But the police and the prosecutor had more interest in gang activity. Marc identified Derrick Norton and the police arrested him for the murder of Joey Pete. Derrick confessed and coughed up the names of his gang members and the other crimes they had committed. Marc didn't have to testify against any of them.

"You were good in math and biology," Mr. Parsons, the juvenile officer said.

No one had ever noticed anything good about Marc. Marc hadn't noticed either.

Henry Parsons was black. Marc hated him.

Over the course of a month of sessions with Mr. Parsons, a portly man with a graying, reddish Afro, who viewed his captives with unwavering boldness, unraveled a plan. If Marc would go to school, work hard and get good grades, he would become eligible for a special grant that would send him to college. As a late teenager, Marc's only alternative might be jail time. His charge had been reduced from selling drugs to possession.

Marc graduated at the top of his class, the first black student at his high school to seize that title. He poured all of the ingredients of his past into his studies in medical school, and once again, graduated with honors. Mr. Parsons came to Marc's graduation from medical school. No one else came. Mr. Parsons hugged him and said, "I'm so proud of you son."

Five years ago, Mr. Parsons passed away. Marc went to the funeral. He learned from Carolyn, Mr. Parson's daughter, that there hadn't been any special grant. Henry Parsons had used inheritance money to pay for Marc's education himself.

Marc's empathy for people and his quiet, humble demeanor attracted Rochelle when they met in the emergency room. As the rage of his youth had fallen away, the kindest, gentlest soul that she'd ever known emerged in its place, and stayed. Marc never fully embraced what he had achieved. He seemed awed, like it all might break and crash to the ground if he tried to touch it. He even refused to drive the Jaguar. "That's too much for me baby," he said.

Rochelle had come from a different type of home. Her father was the pastor of the local Methodist church, a position he'd held his entire life. Her mom stayed home and worked on crafts with other ladies from church. They sold their potholders, baby booties, and quilts at local craft shows and the annual church bazaar. Rochelle had two siblings; an older sister, Rhonda, and a baby brother, Joseph. Her family didn't have monetary riches by any means but they had a certain day to day comfort that Marc had never known. Rochelle couldn't understand what it meant to be Marc. She was no more capable of feeling it than the Sun is capable of changing places with the river.

Marc had been plucked out of the heaving torrent of the inner city. He had hoped to complete his internship at the hospital where he and Rochelle met and then go back home to set up his practice there. But the resentment at home proved intolerable. The people refused to come to him for medical care. The night he made the decision to leave, he said, "Rochelle, I feel like an oddity. I'll never fit in. Not with us. Not with them. They need me in the inner city, yet they don't want me."

When Community General Hospital offered him a residency, he'd nearly collapsed under the weight of the decision. Only a traitor deserted the brothers and sisters in the inner city. He had vowed that he would never do what so many did: reach success and then leave. But he did.

Rochelle supported his decision. "You are a fine doctor. You have to go where there is a position for you."

Marc worked hard to prove himself at Community General, much harder than any white man had to do. The care of his patients absorbed him. Patients and worried family members could call him at home at all hours of the night, and he'd be there for them. He'd listen. Only Rochelle knew that he'd remain awake for hours thinking about them.

Marc never had a hobby. When he said that he'd like to move to the country, near a lake, so that he could fish, Rochelle would do nothing to deny him that one special request. He hadn't been out on Lake Luffit once.

Rochelle kissed him on the forehead. She kissed the scar and turned out the light.

Rochelle awoke the next morning, thinking, *I'm getting too old to deal with this.* She didn't want to return to the barn. But she thought of Safiyyah. Two people caring for her and sharing the responsibilities were best for the horse. *What if Hanna decides not to return and I don't either? What happens to Safiyyah?*

CHAPTER FIFTEEN

HANNA USUALLY PLAYED music at the barn everyday. Rochelle only heard it when she came through the door. Bach, Mozart, or the notes of another classical composer wafted out in soothing or dramatic tones from the CD player. But this music, pounded from the barn clear to the driveway.

"No, no, no," Rochelle said when she got close enough to recognize Marvin Gaye's smooth voice sifting through the lyrics of *Grapevine*. "She didn't. Please, someone, tell me she didn't." She wished she'd stayed home in bed.

Rochelle didn't know what to say. She'd dealt with this before: white people, so determined to prove they aren't racist, have to show you their interest in all-things-black. They would be all nervous and smiley. She expected Hanna to do the same. Perhaps she'd proudly ask (as if Rochelle hadn't noticed) "What do you think?" But Hanna continued pulling on the strings of the hay bale she'd heaved down from the loft, coaxing it across the floor, all the while bobbing her head in all the right places in time to the music.

Rochelle let her backpack fall to her feet. "You didn't have to do this."

Hanna jerked upright, spun the braid behind her. "I didn't have to do what? Bring Marvin Gaye with me? Did you think I did that for you? Now it's my turn, Rochelle. You had to ruin this moment. You've probably ruined the day. I came out here happy as a clam with my favorite music."

Rochelle plunked down onto a hay bale, deflating as she went down.

"Yes. That's right," Hanna said. "It's my favorite music."

"But you're a classical flutist."

"I *play* classical. I *listen* to Motown."

Sometimes it irritated Rochelle when white people gushed over black music. She surmised that they said they liked it because some of them had to prove, to none other than themselves, that they aren't racist. "Why didn't you bring it before?" she asked.

"Because I didn't want you to think I was doing it just for you and I didn't think you'd believe me. That's what some white people have to deal with, like we don't deserve the music, like we don't understand the music, like we're doing it just to prove we aren't racist." Hanna bellowed over the top of Marvin Gaye, sharply enunciating each word, her arms open with hands out to the sides. "Not everything has to do with race, Rochelle, not . . . every . . . single . . . thing!"

Hanna eased down her own speaking volume. "This time, this time, it's got nothing to do with race. I know how difficult it was for all of those musicians. I've read their stories and I know what they went through."

No you don't, Rochelle thought.

"I can't take away slavery. But I didn't enslave your people. My people, my family didn't enslave your people. I can't take away ugly attitudes cops might have and I can't stop being white. But this time, this one time, I will stand toe to toe with you on the exact same turf where no racism exists and tell you that I love them. I love all of them. I love them because of their music, for the sheer brilliance of their work. When Motown ended I cried for days. I played classical music as a kid but my heart beat to Motown. So I don't care if you don't like it that I love Motown. It doesn't change it. You'll not take that away from me, Rochelle. You'll never take that away from me!

"Maybe you wish I was a black woman who found a starved horse and maybe I do wish it was a white woman because things wouldn't be so awkward. I wouldn't feel like I'm walking on egg shells. We'd both have the comfort and ease with our own people and we'd never have to discuss race or tiptoe around it. But *this,* Rochelle, *this* is what we got," Hanna said, out of steam. Her lip trembled. "You got me."

The CD player said, "Click." Marvin was done singing for the day.

"I'm sorry. I'm really sorry about slavery," Hanna said. "I'm sorry that Africans were brought over here, not to follow their own dreams, but to be workhorses for the dreams of others. I'm getting it. I'm trying to get it. I may not have always said the right things and I'll still screw up. But I don't *want* to. Can't that count for something?"

Rochelle had white friends scattered here and there throughout her life. She even dated a white boy for a while in high school before she met Alonzo. She hadn't had a best friend, other than Marc, since her teens. She'd never had a white girl as a best friend, never would have picked a white woman to be her best friend, and she wasn't sure she liked it now. But in the dim light of a lonesome barn, over the days and weeks they'd spent together caring for a neglected horse, that's what brewed. It must have been a mutual feeling, because both came back to the barn. And no—it hadn't just been about the horse.

Hanna dropped both hands down onto her hips. She put her butt down on the hay bale that she'd left in the middle of the aisle, the one she'd been tugging on. Rochelle remained seated on the bale that had already been pushed up against the wall. Safiyyah peeked over the stall door wanting *her* hay.

"Did you bring anyone else?" Rochelle asked.

Hanna fumbled in her bag. She picked up one CD, dropped it, picked it up, and dropped it again. At first, Rochelle thought it funny watching Hanna squirm under her scrutiny. Then she wished she could wave away the heavy awkwardness that had settled on Hanna. Rochelle didn't want to make her feel that nervous.

Hanna fashioned a pinched smile. She held the CD up in her fist at last. Triumph. "Smokey," she said.

CHAPTER SIXTEEN

"YOU'RE QUIET TODAY," Rochelle said. She poured fresh water into Safiyyah's bucket. She patted the mare on her neck and told her "good girl." Her breath swirled up in a white plume as she spoke. The frost of winter had arrived.

"George's mom called. She wants to go to Belgium and to Germany and she wants George to go with her. She's a camp survivor."

"Camp survivor," Rochelle said, "as in, concentration camp survivor? Was your family impacted?"

"No. It didn't touch us, no one in my immediate family. But George's mom and dad are both camp survivors. Dachau."

"Wow."

Hanna forked out three flakes of hay for Safiyyah. She carefully unwound a few pieces of straw from the horse's mane. She didn't want to break any of the long, silken hairs by pulling on them. She pushed her hand up into the mane to bump into the blue bead.

"There's a new Holocaust memorial being dedicated and they want to go. George is quite involved in Holocaust things. Before we moved here we used to go home to see his parents and spend a few days with them for any memorials and services," Hanna said. "And now they want to travel to Europe."

"Is he going to go? Will you go with him? I can manage the chores here."

"No. George can't break away right now. And I wouldn't go. Period."

Hanna said it with conviction. Rochelle became speechless and uncomfortable.

"George preaches over and over, that it was the single most catastrophic event in the history of mankind. That it so profoundly influenced, and still influences, every human on this planet, that I just can't delete it. It's not that I'm trying to delete it. I just don't want to be confined by it. Does that make any sense?"

Rochelle didn't answer. She listened.

"I'm the worst Jew for feeling this way. George doesn't understand it." Hanna paused. She twiddled the lead rope. "Whenever a new movie or a new book comes out about the Holocaust, I kind of get angry. I get angry because it happened. I get angry because I want it behind me. Sometimes I don't know why it makes me angry. I just don't want to talk about it, live it everyday. It's part of my history as a Jew, but it's not my personal history. I want it to be history. Not *now*. I refuse to let it shape who I am. It really scared me when I first learned about it as a little kid. Sometimes I used to have nightmares about the sound of boots stomping behind me and I could never run fast enough to get away. But then I'd wake up."

"Hanna, sometimes you can't just dump things in the past and leave them there, like they never happened. Sometimes you *do* have to face what's happened."

Safiyyah turned two small circles with her knees and hocks buckled and eased her body down onto the straw, as if to get the best seat in the house. She pricked her ears forward, attentive to her two pals.

"And isn't remembering it supposed to remind humanity to not ever do that again?" Rochelle said. "And there are still people grieving, like George's folks."

"I just don't want it to be what defines me, identifies me."

"But you brought it up." Rochelle flicked a spider off Hanna's head. "Chaff," she said.

"That's because I always feel like crap about it, and normally, I don't have anyone to tell that I feel like crap. I'm not good at being Jewish. George is good at being good and good at being a good Jew. I'm only good at being me and some days I have no clue what that means. I guess it means I'm selfish. I always do exactly as I please. Fortunately, I don't think I ever hurt anybody, or do anything bad. For example, if I wanted to eat this whole bag of M&Ms I would do it and never offer you one. It's only because I want to offer them to you that I will. Do you see what I mean?"

Rochelle shook her head, no, thinking, *getting weird.*

"I don't rob banks because I don't want to," Hanna said. "But if I wanted to, I would. George likes to tease me about that. He says that if I decided to rob banks, I'd be the best bank robber the world had ever seen."

At last, an opening, and Rochelle intended to charge through it. Hanna used the word 'tease.' The boulder weight of the conversation might be easing up.

"Girl, you are wacko," Rochelle said. "You know you are a wacko woman. You do know that, don't you? Honestly. Robbing banks?"

Hanna bumped her head back against the wall. "I suppose some would say so." She laughed. "I think wacko woman fits."

"If you do decide to start robbing banks, don't take me with you, okay?" Rochelle said. She had no intent to set one foot into the Holocaust.

The two barn mice ventured out into the open. Ting had no interest in mice, only in moths. He sat near the mice and watched them as they went about their mouse errands.

Hanna opened up the bag of candy and offered it first to Rochelle, grinning at her hospitality. She poured each of them a cup of coffee from the elderly Thermos that George had won at a bingo game with his mom when he was fourteen. Amazing it still worked.

Dachau. Rochelle itched to type a search into the computer right then. But she'd wait until she got home. She would learn that the camp conducted experiments on Jews. They used them for freezing experiments, high altitude experiments, malaria experiments, and tuberculosis experiments. She would learn how the Nazis worked the Jews to death and viewed it merely as production loss since a never ending supply of laborers came into the camp. She would learn that tens of thousands of people had been murdered there, that it had a crematorium on site, and that near the end of the war, thousands of prisoners were forced on a death march. Americans intercepted the march and also freed those left at the camp, in April of 1945.

Were George's mom and dad victims of those experiments? How many people did they see die beside them? Were they on the death march?

Rochelle filled the marble sink in her bathroom with warm water to wash her face. She accidentally dropped the cap to her cleanser bottle into the water. She plucked it from the surface before it filled and sank. But the water remained disturbed and carried ripples to the edges of the basin.

Some would refuse to embrace the truth.

Some would refuse to pick up a basketball.

> *Run child, run*
> *Run fast as you can*
> *Run from the ovens*
> *And run from the sheets*
> *Unwanted unwanted*
> *They catch you*
> *They stomp you*
> *They crush you*
> *And bleed you*
> *Barb-wire you in*
> *They hold you and mold you*
> *Disposal disposal*
> *And never let you go*
> *Run child, run*
> *Run fast as you can*
> *Take here your ticket*
> *And spin with it all*

They catch you
They grind you
They cook you
They eat you
Told you and scold you
Never set you free
Try child, try
Try fast as you can

CHAPTER SEVENTEEN

"I BROUGHT MUSIC," Rochelle said, two nights later when they met to do evening chores. "I think you'll like it."

Hanna sniffed the air. "What do I smell burning?"

"I found a few ratty old hay bales. I put them in the middle of the paddock and I'm burning them. They're smoldering."

"Safiyyah isn't afraid of it?"

"No. She just watched me. Don't worry, no one can see it."

Rochelle put the CD into the player and punched the play button.

"What is it?"

"Music from Africa."

The drums exploded and seized Hanna. Their soul-taking and soul-lifting power filled her mind and her chest with deep, resonant vibrations.

Rochelle rapped out the beat against her thighs. She swayed low and turned and pivoted. She cranked the volume up and motioned for Hanna to follow as she walked backward, gesturing that they needed more room. Safiyyah followed them. She wouldn't miss out on anything that they could do together.

Hanna lifted her face to the sky. The stars appeared in the lavender dusk. The last rays of the sun shone through Safiyyah's flagged tail as the mare trotted in circles opposite them, around the fire, and with them. The dust rose from the ground. The fire, like an offering, lifted the smoke to the heavens. Hanna closed her eyes.

The warmth, the sounds, the night of another place, another time; another continent stole her away.

Drums beating in the moonlight, faster, faster, lions watching in the firelight, savanna song, Sahara song, blood song, Nile song, white horse dancing in the moonlight, swirling, trotting, dancing around the fire, spinning, spinning, twirling, twirling, letting go, letting go, dancing in the dust cloud, dancing in the firelight, dance of anger, memory fire, dance of answers, dance of truth.

Drums pounding, dancing faster, faster, not here, not here, someplace else, someplace free, someplace dancing on the clouds, dancing on the savanna, spinning low, spinning high, twirl it all away, blood dance, smoke in the moonlight, eyes watching, feet moving, white horse, faster, faster, must go faster, faster in the dust, fast as the drums, twirl the pain away, twirl for him, twirl him gone, gone, gone away, twirl it away, dance of freedom, dance of joy.

Free in the dark, free in the fire, free in the drums.

The only light on in the home was the bedroom light upstairs. George parked the Lexus at the garage door and left it out for the night. He walked into a quiet house, slipped off his oxfords, and padded up the stairs.

She'd showered. She sat on the edge of the bed with one leg curled beneath her and the other, just the toe, swirled in the carpet fibers. Her loose hair enclosed her, a tawny satin cape that shimmered in the tender light.

That hair. Whenever George held her and kissed her, he sank into it. It hung just below her buttocks and was so thick that it took a full day to dry when she washed it. In their youth she'd worn it free. As she and George settled into marriage and a comfortable routine, things changed. One day, she braided her hair into a single huge rope at the back of her head. A few days later she braided it again. Eventually, it was always confined in a braid. But not tonight.

Hanna, surprised, yet expecting him, cocked her head over her shoulder, casting that sideways peek through her hair.

He'd wanted to ask her about the can of Friskies at the bottom of the grocery bag forgotten on the counter. Maybe she'd bought it for Rochelle. *Yes, that's it. They must have a cat.* But when he walked into the bedroom, all reasoning, all thoughts, whittled away. His gaze lingered on her naked body. She would be fifty-one soon. But he saw the same young woman he'd fallen in love with years ago. She moved toward him with seductive steps. Her emerald eyes blazed into him and she breezed into his arms. She kissed him sweetly, yet it was a kiss heavy with promise. Most times, nerves got the best of her and she giggled. But not tonight. She loosened his tie and unbuttoned his shirt. She kissed his mouth, his neck, and her lips swept down to his chest. George pulled her up to him and he kissed her with unrestrained ardor. He thrust his hands through her hair and drank in the scent of her; the clean, fresh smell of the recent shower mixed with vanilla body mist. Her hair, dry and messy, smelled of dust and wood and . . . *charcoal?* He buried his face into it, transported somewhere else, somewhere wild.

George Tauber turned over in his king-sized bed, rubbed his eyes, and peered into his wife's face. She still slept but began to stir. He kissed her. And he remembered. "That will go down in history as the single most amazing night of my life," he whispered, "ever." He said it low enough that she didn't hear him, yet he wanted it to penetrate. He wanted her to know. He kissed her on the forehead. He watched her sleep. She loved him. He knew that now. He'd believed that she blamed him for causing her so much pain. She'd rejected him sexually so many times, rejected his masculinity, and that ruptured his identity. A wretched sliver, it had become imbedded into him. But for Hanna to love him like she had in the night, to touch him the way that she had, and to allow him to touch her in the way that he had, gave him proof enough. Proof enough to split his doubts. Proof enough to carry him on.

"I love you," he said when she opened her eyes to see his lashes just inches from her face. He kissed her on the cheek. His words filled her as the finest music. He'd said it. He said, "I love you." She couldn't remember the last time she'd heard those words.

"What time is it?" she mumbled. Her brain tried to chase sleep out of her bones.

"I don't know. Does it matter?" George said. Some things never change.

"I've got to get to the ba . . ." She stopped her sentence. She'd almost said that she had to get to the barn. She covered it and said, "Breakfast. I have to get to the breakfast."

George burst out laughing. "I don't think we're going to starve."

He kissed her again on the mouth. He moved his body over and just above hers, ready. She lifted her hands up. Her fingers fanned across his chest and moved like feathers down to his hips. They made love again. And then again.

CHAPTER EIGHTEEN

"SHE'S LOOKING GOOD. Don't you think?" Rochelle said. The mare's ribs were only visible now when she took a deep breath. Her flanks had filled in and her attitude seemed to send the years running backward. "She's sassy now."

Safiyyah's feet would never be sound. She would always be 'gimpy' as Josh said. But she had become living definition of the word, joy. She cantered everyday with her tail held high over her back. And always, she glided into that magical, airy trot.

On a brisk afternoon, Safiyyah snorted and pranced away from them. She raised and lowered her head, up and down, up and down. The veins bulged all over her body.

"What's up with her?" Rochelle said. "She's upset, like she's afraid."

Safiyyah wouldn't let Hanna touch her. The mare snorted and trotted away, blasting from her nostrils. Safiyyah steadfastly scrutinized the back fence and some creature crouched next to a gathering of ferns near a fence post. Hanna snuck up to this creature. It didn't scamper into the brush. As she got closer, she yelled at it, but the critter didn't run off. Hanna inched forward until she was standing right over it. She bent over the creature and then whooped with laughter. "You silly goose, it's just a bird's nest!"

Hanna picked up the abandoned nest. It had fallen from the blue spruce tree just on the other side of the fence rails. She handed it to Rochelle. "Can you imagine being afraid of this?" Hanna said.

Rochelle examined the nest, turning it over in her hands. It had been built of grass, a few twigs for added stability, horse hair, and black yarn. She held it out for Safiyyah to examine. The mare sniffed it but refused to take one step closer to the dreadful object.

"Look at her. She's leaning so far forward to check it out, she's about to fall over, but she's not going to come anywhere near it," Rochelle said. She flipped the nest over quickly and Safiyyah spun away, bucking and squealing. They laughed so hard that their jaws and their sides cramped. Safiyyah kept herself at a safe distance in the far back corner of the paddock. She wasn't coming anywhere near them until they got rid of the dangerous thing.

Hanna put the nest outside the front door to the barn so that Safiyyah would never have to see it again. Ting Tang waltzed by, took a whiff, and carted the nest off as the true prize it was. Once Safiyyah was convinced that the wretched object had disappeared, she inspected her yard to make sure it was safe, and then jogged into her stall.

"Oh, Saffy . . . you are so silly," Hanna said.

"What did you just call her?"

"Saffy."

"We gave her such a gorgeous name and now you are calling her Saffy?"

"Yep. And it gets worse," Hanna said. "I also call her Saffy Taffy."

"That's awful! She has a beautiful name . . . just be quiet. I don't want to hear anymore," Rochelle said.

"And . . . Taff Taff."

Rochelle put her hands over her ears and started to sing.

A few days later, Rochelle made a troubling observation. "Did you clean the paddock this morning?" she asked. "Because it was my turn." They took turns making sure the stall was clean. They picked the poops out of the paddock and tossed them over the fence into the woods.

"No, I didn't. I thought you already did. There weren't any poops, not in the stall, and not outside."

"That's odd," Rochelle said. "She usually goes a lot in the night."

Safiyyah gathered her legs close together. She pawed, dropped to the ground and rolled. She stood up, and minutes later, rolled again. She came into the stall and threw her body down onto the straw.

"This isn't like her," Rochelle said.

The mare got up and went out to the paddock. They followed. The horse rolled again. She kicked at her belly. She put her ears back and barred her teeth at her left side.

"I don't think this is good," Rochelle said. "Something's wrong."

Hanna ran to the stall and revved up the lap top. "It sounds like it might be colic. It's an emergency. She could die from it."

"We've got to call a vet," Rochelle said.

"No!"

They effectively convinced themselves why they shouldn't call. "We don't own her." "We're not the ones to authorize treatment." "The vet would refuse treatment anyway if the owners aren't here." "Who would we call on such short notice? It's not like we've got a rapport with any vet."

They watched. They tried to pet her but Safiyyah kept her ears pinned and avoided them. The horse began to sweat. Her breathing became fast and forced. She got up and down, rolling and kicking and biting at her sides. They tried to stay beside her to comfort her, but they only shuffled around in circles as the horse dodged away from them at every attempt.

Rochelle poked at the numbers on her cell phone. "I'm calling Josh. He'll know what to do."

Hanna fiddled with pieces of hay, stacking them and then breaking them off in small sections while she listened to Rochelle's conversation. Ting Tang batted at the pieces of hay as they fluttered down.

"What did he say?" Hanna asked. She twirled the kitten's left ear.

"He said he can't come out. He said it definitely sounds like colic, said we *have* to call a vet. He said this is serious. She could die, Hanna. Even with treatment she could still die of this."

"What else? What are we going to do?"

"He said to walk her. Keep walking her. She can lie quietly but if she thrashes around make her get up and keep her walking. We have to try to get her to drink water. He said she has to pass manure. She's probably impacted. He kept saying over and over that we need to get a vet out here."

The retired emergency room nurse took charge. "Here." She dropped the lead rope. "You walk with her. I'm going to run home." She bolted out of the stall. Dumbfounded, Hanna followed her.

Rochelle pointed and ordered Hanna back into the barn. "Go! Go walk the horse." Then she sprinted to the road.

"This is bad," Hanna said. Sweat dripped from the mare. Her nostrils flared bright red on the insides. She shivered and steam rose from her body as her body rocked forward and back from the force of her breaths.

There was no time for tears. This was far too serious.

Safiyyah thrashed on the ground. She twisted from side to side and almost struck Hanna with her flailing hooves. Hanna yanked on the lead rope. She hit the mare with the end of the rope. The horse lurched up and onto her feet but hovered on bent legs as she prepared to sink again. They battled. The horse tried to throw herself on the ground. Hanna's now-loosened hair stuck to her damp face as she fought to keep the horse on its feet. She unzipped her jacket, wrestled out of it, and used it to whip on the horse to keep her up.

"No! It won't happen. I won't let you. Come on, you're going to walk!"

Hanna pulled on the rope. She coaxed the mare forward. She rammed her body into the side of the mare to thwart her attempts to drop.

Rochelle gasped when she reached the stall door. Safiyyah and Hanna panted, drained of all strength. Dust stuck to their wet bodies. Sweat streams zigzagged down Hanna's arms, her face rigid with panic. Rochelle knew well this level of despair, uncertainty. She'd seen it so many times before: the police officer, shot in the stomach, the boy; his body riddled with metal pieces after a lawnmower exploded, a new mom with a breech birth, and their loved ones. All searched for answers, searched for miracles, and searched Rochelle's face as she walked into the room.

"Where did you go? You left me here alone! This is awful!"

"She has to drink," Rochelle said. "I got an idea. I ran home and got table salt and a turkey baster. I'm going to mix the salt with water and squirt it into her." She poured the whole canister of salt into a bucket and swirled it around in the water.

At first their attempts to get the fluid into Safiyyah ended as sloppy disasters. The mixture ran out of the horse's mouth and into the straw.

"I'll hold her head up and you squirt it in," Hanna said. She put her hands under the mare's jaws and strained with all her might to lift up. Her arms shook from the weight of the horse's head. "Squirt it in, now!"

Safiyyah wrenched away. She'd had a taste of the awful concoction and she wanted no more. They tried again. Rochelle put one hand on top of Safiyyah's face to steady her head, and with the other hand, squeezed the bulb of the turkey baster. "It went down. It went down," Rochelle said.

Rochelle dipped into the bucket again and sucked up the salt water and squirted it into Safiyyah's mouth so many times they lost count. Each time the horse clamped her jaws tight but the fluid went in her and not into the straw. They backed away from her completely exhausted. The mare continued to kick at the vicious thing that attacked her belly. She angrily swished her tail from side to side. Her ears lay flat back against her head.

"She's had a lot of salt. It should make her want to drink," Rochelle said. "But I want to give her more." Safiyyah reared and ripped the lead out of Hanna's hands and whirled around to the wall. They cornered her and caught her and they plunged the remaining salt water into her.

When they released control of Safiyyah's head, she fell onto the straw. Hanna, breathing hard, cranked on the lead rope.

Rochelle touched Hanna's arm gently and shook her head. "She's lying quietly now. Remember, Josh said to let her lie if she's quiet. She's got to be tired."

The air hung heavy with sweaty humidity. They gulped air and staggered from spent strength. The reprieve didn't last. Safiyyah thrashed again. Hanna jerked on the lead rope. Rochelle lashed the mare's hips with another rope and she jabbed her toes into the horse's flanks. Covered in foamy sweat, with straw stuck to her, Safiyyah rose to her feet. Her head slowly descended to the straw and she sank onto her side. She moaned and extended her neck out in front of her. The mare's body spewed a warm fog that filled the stall.

The women sat on the sofa, muscles quivering from over-use, their breathing irregular. They didn't speak for a lifetime of minutes.

Please, please, Lord, make her be okay.

Please, God, let her live.

The kitten torpedoed into the stall, bounced against the far wall, and barreled right back out of the stall. Moments later he came back and landed on Rochelle's lap. He kneaded her with his front paws and purred.

"She's been lying quietly for an hour now. The worst might be over. Let's hope so anyway," Rochelle said.

Dusk had fallen by the time they headed home. Rochelle had driven her car from home to get back to the barn with the salt mixture, not just forgivable this time, a true blessing. Neither of them would have had the strength to walk home.

Spent from a battle that had consumed a large part of the day, morose thoughts plagued Hanna's mind. *She's dying. She'll be dead in the morning.* And Hanna didn't sleep that night. She stayed awake as chills lapped over her. She squeezed the bedding in her fists. It was the only thing she could do to hold her in place and keep her from jumping up and running to the barn"

What's wrong, baby?" Marc asked. "You seem troubled tonight." Rochelle seldom cried. But his gentle words, his masculine tenor, and his strong arms around her, brought the tears into the open.

He held her. He didn't pry. He knew when to ask and he knew when to just hold her. Marc was good at that.

Almost. Rochelle almost told him the whole story. But there had been that glimmer of hope that caused her to check her words, and keep them, until morning. And when morning came, the notion no longer tasted good.

They met in the road. Their stomachs growled. Neither had eaten supper or breakfast. They lumbered down the path. Doom led the way.

Rochelle cleared her throat. She prepared to say that she would call Josh to find out what you do with a dead horse. Hanna planned to tell Rochelle that she would cover the cost. But the good morning whinny sailed out to them and chased those thoughts away. As usual, she told them to hurry. They ran.

Safiyyah's head hung over the stall door to greet them, just as it did every morning. She wanted breakfast. But she'd have to wait for all of the hugs and kisses and the pats and gushy words to dwindle.

They stayed tight beside her as she ate. *Had she really been that sick?* The dried swirls of sweaty horse hair crusted over her body served as the stark reminder of the truth.

After she'd eaten, Safiyyah went out and pawed the ground and rolled. She clambered to her feet and shook her body. The women rushed over to her. They were prepared to do it all over again.

"That looks normal, like what she does each morning," Rochelle said. "I think she's okay. Remember, if they shake after they roll, that's a good thing. She looks like her old self now."

When they returned to the stall to pour coffee, Rochelle asked, "Why are you so quiet?"

"I have to come clean," Hanna said.

Rochelle rolled her eyes. "Here we go. Okay, what?"

"This is the most selfish thing I've ever done. I didn't want to call the vet because I didn't want our secret to be out. I was afraid they'd take her away from us. I feel awful about it. I risked her life just so that I could keep her."

Rochelle sighed. She nodded her head. "It wasn't just you. I could have called, too."

"We did a very, very bad thing. We've got to make a pact that we never do this again, okay? Hanna said. "We have to promise that from now on we always do what's right for her. Always."

"Always."

CHAPTER NINETEEN

A WISP OF something stuck to her forehead when she walked in. The single strand of cobweb split the moment she touched it and the severed end swayed and buoyed. The silk line fishtailed down, bobbed up, jerked down, swirled up, lower and lower each time, ghost-like on its way, as it fought to stay afloat. She watched; disheartened and almost grieved to see it come to an end. But she was unable to repair it. It dissolved into the dirt as if it had never been formed.

Hanna searched for the spider. *It's impossible. How did he do it? How did he make a cobweb that spanned the length of the aisle? It's over eight feet wide.* She wanted to see the powerful tiny guy who had done the impossible. But no spiders appeared for her. She wondered if they knew her; knew that she hated them and that she was the one who demolished their homes with her broom. She scanned the eight foot span. She'd never paid them any attention, other than to squash them. She'd certainly not paid any attention to the intricate details of their homes. Spiders and their webs existed only to be whisked away with a broom. They'd been busy during the day, as always, making more webs. Yet, she couldn't find one spider. She surveyed the eight foot expanse. *How did he bridge this distance? Impossible.* She put this in her mental file of things to ponder at some time in the future because, just then, Safiyyah nickered.

"Did you see that it snowed a few flakes early this morning?" Rochelle said when she joined Hanna in the barn for chores.

"We're going to have to dress warmer." She came into the barn with a fake fur hat on her head. She left the strings, with fake fur balls on the ends, untied.

"That's a really dorky hat, Rochelle. You look like a cartoon character, like Elmer Fudd, or someone like that. You should cut the strings off if you're not going to tie them. Even Elmer didn't have dangling strings. That reminds me. Look at these fancy boots I got. You're so right about that resale store. I'm glad we went there the other day to check it out." Hanna lifted up her left foot to model the used boot.

"Girl, you think my hat looks bad? Compared to those boots . . ."

"I also went to the feed store. I got her this blanket. She's grown winter hair but it doesn't look like enough to keep her warm."

Rochelle inspected the plaid blanket. Shades of blue of course. "It's pretty. It should keep her toasty."

"I brought more blankets for us, too. It is getting colder by the minute. And I got something else. I heard a few old guys in red suspenders in the feed store talking about hitching their teams to pull logs out of the woods. One of them said he'd get this stuff. He said it would keep the chill away and they all laughed about it. So I went to Dunham's and got some for us. Here." Hanna offered the glass bottle to Rochelle.

"Hmm. Pucker," Rochelle said. "It's green. Looks like mouthwash. Are you sure we drink it?"

"Yes, we drink it. The clerk said this is the right stuff. They had several flavors so I got this one. Apple flavored."

"What are you thinking? This is alcohol."

Hanna huffed. She fluttered her lashes. "Oh, I didn't know." She fetched a carton of Dixie cups from a plastic grocery bag. "Who said we can't have alcohol? We're adults. We don't need to drink the whole bottle. But I want to try it. It sounds like it's *the* drink of horse people."

Red suspenders, Pucker, and Hanna Tauber didn't quite seem to fit together. But Rochelle, game for it, said, "Okay. I'll try it."

The early dusk that comes with winter; the dusk that sneaks up and chases away the warmth of the summer sun, arrived in its perfected, sly fashion that late afternoon. They wrapped themselves up in their Mexican blankets and sat on their Mexican wrapped sofa. Hanna cracked open the bottle of Pucker and poured it into the cups, about one quarter full.

"To horses," she said.

"To Safiyyah," her partner said.

They tapped the cups together and crushed in the sides of the waxed paper goblets. But the dented cups stayed just stiff enough to do the job. Rochelle sipped the peridot-green fluid. "Hey, this isn't bad," she said.

They sat on their sofa with their bodies yoked together, bundled in their multi-colored blankets, and drinking Pucker from paper cups. Ting Tang drooped himself around Rochelle's neck and she wore him like a fur collar. The cat half-heartedly swatted at the fur balls lopping from the hat. He never did claw one. He just batted at them in slow motion, half asleep. Hanna sat with her legs sprawled two feet apart to better admire her new boots.

"It wasn't such a wacko idea after all. I like it, kind of sweet, kind of sour," Hanna said. "Guess that's why they call it Pucker. Do you want more?"

"Sure," Rochelle said. They filled the cups two more times.

The stall smelled like a spiked cider mill. And the temperature dipped low enough that they could see their breath.

"Pour me a bit more," Rochelle said. "We should sing."

"Okay."

"What should we sing?"

"I don't know. It was your idea," Hanna said. "We should sing a song with a horse in it."

"There's no songs with a horse."

"*Jingle Bells.*"

So, they sang it. They sang *My Guy.* They sang *America the Beautiful.* And when the Pucker petered out and the bottle ran dry, they went home.

The creased brow on George's face told Hanna that a courtroom worthy question would soon follow. "It's dark. How come so late getting home?" He'd thrown a sandwich together for supper. "I was really worried, Hanna. I don't know where you go. I don't know where to look for you. Did you eat? What's going on?"

"Oh, we were just hanging out, spinging spongs. I mean, singing songs."

"Have you been drinking? You're kind of goofy tonight. What's up?"

At least he'd followed the first question by running it right into the next, so answering the second question wasn't a lie. She just didn't answer the first. After all, a paper cup of Pucker, or four, wasn't the same thing as drinking. Really.

"Oh, I'm fine sweetie." She turned her back to him and forced her chin to perch on her chest. She didn't chance breathing on him. "I think I'm just tired. That's all."

"What's wrong with your neck?"

"Nothing."

Pause.

"Well, what *did* you do today? How far are you two walking now?"

"Oh, still about the same." She tussled with her nightgown. Her arms got stuck in it. George positioned an armhole for her.

"We have lots of good conversations," she said.

"I'm glad to hear that. I think she's good for you. Why don't you invite her over for dinner?"

"She'll never fit at the table."

"What *is* the matter with you . . . why don't you invite them over for dinner?"

"Who?"

"I *thought* we were talking about Rochelle."

"Don't be so . . . so . . . imcrugable."

"What? That isn't even a word. Did you mean incorrigible?"

"I meant what I said. It should be a word. And that's what you're being. You are."

George laid face up in bed, feigning sleep, but pondering, *where did my wife go?* Just that morning she'd galloped through the back door and announced, "Look what I got!" She proudly held up one dilapidated cowboy boot in each hand, as if they were medals won in marathons. The toes molded into channels across the tops and curled, like skis. The once suede leather shined smooth from eons of hard use. They were at least two sizes too big for her.

"Got 'em for fifty cents at the Goodwill!"

Hanna Tauber at the Goodwill, George thought. *Hanna Tauber at the Goodwill?* Too much to handle at that hour, he gave in to sleep and delved into a raucous round of snoring.

CHAPTER TWENTY

SAFIYYAH HAD TRANSFORMED. The old Safiyyah; the one shrouded in starvation and sadness, had gone away. The new Safiyyah thrived on the attention she received from her two ladies and especially from the one inch cubes of apple that Rochelle cut up for her. She packed on the pounds and her feet appeared more normal looking after each trim. She gave up whatever a horse might do during her day to lounge in the stall with Hanna and Rochelle. The horse listened to every conversation and included herself in all that they did. The boundaries had become blurred at some point, and it was no longer two women and a horse, but three friends.

Hanna and George invited Rochelle and Marc over for a movie and snacks. And then the foursome alternated between the two homes for movies and dinners. One Sunday evening in November, the heady aroma of garlic drew Hanna into Rochelle's house. She double-timed it to the kitchen and found lasagna, cheese stuffed tortellini, garlic bread; all made from scratch, and salad. Rochelle opened a bottle of Chianti. She giggled. "I think we'll use these . . ." She put a box of Dixie cups on the counter in front of Hanna, who choked on laughter and said, "I'm going to pee my pants!"

Rochelle snorted and whispered, "Shhh."

The men didn't come into the kitchen. They'd grown accustomed to the antics. They no longer bothered to check out the fuss, no longer said, "Hey, can you guys tone it down? We can't hear the game." They grabbed the remote instead and turned the volume up.

A week before Thanksgiving, Rochelle sat on the barn sofa in tears. Marquitta would not be coming home, not for Thanksgiving, and not for Christmas. Hanna put her arm around her, tried to comfort her, and tried to offer suggestions, although Hanna had never considered herself a pro in the art of consoling.

"Can *you* go see *her*?"

"No! Not now!"

"Could you have Christmas at another time?"

Rochelle bawled all the more at that idea. And she cried every day until Hanna suggested that they decorate the stall with Christmas lights. That fun task was the only pastime that curtailed the tears. They hung flashing lights, 'nervous lights' Hanna called them, up and down the wall behind and around the sofa. They put red bows on the feed cans, the door handles, the stall door, and on the horse. They used paper clips to hang satin balls from their pierced ears and they laughed until they cried over that one.

Thanksgiving and the December holidays passed. Rochelle and Marc went to George and Hanna's for each special day. George's mom and dad went to Florida. Rochelle's parents didn't want to travel, so Rhonda and Joe went to see them. Marc couldn't break away. So it was just the four of them; Rochelle and Marc, Hanna and George. Hanukkah and Christmas came during the same week. Hanna gave Rochelle a white china Pegasus figurine. "Can you guess who it is?" Hanna asked, as if Rochelle wasn't capable of arriving at the correct conclusion herself.

Rochelle gave Hanna a CD of the African music. Hanna played it at home once a week and danced to it. And much to George's pleasure, this usually ended with lovemaking.

On the afternoon of the Super Bowl, Hanna and Rochelle bundled up to go do evening chores. They had made popcorn, filled Tupperware with chips and pretzels, double checked that enough Miller bottles chilled, and received clearance at that point to go.

"We're going for a walk."

The volume on the television went up.

"I don't see what they get so excited about. I don't even know who is playing. I think it's the White Sox," Hanna said.

"That's baseball."

"Football, shmootball." Hanna smashed a knit hat down onto her head. "I just don't get it, a bunch of adult men watching a bunch of guys whacking a ball."

"They don't whack it. They kick it." They walked out of Rochelle's back door and into the silver air.

"Whack it, kick it, it's of no consequence to me," Hanna said. She squinted sideways at Rochelle. "You're laughing at me. You think I don't know, but I do. I can see you laughing. And I know why you're laughing. You think I don't know. But I know. You'll never admit why, but I know."

"All right, all right! What do you expect?"

"The only time I paid attention to football was back in the '90s, just to watch the show that comes on in the middle. That's it. I have no interest in the Super Skillet, as I tease George," Hanna said. Her voice softened. "It was '93. Never forget it."

A brilliant male cardinal coasted down from a tall pine, gliding on outstretched wings. He landed on a snow covered bough. His legs disappeared deep into the fluff. Silver clouds, a silver sky, and a bright red bird on a green tree in the silver snow. The air tasted silver. It smelled silver; a splendid, silver winter.

New snow covered Safiyyah's Road. And for the first time there were tire tracks in the snow. The tracks went right to the driveway of the barn. Rochelle and Hanna bent over at their waists to get a better view. The tracks went in about a half car length. It appeared as if the vehicle had backed out, maybe because the driver didn't want to chance getting stuck.

"Strange," Rochelle said.

Hanna's pulse increased.

"Maybe they just needed to turn around," Rochelle said. "They didn't go in far and they didn't get out of the car. No footprints."

Hanna's stomach headed over Niagara Falls. She said, "I hope no one messes with her," and held herself together.

"It is a public road, Hanna. But I think we're okay. I think they just needed to turn around." Rochelle wondered if she had disguised her own worry. She knew that Hanna, so concerned, could make herself sick over it.

February seemed to have no end. The cold and snow fell every day. The county did plow the back roads. The road commission drivers pushed the last hard-packed heaps of snow all the way up to the top of the post, but they always left the "ROAD ENDS" sign visible.

The two-track proved rugged after a fresh snow. But after a few passes they had a new path tamped down that remained firm for several days, at least until the next snowfall.

One afternoon in late February, when George was home alone because Hanna left to go grocery shopping with Rochelle (always with Rochelle) the phone rang. The machine didn't pick it up. Even though he had the toaster in pieces on the kitchen table trying to fix it, he answered the call.

"Is this the Tauber residence?"

"Yes it is."

"Is Hanna in?"

"No. She's out right now. Can I take a message?"

"This is Shelby's Feed and Grain. I'm calling to let her know that the horse vitamins she ordered have come in."

"Horse vitamins?" The perplexed man gathered himself. "You have the wrong number. We don't have a horse . . . not that I know of anyway!" He laughed at the idea. Quite the quipster.

The caller paused . . . a long pause. "I'm sorry. I must be mistaken." But she knew it hadn't been a mistake. She did not call the number again.

That evening, George sat at the table reading through case notes for the following morning. He waited for Hanna to join him with the stew she'd let simmer all day in the crock pot. She had just scooped out a bowl for George and headed across the kitchen to bring it to him when he spoke.

"Some feed store called today to tell you your horse vitamins are in."

Carrots, celery, onions, potatoes, and beef hit the linoleum as a flashflood. But the bowl didn't break. It rolled under the table and oscillated faster and faster, lower and lower, until it wound itself down and smacked the tile. The nasty accident proved to be a diversion, if only for a few minutes, while George and Hanna swabbed up stew.

"Horse vitamins!" She acted surprised and bewildered. But was it good enough?

"Yeah, that's what I said. What a hoot. I wonder how they got our number."

No comment.

I should just tell him the truth. But she spooned out another bowl of stew for him instead.

After supper, George kissed his wife on the cheek. "I have to be in court early. I'm going up now to take a shower."

"Okay dear, I'll be up soon. I'm going to call Rochelle."

"You just saw her a few hours ago. Why do you need to call her?"

"I just do."

"If you say so. See you in a bit." Up the stairs he went.

"Girl, you are not going to believe this," Hanna whispered. She told her about the vitamins and about the stew bomb.

"I can swing by Shelby's tomorrow and pick them up," Rochelle said. "I think we're at the point we talked about when this all started, that once Safiyyah got healthy and looking good we'd tell . . ."

"Not yet, okay? Not yet."

"But when?"

"Let's wait until she's lost all of her winter hair and looks even prettier. How about we wait until April?"

"April it is. But we're going to stick to it. I'm starting to feel really guilty. Like I told you, we can't keep this a secret forever," Rochelle said.

George crawled under the covers and wondered what kept his wife. He thought about picking up the phone, just to see. *No, she isn't still on the phone. Can't be. She's probably cleaning the kitchen.*

"Rochelle says to tell you hi," a chipper Hanna said as she came into the bedroom and sat on the edge of the bed.

"Have you been talking to her all this time?"

"Yes."

It hit George hard. The idea that anyone could talk on the phone for that long, hit him hard. "It's been over an hour. How can you talk to her for over an hour? You just saw her. What can you possibly have to talk about?"

Hanna stopped unbuttoning her blouse. No one had ever asked her such a dumb question. Her eyes searched inside the top of her head. *Men, they just don't understand much of anything.*

"We always have stuff to talk about."

"I don't understand that."

"I know you don't. You're a man."

He pressed back against the pillows, his body trying to convince him, "Enough, can't we just go to sleep?" But his mind resisted. *That book about Mars and Venus is true. They are from another planet.* When she wiggled into bed tight against him, he held her in his arms and kissed the back of her neck. *But she smells so good.*

CHAPTER TWENTY-ONE

TIRE TRACKS AGAIN. Tire tracks in the fresh snow proved that someone had pulled in over a car length into the driveway to the barn and then backed out. Had they noticed the packed snow trail from the countless trips to and from the barn? The footpath had been mashed into place, leaving no doubt that someone used it on a daily basis. But did it matter to the driver of the vehicle?

"Probably just someone turning around," Rochelle said.

"Let's hope so. But I'm beginning to worry."

Tire tracks never appeared in the snow again.

In March, Safiyyah had another bout of colic. She fussed and refused to eat or drink. Rochelle made the salt cocktail. Hanna held the horse's head up and they forced her to guzzle the brine. They honored their pact and called Dr. Huffstead. Hanna walked Safiyyah around her large box stall, one hand held the lead rope, and the other remained locked around the blue bead. Rochelle told Dr. Huffstead the horse's symptoms and vitals. She told him about the salt mixture.

"When's he going to be here?" Hanna asked.

"He's not coming. Not yet anyway. He said it sounds like we're doing everything right and he'd prefer to just be ready to come out if she gets worse because he's in the middle of a difficult calving. He said that giving 'salt slurries', as he called it, is a great idea. He said her vitals are actually quite good and that this is probably a mild colic we caught in time and that she'll come out of. But he said since she's had colic previously, combined with the fact that she's an old horse, she might continue to colic more often. He said eventually she could reach a point where she doesn't get better and has to be put down or dies from it."

But Safiyyah recovered again. She bounced back strong and happy.

Winter strayed and began to depart. Spring began to tiptoe in. The days got longer and the snow began to melt. Safiyyah started to shed her winter hair.

"I've never seen so much hair come off an animal in my entire life," Hanna said. "I had no idea a horse shed this much. We could make a coat out of her old hair."

They loved to brush her. The mare's petite size enabled them to stand on opposite sides of her body, currying her, yet, still see each other from about chest up, like chatting over a breakfast bar. Hanna poured coffee into Rochelle's mug across Safiyyah's back. In between sips they rested their mugs on her now-amply-filled-in broad back. The horse never cared.

Safiyyah's ribs and bones, once so garish, had padded over. Josh cautioned them about letting her gain too much weight. "Her joints crackle from arthritis and she's got those bad feet. Shouldn't carry too much weight. Makes all that worse. You wanna be able to just feel ribs when you press on her but you don't wanna see ribs."

Each morning after they fed her, Safiyyah trotted and cantered and pranced along the fence line with her tail raised over her back, her neck arched, and her head lifted high.

"She knows she's beautiful again," Rochelle said. "She takes my breath away."

And the horse pranced with her knees higher and with more fire when they stopped to watch her, praise her, and tell her she was the most beautiful horse ever.

As spring began to awaken in earnest, it became sweatshirt weather, not winter coat weather. And rain replaced the snow. Safiyyah preferred to stay in her stall when it rained.

"She's become just like us," Hanna said. "I think she'd drink coffee if we offered it to her."

The rain made mud. One day, tire tracks appeared again. This time, they went all the way up to the cabin. The sight of the tracks propelled both women into that shaky, sickly feeling of panic that lodges somewhere between your throat and your stomach. But as they studied the tracks, it didn't appear that anyone had gotten out of the vehicle and walked around. It had pulled in, made a thirty foot circle between the cabin and the barn, and gone right back down the driveway to the road. They didn't say anything as they tended to Safiyyah's needs. The level of their camaraderie, and ability to read unspoken language, had so matured that they seldom had to speak during chores anyway. But the atmosphere in the barn after seeing the tire tracks clasped each of them silent, like a heavy overcoat restricts movement.

CHAPTER TWENTY-TWO

HANNA HAD GONE up to the loft to pitch down a bale of hay and a bale of straw. Rochelle had just given Safiyyah her grain. She held the bucket in one hand for her and massaged the mare's ear with the other hand.

"Rochelle! Get up here, now!"

Rochelle climbed the loft steps two at a time. "Now what? Why do you always do this to me!"

"There's a door here. I grabbed one bale of straw and pulled on it and that whole row against the wall fell down. And there's . . . this door."

A wrought iron slide bolt held the knotted-pine door closed. Rochelle rocked it back and forth and it shifted to the side while the bone-dry hinges screeched.

"There's a light," Rochelle said. She tugged on the shred of baling twine dangling almost in her face. The 40 watt worked.

The room smelled of must and antique things. They waited in the doorway until their vision adjusted to the weak light. Objects lined the wall on the right; each mounted and covered with a blanket, decorated in cobwebs. With the smallest pinch she could make, so as not to touch a web, Hanna tossed one of the blankets off and to the side. "A saddle," she said.

Once they'd pulled off all of the blankets they counted twelve saddles. With intricately tooled leather, suede seats, and engraved silver plating on the horns, cantles, and skirts, the saddles appeared more art than tack.

"These are gorgeous," Hanna said. The tarnish came off as she rubbed the silver cap on one saddle horn.

"And very expensive," Rochelle said.

"I wonder what they're doing up here behind a wall of straw."

"Probably stolen," Rochelle said.

"Look. There's a chest of drawers," Hanna said. And without hesitation, she grabbed the dust-covered knobs and wiggled the top drawer up and down to free the dry, stiff wood. "Empty," she said, when the drawer opened. She opened the middle drawer. "Empty." But when she pulled on the bottom drawer knobs, she smirked. "Bingo."

The drawer bent under the weight of packed papers; stained and curved to the shape of the stack. Hanna plopped down onto the floor in a puff of attic dust and sat cross-legged. Rochelle knelt next to her. They rummaged through the contents. Hanna pawed through the papers on the right side of the drawer and Rochelle sifted through those on the left.

Hanna jerked to attention. With military reverence, she passed a parchment document, embossed with a gold seal, to Rochelle.

Rochelle blew the dust away. "This is the registration certificate to an Arabian horse. It's for a bay gelding." She put the document off to the side on the floor and they dove back into the drawer.

Once again, Hanna became quiet and still enough to hush crickets. She rose to her knees.

Rochelle abandoned her quest to pull more papers out of the drawer. "What have you got there?"

Hanna cupped one hand over her mouth. In her free hand, she held a tattered newspaper article. She slowly, resolutely guided it to Rochelle's hand. Rochelle took the paper.

"My God . . . it's Safiyyah," Rochelle whispered.

They huddled over the crisp newspaper clipping and read the tale of a champion Arabian filly that had come up missing during

151

a business deal gone sour . . . twenty-nine years ago. The cracked, moisture damaged article, with smeared and chipped off print, still held the image of a dark gray Arabian with four perfect socks. Unmistakably: Safiyyah.

They didn't even try to talk. Engrossed in trying to read each word of the messy print they didn't hear Safiyyah nicker.

They could just barely make out the partial name of the rightful owners: "VanderZ . . ." The last letters of the name had worn away. The rest of the article referred to the people with that name as, "the owners."

They didn't hear the hello nicker again. They didn't hear the steps groaning in protest under the weight of three hundred pounds. But they did hear the roar.

"Police! Freeze!"

Hanna rolled back onto her buttocks with such force she heard the vertebrae collide. She shoved the newspaper article inside her sweatshirt, tight against her chest into a bra cup.

"Don't move!"

He roared again. "Put your hands on your heads. Now! And slowly, slowly, turn around."

With shaking hands locked onto their heads, they inched around to face the officer. Filled with fear, they blinked at each other. *God, help us.*

Deputy Charlie Kompoltowitz, 'CK' as they called him, had never nabbed two such criminals in his life. A white woman and a black woman, both in their late forties, maybe fifty, they didn't resemble his usual burglars. But he'd staked out the place long enough to know that they were the perpetrators he'd been observing.

CK hit six foot four and weighed almost three hundred pounds. Thirty-five years old, he'd developed a beer belly, though he never drank beer. It was pizza that did it to him.

He evaluated his catch. Dust covered their faces and dust hovered around them, blue in the poor light. The women shook so much that the floor boards quaked.

The stair steps growled again, but this time under the weight of quicker and lighter steps. A petite female officer fluttered into the loft. "Well, well, look what we have here," she said.

"We caught 'em," CK said to his partner. "Search 'em."

Deputy Wilcox patted Hanna down and then Rochelle. She shook her head and backed away. "Clean."

"Okay," CK said, "you can put your hands down. Who are you? You first," he snapped at Hanna.

She didn't mean to be rude. She just couldn't speak.

"Who *are* you?"

Rochelle whacked Hanna on the arm. A few nonhuman sounding chirps came out of Hanna's mouth. It took several more attempts before those sounds formed discernable words.

"Ha . . . Han . . . Hanna Tauber."

"Where do you live?"

Rochelle punched Hanna again to prompt a response.

Staccato, she tried again. "515 Stormy Drive, Stony Drive, here, in Lake Luffit. My husband is George Tauber, an attorney."

"Your husband is a mouthpiece, an attorney? Tauber is the name, correct?"

"Yes."

Turning to Rochelle, the sharpshooter asked, "And you?"

"I'm Rochelle Harris. I live at 112 Feather Lane."

"Do you have ID?" Deputy Wilcox asked.

Rochelle's breathing stopped. Hanna's head filled with pudding. Her stomach filled with bricks. They never took ID with them on their walks.

"No," Rochelle said. "We walk here twice a day and I don't carry ID with me. Do you, Hanna?" Hanna shook her head.

"You're both under arrest," CK said.

"For what?" Hanna said. Rochelle punched her again.

"Ouch! Why do you keep hitting me?"

"We can explain this," Rochelle said.

"I'm sure you can. But we're taking you down to the station. I'll read you your rights when we get in the car and we'll have an opportunity to talk about it if you want. Cuff them, Jill."

Deputy Wilcox unsnapped a case on her belt and removed shiny steel handcuffs. "I think we can cuff them in the front." She brought Rochelle's wrists to the front of her body and secured the cold metal rings, one on each wrist.

CK snapped his handcuffs onto Hanna's wrists in the same fashion. "Let's go," he said. He motioned with his chin to the stairs.

CK guided Hanna by holding on to her left arm as the four of them began their descent down the steps. "Let's put both in my car," he said.

They assisted the women into CK's patrol car. Deputy Wilcox said, "I'll meet you back at the ranch." She left in her patrol car.

Hanna had never been in a police car in her life. Rochelle had never been in a police car in her life.

This can't be happening, Rochelle thought.

I'm going to pass out, Hanna thought.

It was after nine o'clock and stars salted the dark sky. The patrol car blinked and bleeped with oodles of lights and gadgets. *Looks like the inside of a spaceship*, Hanna thought, though she'd never been inside a spaceship, either.

CK picked up a radio microphone and alerted the dispatcher on the other end. "I'm en route, with two."

"Ten four."

Hanna never understood, and never cared, why she did what she did next. First, she asked CK, "I thought you guys had to have a screen separating the front seat from the back seat. Why don't you?"

"Our department doesn't use them," he said, turning back to look at her. *Is she gonna try to book?*

"Then here, take your old handcuffs." She tossed the empty handcuffs over the back of the front seat. They made a heavy crunching sound as they hit CK's paperwork when she dropped them. She jerked back and pegged herself against the seat with her arms folded across her chest.

Rochelle, wide-eyed, gasped. "What is the matter with you?" She snarled. "You're going to get us into more trouble."

In thirteen years of law enforcement, CK had seen most everything, several times over. Never, had anyone been able to yank themselves out of handcuffs. Many had tried. Drunks fought and fought against the metal, bruising themselves, until finally giving up and sitting quietly. No one, not even other small women, had been able to slip them off and ditch them.

CK opened his door and got out of his patrol car.

He's going to kill me now.

Rochelle glared at her: you're dead.

CK opened the back seat door. "Give me your wrists."

Hanna heard herself swallow. CK heard it, too. She offered both wrists. He fastened a plastic cable around each wrist in a loop and pulled it snug, but not painfully tight. "You won't get out of that." He got back behind the wheel.

Hanna scowled at her crossed over wrists and at what appeared to be not much more than a glorified bread tie. Just to be sure, she tugged against the taut binding. She would not get out of it. Hanna could feel Rochelle glowering at her.

"What?" Hanna said.

Rochelle hissed.

"I didn't want to wear them."

Rochelle rebuffed the comment by scowling at the roof of the patrol car. She snapped her body back against the seat.

"I have to ask you not to talk to each other, okay?" CK said. He knew they weren't practiced criminals. He could hardly wait to hear their story.

CK read each of the women the Miranda warning. "Do you want to talk to me now?" he asked.

"We didn't do anything wrong," Hanna said. "You shouldn't be arresting us."

"Do you own that barn?" CK asked. A smidgen of sarcasm tossed out with it.

"Well, no," Hanna said.

"You were inside the barn. That's breaking and entering, unlawful entry. What were you doing in there?"

"Did you happen to notice the horse in the stall downstairs?" Hanna asked.

"Yes, I did. Is it your horse?"

Silence.

"Is it your horse?" CK asked again, with more gusto.

"No," Hanna said. "But we found her. She was starved. We saved her life and we go down there twice a day to care for her. Her name is Safiyyah. At least *we* call her Safiyyah."

Feisty little broad, he thought. He didn't want them to see the grin. He kept his head down as his pen scratched disheveled notes that only he'd be able to read later. "Did you know Roger Durfee?"

"No," Hanna said. "When we first started going there, the place was abandoned, except for Safiyyah. We heard at the feed store that he died. Most of his horses were put down, some got a home; others went to slaughter. Did you know that? But not her, she was spared."

"I knew he had horses that that animal control took. I was there that day. I don't know how we missed this one. She must have been in the barn or in the woods, hidden somewhere."

The deputy adjusted the rear view mirror so that he could see Rochelle. "What do you have to say about all of this?"

"It's true, Officer. We both had been walking down that road when we found the horse months ago, end of summer, close to fall, and started caring for her."

"No, no, no," Hanna said. "I walked. You rode a bike."

Rochelle hoped that her earnest expression conveyed, *I'm trying, Officer. I really am. She's a nutcase.* Rochelle smacked Hanna with her bound wrists.

"Why didn't you call us or animal control?"

"We've been so afraid . . ." Hanna began, "I mean, after we learned that some of the other horses were sold for slaughter, we couldn't bear to think of that happening to her. She's the sweetest thing. She didn't deserve any of the bad stuff that happened to her."

CK tilted the mirror again. He could see both of them. Tears they didn't even feel at the moment had trailed down all four cheeks, leaving shiny tracks in the dust. CK wasn't a stupid man. The tears weren't because they sat handcuffed in a police car. The tears belonged to one small white horse and what fate held for her.

"Am I going to be able to call my husband?" Rochelle asked.

A wrecking ball slammed into Hanna's stomach.

"What do your husbands think of all this? Especially you, since your husband is an attorney. I can't believe he'd go along with this."

"They don't know," Rochelle said, meekly.

CK abandoned the rear view mirror. He swiveled his head around and twisted his body to look at them. "Huh?" But then it dawned on him that this would be a lengthy and complicated story. "We can talk about it at the station," he said. He put the car in gear.

The patrol car turned out of the barn driveway and onto Safiyyah's Road. Hanna strained her neck to peer down Stony Drive. She could just see the living room window. The lights were on. *He's home. He's home and he's worried sick.*

CHAPTER TWENTY-THREE

THE AUTOMATIC OVERHEAD garage door at the sheriff's department opened for the patrol car and then encased them with a horrendous thud. Surely, no one ever escaped from such a fortress.

CK opened the door for them. "Get out."

They couldn't get from the garage into the building without another deputy on the inside pushing buttons to unlock the first of two doors and again for the next metal door.

"Got a couple of horse rustlers," CK said to the door guard. He ushered Rochelle through a lobby and into a back room. He checked behind him to make sure that her accomplice was still in tow.

CK used a tiny key to unlock the handcuffs on Rochelle's wrists. She rubbed them. He thumbed through his paperwork.

"What about me?" Hanna asked.

He sorted through a few more papers. He left the room and returned with a cup of coffee.

"Excuse me, what about me? Don't you want to take these off me, too? Please," Hanna said.

He stirred his coffee, took a sip, added another pack of sugar, and stirred it again. One more taste and he got up and cut the plastic cuffs off Hanna's wrists with pocket nippers.

Next, they handed over the belongings in their pockets: one phone of Rochelle's and six pastel green objects and two pink from Hanna's jacket pocket.

"What are those?" CK asked, but not soon enough.

"Mints," Hanna said. She popped them into her mouth and ground them up.

Rochelle shook her head. She slugged Hanna in the arm. "Stop with this sassing."

CK told them to take off their shoes. He gave them brown one-size-fits-all slippers and escorted them down a hallway, bright with 100 watt bulbs overhead.

Hanna balked at the opening. "That's a jail cell!"

"What did you think we have in a jail? This is where we put criminals," CK said. "Get in. I'll bring you a phone so you can call home."

They stepped just enough inside the cell so that the barred door swung shut with a torture-chamber clang, securing them. Hanna walked over to a gray cement bench, built into the wall so that no prisoner would be able to pick it up and throw it. "I'm not going to talk to him."

"Who aren't you going to talk to?" Rochelle asked.

"George. You can talk to him."

Another deputy, a heavyset female with Dolly Parton hair, wearing cat-eye glasses, brought them a portable phone. She waved the phone. "Who wants to go first?"

"I think you should call George first since he's an attorney. Marc might not even be home from the hospital."

"Hospital?" the deputy asked.

"Yes. My husband, Marc Harris, is an oncologist. He's been at the hospital all day. Come on, Hanna, call George."

"I'm not going to call him. You call him."

"You want *me* to call *your* husband?"

"Yes."

"That's crazy," Rochelle said. But she knew she would be the one making the call. She thanked the deputy and took the phone.

"George? This is Rochelle. Hanna and I are . . . it's like this . . . Hanna and I are in jail. No, no, it's not a joke. We're locked up in the county jail." She couldn't think of anything else to do as proof, so she tapped the phone on a metal bar. "Did you hear that? That's a metal bar. I know . . . you may not believe us . . ." Rochelle lowered the phone to her side. "He hung up. He said he would call here."

Hanna stuck her left index finger into the mortar line of the middle cinder blocks and drifted along the wall to the back of the cell tracing the mortar line as she went. She wanted to put as much distance between her and that phone as possible. She hummed.

The big-haired deputy came back to the cell. "Your husband called the main line. He's going to call you back. I would suggest you answer it. Boy, are you in a mountain heap of trouble, missy.

Hanna winced with locked teeth. Her face warped when the phone rang. The ring sounded angry.

Rochelle passed the phone to Hanna without answering it. "It's for you."

The syrup ran thick. "George?" She batted her eyelashes. And then the explosion occurred. Hanna rocketed the phone out at arm's length. He yelled, but Rochelle couldn't make out any of the words. Hanna maintained an unbroken grimace. Ouch.

George had yelled only one other time in all the years she'd known him. In twenty-five years he had yelled at this moment and that one other time, the day she washed his Corvette.

She meant to do him a favor on that warm, overcast June day. That evening, they would celebrate their engagement at a party with their parents and closest friends.

"I'm going to wash the 'Vette today," he said, "so that we go in style. But first I'll go get the things my mom needs for that salad she wants to make." Then he left, driving Hanna's Camaro.

She probably should have known not to mess with the Corvette. The exalted car crowned the summit of all things important to George. Before they met, she'd seen him driving around in the vintage sports car. On their first date, however, he picked her up in a beater LeMans that had a leaky windshield. "The 'Vette never sees rain," he explained, as if a completely normal standard by which to live. Sometimes, it even snowed inside the LeMans.

On the few dates that she did get to ride in the special car, he always parked it at the farthest edge of the parking lot. This forced her to hike agonizing miles, usually in stilettos, with her hair blowing in every direction so that she couldn't see in front of her, to reach their destination. Her hair would be a twisted string mop disaster by the time they made it through the doors of the theater or restaurant. But Hanna loved George and she grew to love the Corvette, too. A woman felt like royalty riding in the car with the fire engine-red paint job. She even named it. Horatio.

On that fine June day, she only wanted to do him a favor. She'd wash the car for him. She got the special soap that George used only for the special car and she got the special wash cloths. She got the special bucket that had been scoured so that "not one grain of sand is in it to even threaten a scratch" and she filled that special bucket with water of the special temperature.

Tiny bumps ran all along the bottom half of the shiny body of the car. "Bitty stuck bugs," she said. And that's when she went into the house to get the Brillo Pads.

By the time George came home, Hanna had gone into the house to gab on the phone with her bridesmaid, Josie. The painful screams, like those of a wounded animal, like the sound of a shrieking banshee, of a train wreck, all at the same time, blared as a foghorn into the house. She ran to the horrifying wails but stayed in the doorway. George had sunk to the ground beside his car. Two toilet paper rolls skirted away from him down a grade in the cement. Two heads of lettuce, a dozen or so tomatoes, and a whole bunch of loose radishes had gathered around him. What a pitiful sight. George sobbed, "No, no, no." He held his head in one hand and rhythmically pounded a zucchini over and over and over on the pavement with the other hand, each jab losing momentum, like a car on empty, coasting to a stop. The bludgeoned end of the zucchini had splayed to half its length.

George rose to his feet, a panther on the verge of a killing dive for its prey, when she peeked around the doorjamb. He yelled distorted, guttural sounds. The gist of it all, "How could you do this?"

The car had dried. Hanna couldn't avoid seeing the damage; chalky hand swirls gouged into the plastic body. The shine, that brilliant, mirror finish, gone. George ran down the sidewalk whimpering and flailing his arms and his zucchini. Hanna ran crying to call her mom. The toilet paper and all of the tomatoes rolled down the sidewalk to the neighbor's driveway.

"That's one marriage that just went down with the dead goldfish," Hanna's mom, Arleen Glassman, said. Hanna vaulted up the stairs and flopped onto the bed, bawling. She knew that she'd lost George. But of course, that's not what happened. He came home. Though devastated, he hugged her. He still married her. They went to their engagement party that night in the Camaro.

And now, in her jail cell, Hanna listened as George yelled himself out. It ended with a dial tone. "I think he's coming over here," she said.

Fifteen minutes later, George's professional exchange with the deputies aired in from the front desk. *Okay, this is good*, she thought, as she listened to his restored, best courtroom manner of speaking.

"At least he doesn't sound . . ."

"Marc is here, too. I hear him. George must have called him," Rochelle said.

A parade of people filed back to the cell. Once the door opened to release Hanna and Rochelle, they marched back down the same hallway with CK in the lead, followed by Rochelle, followed by Hanna, followed by Deputy Wilcox, followed by George, followed by Marc, wearing blue scrubs. Dolly Parton brought up the rear.

"We're going to one of the interview rooms to talk about all of this," CK said.

They all crowded into a small room and sat at a table in the center. Hanna glimpsed at George's face. It didn't seem to be flushed from anger, more like bewilderment. No—shock. She tried to sneak in another peek, but he caught it, and scowled back at her.

Marc sat quietly and stared at his thumbs. Rochelle fidgeted with her rings and cracked her knuckles. Hanna spun a small section

of her hair round and round her finger. She hadn't done that since
the last time she got called to the counselor's office in junior high
school after she'd accidentally locked Mrs. Baumgartner, the gym
teacher, in the broom closet with her stupid wiffle balls.

"There will be someone else joining us," CK said.

No one else said anything as they waited. Hanna found the
one thing of interest to watch in the room. A coffeemaker on a
back desk spewed out disgusting, gurgling noises, and coffee the
color of tarpaper half filled two pots. *A big, ugly institutional glob of
coffee*, she thought. *Ugly as sin. Ugly as this place. Fits.*

Ten minutes later someone knocked on the door. The scent of
aftershave entered just before he did. A nice looking man, maybe
sixty, came into the room and quietly closed the door. He wore
jeans, a polo shirt, and a black leather jacket. He shook CK's hand
and tipped his head as each person was introduced to him.

"Hello George, good to see you," he said.

"You two know each other?" Hanna asked.

George didn't say one word. Not to Hanna.

"Yes," the man said, and introduced himself. "I'm Matt Ross,
probate court officer." Matt Ross sat down at the table.

"Matt said that he's known someone was going back on
Durfee's property for weeks now," CK said. "It took a while for
Durfee's estate to go to court, but now probate's involved to get
things settled."

"The kicker was the electric bill," Matt Ross said. "At first,
there was no electricity being used, somehow we missed getting it
shut off. Then, power started getting used. It took a while for the
bills to reach my desk."

"So we did a stake out," CK said, "and caught you. Now is the
time to tell us . . . what happened?"

"I go walking down that road twice a day," Hanna said.

"Me too," Rochelle said.

"We both found the horse and started taking care of her. She
was so starved, so thirsty . . . we didn't think she'd even live. She
laid down for days and days because she was in a lot of pain from

her sore feet, but she came around. She's healthy now," Hanna said.

"We saved her life," Rochelle said. "I know we saved her life."

"What were you doing up in the loft?" CK asked.

"We bought grain for her, but there is hay and straw up in the loft that we used. I went up there to get straw for her bed tonight and found the door to that room. I opened it. We found things," Hanna said.

"Did you see all of those saddles up there?" Rochelle asked.

"No," Deputy Wilcox said. She leaned across the table. "What saddles, how many?"

"We counted twelve. They're all on racks attached to the wall. They were covered with blankets. They're absolutely beautiful," Rochelle said.

Deputy Wilcox excused herself and left the room. She came back moments later, whistling. She dropped a manila file on the table right on top of CK's notepad. "I'll bet they're the O'Connor saddles."

"O'Connor saddles?" Rochelle asked.

"There was a major theft a few years ago from one of the big show and breeding barns in the area, O'Connor's place," CK said. "Twelve specially made silver show saddles were stolen. Each of those saddles is worth between four and six thousand dollars. We've always suspected that Durfee knew something about it but when we questioned him he had an alibi that checked out."

"That's not all," Hanna said. She tugged under her sweatshirt and plucked the yellowed newspaper article from under her bra. She unfolded it and placed it in front of her. She slowly pushed it toward CK with her index finger.

CK opened the fragile sheet and scanned the print.

"It's Safiyyah," Hanna said. "We know it's her. We gave her a bath and she has those exact white markings."

"It's not just the saddles. She was stolen, too," Rochelle said.

Silence fell into the room. Roadblock silence.

Rochelle wondered how Safiyyah would get fed in the morning. Hanna stewed over when and where they would take the horse.

And CK asked himself, *how'd we miss all this?*

Marc sat heavy in his chair, exhausted from two extensive surgeries that day. Yet he managed to stifle the laugh that began to percolate. George thought that not much in his life appeared logical anymore. And George needed logic, like a motor needs pistons to fire properly, George required logic. Deputy Wilcox tapped her foot against the floor and rapped the table with an ink pen in anticipation of calling the O'Connor's to tell them that their saddles had been found.

Matt Ross spoke first and broke through the barrier. "What we've got here, then, are a couple of ace sleuths who have solved not one, but at least two crimes. I'll not be the one to press charges against them. Furthermore, my daughter, Emmy, wouldn't be too thrilled with her old man if she knew I'd pressed charges against two women who saved a horse's life. She and her husband have racehorses and they've done a few rescues, too."

Matt Ross got to his feet. He twisted his back left, then right, to knock the kinks out.

"CK," he said, "I'm out of here. I'm going home. Just let me know when I can get back to Durfee's place. I think we've got a buyer for it." Matt issued a global, "Goodnight all," and left.

"You heard the man," CK said. "You're free to go." He'd hoped all along that it would work out exactly so. "In this instance, we won't book you if we have no victim of the alleged crime and no one wants to press charges. Matt's a good guy."

"What happens to Safiyyah?" Hanna asked.

"We have to try to get her back to her rightful owners, if they're still around, and if they want her back," he said.

"What if they don't want her or you can't find them?" Rochelle asked.

"Looks like you got yourselves a horse. I can't figure out much from that old article, but we'll do some checking."

"If you find them, can we call them?" Rochelle asked.

"Sure. I don't have a problem with that."

They walked out of the sheriff's department to go home under a cold, makes-your-bones-hurt kind of darkness. Midnight. Before they split up, Rochelle and Hanna hugged. *We're in this together. Stay strong.*

CHAPTER TWENTY-FOUR

THE RIDE HOME passed as one of the longest, most lonesome fifteen minute chunks of time in all of Hanna Tauber's life. He didn't speak. She didn't speak. George pulled into the driveway and they got out of the Lexus and walked into the house in stormy silence. Hanna went up the stairs to the bedroom. George went to the kitchen.

She scooted out of her jeans and dropped them in a mound on the floor. Then she sat on the edge of the bed.

I wonder how Rochelle is doing. I should call her. But she knew George would get even more upset with her if she made the call. *How is Safiyyah doing? My life is ruined. My marriage is over.*

The stairwell light switch clicked. George would be in the bedroom in about four seconds.

He spoke sternly. "Hanna, we have to talk about this."

"What do you want to know?"

"My wife just got arrested for breaking and entering and has been keeping this secret from me for months . . . and she asks me what I want to know? What is the matter with you? What's happened to you? I don't even know you anymore."

"It's not like you just found out I've been working as a stripper."

"I don't believe this." He jerked the tie from around his neck, wadded it in a ball and tossed it at the dresser. He took off his jacket, wound it around and around in his arms and hurled it into the closet. "Hanna, I'm an attorney in this town. My wife has just been arrested. Don't you get it? Does that mean anything to you?"

"I'm sorry. I'm really, really sorry." The tears would leap weir soon enough.

"But it's so much more than that. Why? How could you keep this from me for so many months? I'm your husband for crying out loud. We're supposed to share things . . . here you've been leading this secret life, disappearing to go for these walks, breaking into someone's barn . . . and a horse! Why didn't you tell me about this?" Visions of mud-caked shoes, cowboy boots, horse vitamins, and a tipsy wife flashed through George's mind. "Why, Hanna? I have to know why I wasn't someone you felt the need or the desire to confide in."

She searched every nook for an answer. She came up with, "I don't know."

"You don't *know*? That's the best you can do? It's not good enough. I need to know the reason."

"Does everything have to have a reason? Because I truly don't have one."

"This isn't normal."

Her response hit him like shrapnel. "What is normal, George? Tell me! What . . . is . . . normal?"

It coursed up through her body: old, buried, foreign, yet known; it pushed up to the surface. She tried to swallow it away, down where it all belonged, but it kept pushing.

George had never seen such an explosion. It startled him, paralyzed him, as he watched Hanna. Her fists pounded her thighs over and over, as if machine driven, as if her hands belonged to someone else, she bludgeoned her own body. Her red face contorted as the tears gushed, threatening to drown the woman named Hanna. George, too fearful to reach out and touch her, hesitated. Heat came from her skin and he felt her shaking body in his own chest.

Mere seconds later, he grabbed her and tore her away from the cruelty she inflicted upon herself. He clutched her tight against him, so tight that her arms could no longer swing to drive her fists.

Hot and sweating, Hanna shook so violently that George could barely contain her. His dress shirt and under shirt became wet all the way through to his skin from her tears. Never, could he have imagined that any human being could cry like that. Never, would he want to witness her cry like that again. He held her. He fought to hang on. But terror raged against him and ridiculed him as he began to slip and fall into a dark cavern. His mind strained and he grappled for anything, anything to hang on to; anything to stabilize his manhood. The clock on the stand by the bed became hypnotic as he watched one red digital number convert to the next. Nineteen minutes. Nineteen minutes before the sobs subsided to raspy breaths and the well of tears for all of creation drained its last.

With Hanna held fast to him, George sidestepped to the bed. He guided them both down onto it with their bodies bound by his arms. Still horrified by what he had just experienced, he released his wife in graduated increments. Her head hung. Her nose dripped several times before she wiped her face on the sleeve of her sweatshirt. She trembled. His arm searched behind them. He grabbed her robe and covered her. He pulled a tissue from the box on the nightstand and dabbed her cheeks with it and then pushed it into her circled hand.

She tried to thank him. But no sound formed.

He lifted a few hairs that had stuck to her lips. He caressed her cheek. "Hanna, please . . . please talk to me."

His fractured words, the pain, and the tenderness when he spoke, restored her to him. She lifted the tissue to his face and touched his lashes. The tears hadn't been hers alone. She knew that she had to speak, though she felt numb and ill.

"It's been one of the best things I've ever done."

No. My God, no, he thought. *This is not what I want to hear now! Why are you abusing yourself?* But he listened to what she had to say.

169

Hanna studied the tissue, in tiny, rolled pieces now, as she'd picked it apart. She breathed deeply.

"I love you George. I do. And it's not that I love her more than you."

"Why didn't you tell me?"

"That's the part I'm struggling with now. When you asked me before and I told you I didn't know, I still don't know. I can't put it into words." She ran her hands through her hair. She stopped when they snagged on tangles and wouldn't go all the way to the end. "I'm not so sure that anything in life is simple anymore. There might be a lot more to everything. And then I guess I take that back."

"Explain."

"Maybe things are simple and this great human brain of ours messes things up and makes everything more complicated than it is. I just don't know. I don't know anything."

He pressed her to him again. He kissed the side of her head and lost his lips in her hair.

He said it so softly he wasn't sure if he had spoken the words or if he merely thought them, "You were afraid of losing her."

"Protecting her at all cost was worth the risk to us. I guess that's the truth. It's the best I can explain it anyway." She cleared her throat and blew her nose. "Some of the other horses went to slaughter. Rochelle and I couldn't bear to think of that happening to her. So we made a pact not to tell anyone, not even you and Marc. You should have seen her. I've never seen anything so pitiful in my life. I can't imagine an animal being that starved. She didn't have any food. She didn't even have water. Her feet were in the worst shape. She could barely walk and she almost died. And she loves us. She loves me unconditionally."

"I love you unconditionally."

"No. It's not the same. I'm not so sure that humans are capable of that type of acceptance. Or, we let go of it as we grow up. Think about it. Why do you love me? Why did you ask me out? Because my looks attracted you. We had conversations; we shared values, goals, and common interests. With Safiyyah, there are no reasons.

She doesn't care if I come to the barn wearing no makeup, with my hair in a wild mess. She doesn't even care if I shave my head. She doesn't care that I have a college degree, that I played the flute and entertained audiences. She doesn't see my crow's feet. She doesn't make me feel the need to look in the mirror and worry about my sagging breasts. She doesn't care."

Stumped, George withheld words, but thought, *there is a whole lot more to this.*

"Even if I didn't feed her, she'd still come when I called her and want to be with me. No matter what I did, or failed to do for her, she'd still love me. She's completely incapable of hurting anyone. Yes, a horse could kick you. But that's not what I mean. She cannot and would not . . . hurt me. Rochelle and I sit in the barn with her laptop and we read about horses, other stuff too, but mostly about horses. Safiyyah gave me something to do . . . with *me*. I've never had anything of my own that was special to do. I've never been really good at anything. Name one thing, George, besides growing hair, name one thing I'm good at. But I was good at this. You're good at everything. You're a good Jew, you're a good son, a good husband, a good attorney, you're involved in important issues, everything. This was my very own thing to do. And I was good at it."

Hanna rubbed her face. Her eyelids had swollen so much that she could see them closing in. "I suppose that's not all, now that I think about it. Ever since I was a child," she said, her words broken again, "all I've ever wanted was to be a mom. Safiyyah gave me a place . . ."

Cherise. My God, that's it. George never once lost sight of the baby's beautiful face. He saw her just in front of him every day: in the morning sunrise, in new fallen snow, in front of him on every road he traveled, and at night in his dreams. She lived on in every tear that had just fallen. George knew that now. But not once during that harrowing time had Hanna Tauber ever cried. She'd always been a strong woman. *Right?* He'd been smitten by her, in part, because of that attribute. She amazed him at that time with her strength and ability to go on so soon after Cherise's death. But he knew that he needed to be strong for her. The doctors told him that losing a child, the most heart-wrenching, spirit-wrenching loss, could destroy them individually. It could also erode their marriage. Dr. Shapiro suggested counseling, especially for Hanna, but they never went. When people asked George how Hanna was doing in the days, weeks, and the months after, he had always said, "Okay, I guess." Now, it railed against him because he'd never known for sure. George assigned himself the task of being even stronger than Hanna, so that he'd be there for her, if, or when, she collapsed. To deal with his own grief, he'd thrown himself completely into his law firm. If he provided for Hanna, above and beyond, surely she'd feel secure. And Hanna had her music. Yet, he couldn't remember the last time the flute sang in his home.

"I'm sorry," Hanna said. "I've been rambling. I don't think you can understand all of this stuff."

"Are you saying that because I'm a man I don't understand what it means to be a mom?"

The power that had evoked those words stunned her: she hadn't mentioned their loss.

"Just because so many magazine articles say that men avoid emotion, doesn't mean that we don't feel it. I loved her, too, Hanna. I will always love her."

The stillness in the room swept to the walls and rose to the ceiling. One could hear the books on the shelves breathe.

"You've never said." The lumps rose in her throat again. But she managed to push them down with a series of forced swallows.

"*You've* never said. You're a small woman, but you're so strong. Sometimes you scare me because I think you're stronger than I am. I wanted to be her dad. There isn't a day that goes by that I don't think about her."

Tears began to rise in Hanna again. How could two hearts beat so close, yet so far apart, all these years? How could she have missed those beats right next to her own?

"I didn't know," she said. "You never mention her birthday. I didn't think it . . . I thought you were long . . ."

172

"Every year on Cherise's birthday I spend time outside by myself, with her. I stand in the wind, sunny days, cloudy days, rain, whatever we get, because if she was with me, that's what we'd have. So I spend the weather and the day with her. I tell her I love her and I tell her that I wish I could see her, you know, see how she's doing. Is she pretty? Does she have her mom's hair? Does she have my nose? Did someone build her a house for her Barbie dolls? Did she watch the game last night?"

Hanna's body trembled again, so much so, that the bed shook.

"I thought you blamed me," he said.

She grabbed him. She wept openly and tight against his shoulder. "No. No. Please, no. Don't go there . . . I didn't."

Over two decades of self blame began to flow away, as discarded shells on a beach are drawn back to the sea by the tide. In that instant, each also knew another truth. They must not go ahead with the rest of the conversation, not at this moment. The tide had also carried precious time away. And now, it was too late.

Just like that couple who'd drowned when their rowboat capsized. When their lifeless bodies came to the surface someone said, "Such a senseless thing. Here are the life jackets right within reach." They never searched. They never tried. The lifeline had been there all along and they'd never reached for it. There would be no second chance.

They held each other. They covered themselves with the puffed satin comforter. They fell into sleep, at first charred with nagging images that they had failed at the one thing that set them apart from all other living things—the gift of speech. But as the night carried them deeper, the feather-tip touch of cherubic baby girls and the gentle touch of white horse whiskers lifted troubled thoughts from them. They slept in peace.

CHAPTER TWENTY-FIVE

"IT'S SIX O'CLOCK in the morning," Hanna whispered hoarsely into the phone when she answered it. She glanced at George. He snored.

"Girl, you have got to go out and get the paper," Rochelle said. "See you at nine, usual time, right? We have a lot to do today."

Hanna sat up in bed. George, bundled in the covers, still slept. She shook him. He scratched the stubble on his cheek and rubbed his chapped lips. "Hey," he said.

"We have a cat, too." She leaped out of bed, yanked on the same jeans and pulled a sweatshirt over her head as she went downstairs, socks from yesterday still on.

They had made the front page.

The phone rang. George got it. Minutes later the phone rang again, and then again, and then again. The coffeemaker had just splattered its last drop when George came down the stairs and sat at the table. Hanna put the paper at his place so he'd see it right away. No more hiding. She made a promise to herself that she would do her best to never keep anything from him again. He ignored the paper as if he'd already seen it.

She had terrified him last night. He worried about her and was still horrified by what he had seen. *Did she really punch herself like that?*

"Who called?" she asked, trying to sound nonchalant.

"A lady." He rubbed his eyes, hoping to coax day and normalcy into them. "She wanted to know if you needed hay for the horse."

Hanna placed his coffee cup in front of him. She sat down next to him.

"And then a man called wanting to know if you could use an extra water tank."

She stirred the coffee for him and pushed it closer to him. She'd have held the cup to his lips, too.

"And then another called saying that he'd like to give you cash to use to buy feed." He concentrated on a faint groove in the table. "They all said that they'd read about you and the horse in the paper. Front page."

"I see." She sent a sip of coffee down her scratched throat. "There's an article about it in the paper this morning."

The reporter wrote: "Hanna Tauber, wife of George Tauber, of Tauber Law, and Rochelle Harris, wife of Dr. Marcus Harris, were arrested and released last night for breaking and entering into the barn of the deceased Roger Durfee."

Hanna thought it good that the bitter facts had been addressed immediately in the article. It went on to explain that one starved Arabian horse had been left in the barn and that 'Tauber and Harris' found her, nursed her back to health, and kept her existence a secret. "Tauber and Harris also discovered twelve saddles that had been stolen from the O'Connor farm. The saddles, valued at $44,700, will be returned to Stewart and Claudia O'Connor who were notified late last night that their property had been recovered."

"So now you're a heroine. And you've got fans," George said to the table, a simple affirmation of fact.

She touched the back of her wrist to his warm cup. She dumped it in the sink and filled it again with hot coffee. George didn't like his coffee reheated in the microwave.

"What would you have done if I had told you?" she asked.

It grieved him to look at his wife. Her eyelids were so swollen he wondered if she could see properly, if it was painful to try.

Her face had tinged gray from the late night and fitful sleep. He wondered, too, how badly she'd bruised her thighs. But he knew the horse was most important to her at the time.

"I would have called the police," he said. "I would have had no choice."

"But I did have a choice. I took that chance. You always do the right thing, the legally correct thing. In this instance, the right thing would have been the wrong thing. If I had told you in the beginning, there is no way you would have agreed to keep this a secret. There is no way you could have. They would have come and put her down right then or taken her away. A thirty year old horse in her condition doesn't get a good home. She could barely stand. They would have just put her out of her misery. There were bales upon bales of straw stacked up in front of the door in the loft. No one would have found the door for God knows how long . . . long after Safiyyah had been disposed of anyway. *Then* someone might have found the newspaper article, long after she'd been destroyed. But no one would have known it was the same horse. Safiyyah is solid white, or so it appears. The stolen horse in the article is dark, with four white socks. Gray horses turn white as they age. You cannot see Safiyyah's white socks until her legs are soaking wet. That's the only way white markings show up on a white horse."

Hanna touched George's cup. Still hot. She pushed it closer to him. "I followed my heart on this one. I would do it the same way all over again."

George nodded to himself, a contemplative nod, nearly invisible, weighing all he'd seen and all he'd heard. He looked up at Hanna. As if he'd relinquished his soul, he said, "Okay." He held his arms open. She hesitated, then stepped in. "I'm sorry, Hanna," George said. "I was hard on you. I may not understand you, but I do love you." He held her tightly, yet unburdened, and with a vulnerability that she'd never experienced before. She pressed his head to her breasts. She kissed the top of his head.

"And I love you," she said. "I don't understand me either. I don't think I ever have. But I won't ever do something like this again. Promise. I'll make it up to you. Think of something, anything, that you would like me to do, and I will do it."

Chaptr Twenty-Six

"You can wipe that wicked grin off your face right now, mister," Rochelle said when Josh came into Safiyyah's stall to trim her feet for the last time.

"This where I find the famous duo, 'Tauber and Harris'? I'm just glad that Durfee got beat for once, that at least one of his secrets and wrongdoings didn't go to the grave with him," he said.

"You knew Durfee?" Hanna asked.

"Sure I knew Roger Durfee. Everyone knew Roger Durfee."

Then Rochelle remembered. When Josh came to the barn on that first day, he'd asked if there was *still* straw in the loft. "You've been here, haven't you? You knew there was straw in the loft," she said. "Why didn't you say something?"

"If you gals wanted to tell me you were caring for a horse of Durfee's, you'd tell me. I knew about the straw, 'cause, hell, I helped stack it."

"Well, I'll be," Hanna said. "Nothing shocks me anymore. Did you trim his horses?"

"Trimmed all of them; thirteen at the time, just once, a few years ago. Stiffed me for the bill, never paid me for the work. Old coot refused to answer the door, refused to answer the phone."

"So then, you know Safiyyah, right?" Rochelle asked.

"No. Never seen her 'til the day ya called me. Always had a gut feeling Durfee had more horses hidden away here. They constantly changed. Never had the same horses for long, except Dice, Quarter

178

Horse stud he had for years . . . and this girl here. He must have had her all these years. He'd get drunk and haul a few out."

"Did Roger Durfee ever . . ." Hanna said, "Did he ever beat them? Did he ever mistreat his horses?"

"No. You know I'll give ya straight scoop. I'd tell ya if he did. Durfee didn't take best care of them, but I never once seen him abuse a horse or a dog."

"It sickens me to think what could have happened to her," Rochelle said.

"Doc would have just put her down right here. She was too skinny for the market," Josh said. "And as much as I'd like to blame Durfee for everything, she's been alone here for a while. Sure, he neglected her. Her feet have been neglected for years, but he did feed her, not enough, but ya gotta remember she'd been fending for herself until you found her. He's still scum."

Hanna pulled the newspaper article out of her back jeans pocket. She handed it to Josh.

"Don't surprise me one bit. That's her alright," he said.

"Do you know who those people are? We can't make out the full name," Rochelle said.

"Holy shit! That's the VanderZahns."

"You know them?" Hanna asked.

"Huge Arabian breeders in their day. Biggest and best years ago, cranking out one champion after the next, like *the* who's who in the Arabian world. Big bucks. And big bucks here I'm guessing." He nodded toward the Arabian mare whose sole mission involved weaving her muzzle through her hay pile to select the tastiest timothy stalks.

"VanderZahn . . . as in VanderZahn Jewelers?" Hanna asked.

"Same."

"Where do they live?" Rochelle asked.

"Hundred fifty miles north."

When Josh finished with Safiyyah's hooves, he packed up all of his tools and wiped the sweat from his face. He put his arm across the mare's back. "Probably the last time I'll see the old lady, isn't it? I'd imagine if any of the VanderZahns still have horses, they're

179

gonna want her back. Guessing this horse was worth a mint at one time. But who knows? Maybe you get to keep her."

Rochelle shook her head, no. Hanna didn't respond.

"Might be the last time I see you two." He doffed his hat to them. "Been a pleasure. Glad to been part of this." Josh knew what was in order and he also knew that he would have to make the move. He opened his arms and pulled the two of them together to his chest quickly. And just as quickly, he released them. He knew they'd get loose eyed.

"You done right," he said. "I'm proud of you gals."

"We'll never forget you," Rochelle said, sniffling. "You're a special man. Thanks for everything."

Hanna dabbed her nose with her sweatshirt sleeve, used the other sleeve to wipe away a tear. "Thank you. Thank you so much for all you did. I don't know what we'd have done without you."

"Glad to be here."

He winked and ducked his brow under that hat. He latched the stall door and turned his back to them.

"Josh?" Hanna said. "One more question."

"Shoot."

"What happened to the dog?"

"Old Bart? Last time I banged on the door to get money out of Durfee, Bart busted his chain, chased me and Regina all the way down the driveway. I took him home. 'Bout a month before Durfee croaked. Figured I'd never get a penny out of Durfee, least I got the best dog I ever had. Sleeps most of the day, but he's a good old cuss."

Josh tipped his hat again. Regina took him away for the last time. His exit hammered in the sad fact that these days had come to an end. Everything ached. To make it ache all the more, as if scripted so, cold drops pelted the ground. Hanna and Rochelle listened to the drops. They watched the wind punch the blue spruce boughs of the tree on the other side of the paddock, the one that the bird built her nest in. They listened to the sounds of the old farm. They heard each other's sniffles.

"Well," Hanna finally said, "we've got to talk. We've at least got to talk about something . . . anything. This silence is driving me batty. How did things go at your house last night?"

"The minute Marc got in the house, he cracked up. He laughed so hard, cracked up so much, he couldn't talk. Tears streamed down his face." She read Hanna's expressionless stare. "What's wrong? Did things not go well with George?"

"No. Oh heavens no. He didn't see any humor in it at all. Neither of us did."

"Marc thought it was serious," Rochelle said "but he said there wasn't much else to do about it, *but* laugh."

That night, Hanna opened a new tub of cherry cordial ice cream. George watched her for a few minutes and then told her that he'd come up with a way that she could make amends, as she had promised, for this transgression.

"I've thought about what you can do, what we can do. I want us to go to counseling. Together. There are lots of reasons we should do this. It's what I want. It's what we need."

She answered by throwing a spoon at him. "Buy me some African drums. They'll do a better job."

The next few days passed in whirls of activity, mingled with tangled-up lulls. In late afternoon on the third day, CK called with a phone number for Inga and Julius VanderZahn.

"I'm proud of you," George said when Hanna told him that she would make the call to Safiyyah's owners. He came up behind her, fastened his arms around her and kissed the curve of her neck. "I know it hurts. But I'm proud of you. I just want you to know that."

In fact, it hurt so much that Hanna couldn't sleep the night before. She envisioned renting, borrowing, even stealing a horse trailer and a truck. She and Safiyyah would disappear, somewhere, any place, but stay here. Rochelle would go with them. Even though foolish and childish to concoct such plans, it gave her mind a project other than steeping in worry.

Hanna hadn't been in the old shed since they'd moved into their new home. It had struck her as odd that it hadn't been torn down when the contractors built the house, because they certainly didn't match. But the shed became a good place for storage. When she opened the door, sunlight danced in front of her. She tapped her shoe on the floor. *Yes, the floor is dirt.* She scanned the interior. She smiled at the large tarpaulin parked against the back wall.

She hoisted a section of the covering. "Hey, you," she said. The Corvette lived here. She lifted the canvas and felt along the body. There were no bitty stuck bugs.

For their third wedding anniversary, Hanna had surprised George by finding the best of the best of body shops that specialized in Corvette restoration. She'd learned a hard lesson: never touch that car without first discussing it with George. So, she'd had to clue him in on the idea of her gift. He insisted on going to see the body shop to meet the man who would do the work and to interview him before he deemed him trustworthy.

Bogart Hartounian, wearing an apricot-colored jumpsuit with satiny lavender piping on the collar, broke into tears and nearly fainted onto the surgery-room-clean concrete floor of his shop when the 'Vette came tooling in. He yowled in a hyena yip. "Vandals! It was vandals what did this, wasn't it?" They didn't dare tell him the truth. Hanna might not have lived another day.

"From vandalism to breaking and entering," Hanna said, out loud. She sat on a nylon fabric lawn chair and admired the perfect red finish on the car. Once in awhile, on clear, sunny days, George would fire up the 'Vette. Occasionally, she went with him. Usually, he went by himself. She surmised that he needed time alone with his shiny car and with his fading youth.

Later in the day, Hanna and Rochelle huddled around Rochelle's cell phone. Hanna pushed the buttons. At first, a woman with a German accent from long ago almost hung up on her, seemed to have second thoughts, and then listened. Perhaps it had been that molecule of grief leaked from the caller that convinced the woman that this wasn't a hoax.

CHAPTER TWENTY-SEVEN

INGA VANDERZAHN CONSIDERED herself the wisest woman ever born. She had persevered, she had survived, and she had lived long and full.

At the age of seventeen she decided that she would do whatever she had to do to get out of Germany. The night before she made this decision, the enemies bombed Leipzig. Inga's home, where she lived with her mother and father, didn't take a hit. But she opened the door in the morning to devastation she wasn't prepared for: the charred remains of her neighbor's barn. All four of their Arabian horses were gone. Inga bristled with rage, the kind of rage that sucks the humanness out of you. Hans and Marie embraced as they stood next to a twisted piece of metal that used to be a gate.

Since childhood, Inga had dreamed of owning one of the beautiful horses with the dished face and the lofty, cascading tail carriage. Hans and Marie let her come over every day to brush the mares and their spindly-legged babies. This year, there had been two foals born, one colt and one filly. They never had a chance. Strange, how growing up in the midst of war, that the proportions of it are smaller as dreams are cut away when you are a youngster.

Inga turned to slip away back to her house. She didn't want her dear neighbors to know that she'd been watching. She noticed a small object hanging on the splintered fence. She thought it might be a poor unfortunate bird, blown up and impaled. But upon closer inspection, she saw the five-day-old filly, Sasha's, thumb-sized ear.

Inga hated the war and how it had changed everything. She hated soldiers. She hated Germany and she hated America. Yet, to America she planned to flee. All of her dreams had been torn away from her in a matter of minutes in the night.

"I refuse to stay in the middle of a war. Germany is ruined and I won't die just because I was born here," she said.

Inga didn't want Hans or Marie to find Sasha's ear. So, she took it home with her. How cold and lifeless it felt. She held it, as if doing so might turn it warm and living again. She sat on the empty rabbit hutch next to her house. They'd eaten the rabbits months ago, even though Fritz and Spot had been pets. Hunger can drive you to such barbarity. The horses always remained at risk of the same fate. Everything about the war confused and angered Inga. She wondered why her house had been spared, why the neighbor's house had been spared, yet, their sturdy, clean barn had been reduced to smoking ruins. She knelt beside the rabbit hutch and dug into the soil with her fingernails. She placed the ear in the hole and covered it up.

Inga checked the calendar she kept in her room. She scanned the past days where she had drawn an X on the day that marked the start of her period. She counted forward. She whispered, "Tonight. I have to do this tonight."

Inga Anne Shultz borrowed one of her mother's evening dresses and her mother's rouge. She fixed herself up to look, so she thought, older her than her years. She sashayed downtown that night. American soldiers lined the streets everywhere as the war came to a close. She chose the smallest group standing next to a mountain of rubble that had been Wirth's Shoe Store. She picked the handsomest young man, the muscular one, with dark hair. Though she hadn't had a lot of practice, she winked, and she strutted on her long legs and won him over. They had sex behind the bushes near the depot. Exactly according to her plans, Inga got pregnant by an American GI.

Bennett 'Bennie' Ellsworth was a decent man. When he learned of Inga's pregnancy, he married her and he took her home to America as his wife, just as Inga planned.

He loved her. And he was all she had in the new country. The last letter she got from her parents told her to not write to them anymore and not to come home. They shunned her permanently because of her 'foolish stunt.' She never heard from them again.

Inga spoke not one word of English and life with Bennie, as a couple, spilled over with almost unbearable difficulties. Inga assumed that by virtue of birth alone as an American, Bennie was rich. She learned the pungent truth the first day in her new home. Bennie only worked odd jobs here and there as a mechanic. The language barrier made their existence all the more frustrating and complicated. But they managed to navigate through these obstacles and found things to enjoy, pennies saved up to buy one ice cream cone, and laughter and dancing in the moonlight, simple pleasures not governed by language.

Soon after the baby came, Inga had to get a job to help buy food and pay bills. She got her first job at the local supermarket. Mr. McGillis, the owner, hired her to stock shelves. Mrs. Martinez, who lived in the downstairs half of the rental house, watched baby Elizabeth for them.

Inga studied and listened to everything that Americans did, and said, to catch on to life here. At night, she practiced English. She spent hours in the library. She checked out every book about horses and she devoured everything she could about Arabians. One night, as she sat in the library with the last book in the building about horses, she said, "Someday, I will have my Arabians. I will get them straight from the desert."

A kind and compassionate husband, Bennie told Inga daily that he loved her. He changed diapers, fed Elizabeth and rushed to her when she cried in the night. He rocked the baby and made her laugh with his clown faces.

But Bennie experienced dark times also; down times that held him imprisoned and tormented. It always happened in the night. If a police or ambulance siren blared in the street outside the apartment, the mattress would begin to shake, and the bed got tipped over and onto its side as Bennie forced his body under it. She would find him; sweating, and hysterical. She would shake him until he started to cry. Then she would hold his head to her chest until the terror subsided. He never told her what gouged the night and his sanity away from him.

One night the sirens wailed. Bennie left the bedroom, she assumed, to get a glass of water. She found him in the morning in the garage with a heavy electrical cord pulled tight down from the rafters around his neck. She had mere seconds to view the scene, because the phone buzzed. She was free to go answer it: she knew that Bennett Ellsworth, her husband of two years, was dead.

"Inga," Mr. McGillis said, with the sound of a cash resister chinging in the background. "I have bad news for you. I have to let you go. I'm sorry, but you don't need to come to work anymore. My nephew came home and I had to give him your job."

She sat at the kitchen table for an hour, like a chunk of rough-sawn wood. She should have been crying. But tears don't exist for situations so horrific. Her arms buried into a stack of unpaid bills. The rent was two months past due and she'd just lost her job. From the bedroom, Elizabeth stirred, calling out to be held, calling out for a breakfast that Inga would scrape together—and calling out for her daddy who hung from the rafters. There was no one for Inga. There were no parents to come over and hug her and no best friends to come running.

She lifted the baby out of the crib and held her close. "I promise you my Elizabeth, we will get through this. Some how, some way, we will make it."

America, in all its greatness, could be the place of broken dreams, if you let it. Inga had not allowed Germany to destroy her. She would not allow America to finish the job.

Yesterday's newspaper sat next to the bills. She flipped it over. That simple flick of her wrist set in motion events that would change the rest of her life. "Julius VanderZahn Elected President of Country Club," the heading on the back page read.

A week later, Inga applied for a job that didn't exist at the country club. But she crossed her magnificent alabaster legs, expertly choreographed, and leaned back in the chair.

The manager, Mr. Sims, tried to avert his gaze. "On second thought," he said, "you might be good for business. Do you think you can serve drinks?"

Julius VanderZahn's wife of eight years had passed away three years ago. On the first night Inga saw him, he relaxed with friends on the outdoor patio of the country club. As she walked past him, her long legs gliding and pushing each hip to the side, her heel just so happened to catch. The martini on her tray tipped over the edge and landed on his lap. Mr. Sims barreled out to the patio, screaming at Inga, and uttering comforting apologies in the next breath to Julius. Inga dropped her tray and burst into tears. Julius arose to put his arm around her so fast that his chair skated off the patio. "There, there now. Don't cry, dear girl. You didn't mean it." And then he addressed Mr. Sims brusquely, "It was an accident, Doug. Don't worry about it."

Julius and Inga Anne Shultz Ellsworth VanderZahn went to the Grand Canyon, to Las Vegas, and to Hollywood one month later on their honeymoon.

Pudgy, short, and forever balding, she liked him. And Julius, seven years older than Inga, loved her. The light of the heavens paled in comparison to his love for her. He also loved indulging her every whim and desire.

Julius owned a chain of successful jewelry stores. He owned half of an aircraft manufacturing company and another company that produced a fruit drink heralded as tasting like berries. Inga thought it tasted more like cucumbers. But people bought it anyway.

Julius purchased four hundred acres and built Inga a mansion, with stables and fencing so extravagant, queens would remove their shoes to enter. They traveled the world over and searched for the exact bloodlines of the Arabian horses that Inga wanted. They made wise choices and only imported breeding animals of the highest quality.

On the morning their first foal was born Inga circled her arms around the wiggly tot's neck. She breathed in the sweet smell of new life. She kissed a tiny chestnut ear and nuzzled his soft, curly mane. That colt, VZA Nile Rain, grew up to be an undefeated champion and *the* most sought after Arabian breeding stallion in the nation. For over five decades, VanderZahn Arabians dominated the horse world.

Julius had been blessed, not with looks, but with gifts of far greater weight and depth. He had a strong, creative mind, a compassionate and generous heart, and he loved Elizabeth as his own daughter right from the start. He and Inga also had two sons of their own; Peter, a flight instructor in Connecticut, and Henry, who taught philosophy at a small college in Texas. Elizabeth lived with Inga and Julius. She managed the farm now. Inga had four grandchildren, two girls of Peter's, and a son belonged to Henry. Elizabeth had no interest in being married, but she'd had a one night stand with a park ranger at Yosemite, got pregnant, and produced Michelle, another true horsewoman born to the family.

Inga's dreams did come true, just not in the way she had envisioned. She never went back to Germany. At times she thought of her childhood home. She wondered if her parents ever thought about her. She wondered when, and how, they died. But she never once questioned if she'd made the right choice. Through it all, she had fallen in love with America. She had been an American citizen far longer than she had been a German citizen. The dreams and the promises that America held came from her people, from their passion, their tenacity, their sense of humor, their empathy, and from the fact that no matter how fiercely they might disagree; their camaraderie always carried them through.

CHAPTER TWENTY-EIGHT

THEY HAD BATHED Safiyyah the day before. Rochelle latched the paddock door overnight so that the horse couldn't leave her stall and roll in the dirt. Every hair on the mare's body shone like satin. They sat on the sofa in the stall with her and waited.

"Remember when she ate the books?" Rochelle said. Her voice faltered, even though she chuckled. "Oh crap. This isn't going to be easy. My emotions are a mess."

"It's going to be okay, Rochelle. You'll see."

"I have to give you a lot of credit. I'm impressed. You're doing better with this than I am. I'm crying and I feel giddy all at the same time," Rochelle said. "Just think . . . this is our last time sitting here with her."

"Everything's going to be just fine."

Moments later Rochelle heard the sound of gears grinding. "That must be the trailer coming down the driveway." She hurried to the barn entrance. "You gotta see this thing," she yelled back. "You won't believe what's in our yard."

A metallic turquoise semi-tractor hitched to a horse trailer big enough to haul elephants rumbled in. The cream-colored trailer had matching turquoise striping on the sides, and fancy scrolled letters: *VanderZahn Arabians*. The chrome hubcaps on more than a dozen wheels sparkled. The driver had just enough room to maneuver the monster and circled it between the cabin and the barn, and stopped it, aimed it at the road.

All this for one horse? Rochelle thought.

They actually came, Hanna thought.

The driver let the engine idle. He opened the door and vaulted out of the cab. The size and weight of a jockey, he wore a baseball cap and a shirt the same color as the semi. His face stiffened as he scanned the condition of the place. But he smiled when he spotted the two women. He walked straight to them and offered a handshake.

"Hi, I'm Corky."

"VanderZahn?" Hanna asked.

"No. Oh gosh no. Corky Garrett. I work for them. This is so exciting. What a story this is. I remember the day the mare left but I'm going to let Mrs. V and Elizabeth tell the story. It wouldn't be right. It's their story. I was a kid back then but I remember. My parents worked for the VanderZahns. We lived in the hired hand's house while I was growing up. Me and my wife live there now. Where is the mare? My instructions were to hustle. We want to get her settled before it's late, so we need to move right along."

Hanna brought Safiyyah out to the trailer. Marc's Suburban pulled up alongside the semi. George and Marc eyed the mass of the colossal rig. George whistled under his breath. As they walked up and down the length of it, in awe.

Hanna held Safiyyah's lead while Corky fitted leg wraps onto the horse. The wraps fastened around each leg with Velcro tabs. He opened up the back door to the trailer and pushed a button that brought down a ramp covered with rubber matting so a horse wouldn't slip. Hanna passed the lead rope to Corky. Her breathe caught as she did so. The finality of that gesture gave Hanna a stinging sensation. Corky walked up the ramp. Without hesitation, Safiyyah followed him in.

"She acts like she's been in it before," Rochelle said.

"Not this trailer. This baby's brand new, the whole thing, tractor, trailer. But she was always good about loading," Corky said. "Follow me." He climbed back up into the cab.

Hanna and Rochelle sat on the back seat of the Suburban. Marc drove. And the trip began.

"Can you imagine what that thing cost?" George said.

"No. I can't even come up with a good guess," Marc said, "into the hundreds of thousands of dollars anyway."

Hanna hummed. George knew that she did that when nervous or happy. He guessed nervousness this time. She had to be sad about losing the horse. Almost no conversation took place in the back seat. George and Marc did all of the talking. They talked about sports, the weather, sports, and more sports. The tires clipped over the seams in the cement freeway. Outside, pines sped past in a continuous chorus line. Maple, birch, poplar, and a few oak trees filled in the remaining gaps. Their leaves were just beginning to emerge, like lace, on the vacant branches. A few pillow clouds clung to the crisp blue sky.

They poured the last of the coffee from the Thermos. George ate the last blueberry muffin. Two hours passed. "We've got to be getting close," he said. "Look at all of this elaborate fencing. We've been passing it for acres."

The turn signal came on ahead and the semi downshifted and then swung left onto an asphalt drive. The driveway spanned at least six hundred feet and swept to a full circle with a fountain in the center. A marble fairy sat on top of a waterfall in the fountain.

"Lordy," George said.

"It's a castle," Rochelle said, "It's a doggone castle."

To most, it did look like a castle. The two story stucco sprawled over thousands of square feet. A flagpole with an American flag the size of Texas also graced the front yard. There was a sunken pool in the distance to the east, and tennis courts off to the west. But to its inhabitants, this was just home.

Corky announced their arrival with two short raps of the horn. He drove beyond the castle to a huge barn the same color as the house, with white fencing attached, and two additional horse trailers parked near a second circular drive.

"And there's the matching *horse* castle," Rochelle said. "This place is incredible. I thought I had a nice home. The barn alone makes my house look like a shoe box."

Corky opened the back door of the trailer and went inside.

Inga and Elizabeth started on the walk from the house down to the barn as soon as the trailer pulled in. They waited just on the other side of the trailer when the back door opened. The horse would exit at any moment and they didn't want to startle her.

A Jew and a Negro, Inga thought. As a youngster growing up in Nazi Germany, she never paid much attention to Jews. That was easy, since all of the teachers made the Jewish kids sit in an isolated area of the room. The teachers spent so much time rearranging kids, Inga thought it the poorest use of a school day. She wished the teachers would spend more time helping her with mathematics. But she was a youngster with only one thing, truly, on her mind: horses.

She'd been just a kid when the war broke out. She was still just a kid when she came to America. It was then that she learned the enormity of what Germany and much of Europe had done to the Jews. She experienced the full gamut of emotions: denial that something so heinous could have occurred, hatred for her homeland, and finally grief for the millions of innocent people murdered. But after Bennie died and Julius came into her life, the horses came. And healing came through the horses.

Inga remembered the first time she saw a Negro. 1936. She and Papa had taken the bus to Berlin to watch one full day of the Olympic Games. The Nazi flags whipped along every street and throughout the stadium. Excitement filled the city. She waited for her father as he watched the track and field events. They watched Jesse Owens win the long jump. Inga had never seen a person so dark. But Papa explained that Jesse Owens, and all Negroes, belonged to a lesser species, just above chimpanzee but well below human, as Adolph Hitler preached. *I don't care,* she thought. She wanted to see the horses. She fretted and sassed until her father relented and took her to the arena where the equestrian teams competed. And she sang all the way home from that trip. Germany went on to win all of the gold medals in the equestrian events that year. And before she gave in to sleep that night, Inga thought about all of the magnificent horses she had seen; the intricate maneuvers they performed in dressage, and the gigantic obstacles they cleared in the cross country and stadium jumping. She also thought about Jesse Owens. He tied his own shoes and no trainer cued him to do it. *He's not a chimpanzee. He's a person.* And that was the end of it as far as she was concerned. She fell asleep, dreaming of horses and gold medals.

A Jew and a Negro, Inga thought again—those she had been told to hate.

The mix of emotions could have burbled longer in Inga's heart. But the miracle that the horse had returned to her after all these years recaptured all of her senses. Would the horse remember?

Three women came up to Hanna's group. "I'm Elizabeth VanderZahn. You spoke with my mother, Inga, and this is my daughter, Michelle."

Safiyyah pawed in the trailer. Her impatience forced brief introductions. She wanted out.

Inga succumbed to emotion and almost allowed herself to break down as the mare stepped off the ramp. Safiyyah whinnied. This was not the dainty nicker that greeted Hanna and Rochelle each morning. The mare called out, trumpeted, from deep inside her body, resonant and full of power. Elizabeth and Michelle burst into tears.

"She used to do that every time we brought her home from a horse show," Elizabeth said.

The mare pricked her ears forward. She raised and lowered her head to better discern the location. She flared her nostrils. She lifted her head toward the barn and out beyond to the lush pastures in the distance. She whinnied again: stronger, louder, longer. A breeze lifted the mare's mane. She breathed into it.

She knew.

The introductions put a face and a handshake with a person already known from the story. Inga, Elizabeth, and Michelle hugged Rochelle and Hanna, solid hugs that arose from the gratitude centered in the depths of their hearts. They hugged Marc and they hugged George. The men fidgeted, as men do, when caught up in an emotional moment with people they don't know.

Elizabeth approached the mare first. She trembled as she touched her face. "Do you remember me, my lovely one?" She spoke as if anything more than whispers would cause the vision to perish. She lifted her arms to put around Safiyyah's neck but tarried then, too. Seconds later, she embraced the mare and cried openly.

No dry eyes. No words. The minutes passed as you might turn the pages in an old photo album. You want to go to the next page, yet you want to stay and linger with the one in front of you before you go on, before that memory comes to a close. There is that part of you that resists lifting the page.

Safiyyah tugged on the lead rope and peals of laughter immediately replaced the tears as she jerked Elizabeth about two feet off the driveway and onto the grass as soon as she spotted it. She grabbed a good mouthful before Elizabeth gently pulled her away.

Swept into the present, Elizabeth gushed, "We have so much to talk about! Corky, walk her to the barn and we'll follow."

It seemed improper to call the structure a barn. It was so ornate, and so spotless, it intimidated most humans. A palace built for horses. Chandeliers in the halls, some eighteen feet up, provided the light, and bronze brick paved the floor. The brass fittings and door handles gleamed.

"This is a horse barn?" George mouthed to Hanna. She whacked him on the arm and growled. "Hush."

Safiyyah stepped onto the bricks. Her head went down and her weight shifted to her hind legs. She took only two steps. Her front legs abruptly bent at each joint and bobbled as she tried to support her body.

A groan erupted straight out of Inga's soul. She instantly put her fingers to her lips. She shook her head. It pained her to see the horse falter. "Take her easy Corky. She's foundered."

"Yes, ma'am."

Safiyyah walked to the first stall on the left with minced, guarded steps. The hard floor hurt her feet.

"She'd been horribly foundered when we got to her," Rochelle said. "Her feet are so much healthier now."

"Yes. I understand," Inga said. But the grief branched thick enough to saw through.

"When she's on dirt she canters and bucks and does this amazing trot," Hanna said. She didn't want sadness to ruin the day.

Corky walked beside the mare with the lead rope relaxed. He let her choose the pace. They all followed and gathered in the stall, deep with fresh pine shavings. Corky slipped the halter off. Safiyyah took a few sips of water and went in search of the fodder waiting to greet her.

"There is something I need to show you," Hanna said. She lifted Safiyyah's mane. "See this bead?"

Michelle gasped. She rushed forward, arms outstretched to reach it, beginning to sob. Her hands trembled as she cupped the blue bead. The other six stayed next to the horse wondering what they should do or say. They stared at the bead. They stared at Michelle and then at the bead again. Hanna had polished the bead with Windex that morning and it flickered like a jewel in the overhead light against the white horse. But Hanna saw it again, as she did on that first day, encased in hair and clay and then soapy when it broke free to glimmer in the sunlight. She'd never forget that moment.

Michelle faced them. She held her hands, as if she prayed, tight to her lips, with her thumbs braced under her chin. More tears brimmed in her lashes and then the tears fell unhindered. "I don't believe it's still there," she said. "I put this in her mane the day she left. That was twenty-nine years ago. I was ten years old. I wanted Scarlett to be my horse so badly but Grandmother said she was too full of fire to be a child's horse. They wanted her to do well at the national show and that meant she'd have to go to the trainer's. When you live on a horse farm, you learn that horses sometimes have to go away."

"What does the bead mean?" Rochelle asked.

"I'd just read about a Bedouin legend. The Bedouins tied a blue bead into a horse's mane for protection and to bring it safely home from a journey. So, on the day that Scarlett left, I took a bead from Mrs. Garrett's craft basket and tied it in there as tightly as I could. It's impossible that it stayed. It's a miracle. There is no way it should be there."

Driven by the ancient desert promise, a child's fingers frantically braided and tied the bead into the mane of a beloved, fiery young mare. Had Michelle cried in those moments alone with the horse before they'd have to part? Had she whispered, "This will protect you and bring you safely home"?

Twenty-nine years.

What could one possibly say?

For the first time, Marc reached out to Safiyyah. He stroked her face gently. George allowed his hand to caress the length of the horse's neck. Neither had ever touched a horse before. Both men stared at the bead again. They scanned the horse and returned to the bead. The story shattered common sense; all order that humans expect the universe to obey.

Drums echoed in Hanna's heart. And in her mind she saw a white horse racing over a dune with a cloudless cerulean sky as the backdrop. She felt the desert blow across her skin. She felt a chill swirl over her, as only the heat of the Sun can send.

Inga knew that she would have to be the first to speak. "Why don't we gather in the Ribbon Room?"

Blue and purple ribbons covered the walls in the Ribbon Room. Shelves built into the fourth wall held trophies of every size and design; made of gold, bronze, wood, and crystal. Decades of awards graced the room. It boasted a dining room set, a sectional sofa, a kitchen with a bar, a huge television, and a fireplace.

"Champagne?" Elizabeth asked. Responding to approval, she poured six glasses of amber brew. She served each guest and then her mother. She poured a seventh for herself.

Rochelle cocked an eyebrow in Hanna's direction: no Pucker here.

"You called her Scarlett," Hanna said.

196

"Yes," Elizabeth said. "That's her barn name. All of our horses have barn names. Her registered name is VZA Desert Wind."

"That's beautiful," Hanna whispered. "Absolutely gorgeous."

And then Hanna and Rochelle told their story. They explained how they had been walking, or biking, near the Durfee farm and how Safiyyah made her presence known, how she managed to make it to the road on her ruined feet. George and Marc heard the full story for the first time, too.

Hanna did most of the talking. She exuded such confidence it astonished Rochelle that she held it together so well.

"Now please tell us the story that we've been waiting to hear," Hanna said.

Inga sat back in her chair as her daughter and granddaughter took up the reins. Elizabeth had her father's wavy hair, gray now, and her mother's fair skin. Michelle wore her black hair pulled back in an elastic band, the no-fuss girl. She had the park ranger's russet complexion.

"The story begins a ways back," Elizabeth said. "My mom and dad had the dream to raise the most fabulous Arabian horses in the world. They searched all over the Middle East for the finest and most revered bloodlines. For years they went to Egypt and to Arabia to purchase breeding stock. Thirty-three years ago they closed the deal on a gorgeous mare in Egypt that they'd wanted for a long time. Her name was Leila and they brought her home. Five months later she gave birth to this spitfire of a filly . . . your Safiyyah. I wanted to call her Windy but Mom started calling her Scarlett and Scarlett stuck.

"Anyway, this was no minor purchase. They paid two million dollars for Leila . . ." Gasps from her audience momentarily interrupted Elizabeth, but she continued. "It was the highest price ever paid for an Arabian, possibly the highest price paid for any horse at the time. It made headlines.

"Scarlett started her show career as a yearling and she won first place in halter her first time out and won Junior Champion and Grand Champion. She beat out all of the adult mares. She never took less than first place and never less than Grand Champion . . . ever."

"What do you mean when you say you showed her in halter?" Marc asked.

"It's a class at a horse show where you don't ride the horse. It's judged on the horse's conformation, correct way of traveling, and on their Arabian type and beauty. In a nutshell, it's a class for breeding animals," Elizabeth said.

"She qualified for the U.S. Nationals at the age of three. Mom and Dad sent her to a trainer they hadn't used before, though he was highly recommended. His name was Jim Upshaw. He came up to get her. We stayed in communication with him all along and then he stopped returning calls."

"We learned that he got into serious trouble with the Internal Revenue Service," Inga said. "He left the country. We heard that he went to Costa Rica. Then it was Venezuela and then there was no news about him at all. The horses he had in training, all belonging to other people, were gone. We drove to his place immediately once we couldn't get him on the phone. Scarlett was gone, too. They did an investigation. Some of the horses were found and reunited with their owners. Scarlett was never found."

"Dad put up a big reward for her but no one ever came forward," Elizabeth said. "Rewards worked for getting those other horses back. Most people responded right away because they had no idea they had a stolen horse. Apparently Scarlett was the only one that got into the wrong hands. We got no response on her. Just like Jim Upshaw, she vanished. Weeks went by, then months, and then years. Over time we had to accept that we'd never get her back."

"I never got over her being gone," Michelle said. "I used to cry myself to sleep at night because I missed her so much."

"Did you know Roger Durfee?" George asked.

"No. We've never heard the name," Inga said. "The police talked to us a few days ago and asked us the same question. But we've never heard that name until all of this came about."

"If only she could talk, say where she's been, what she's done, what she's seen for all these years," Rochelle said.

"I wonder if that Durfee guy, or anyone else, ever bred her," Elizabeth said.

"He had lots and lots of horses over the years from what we've been told," Rochelle said. "It wouldn't surprise me."

"We used to check the registries to see if she had any recorded foals but nothing showed up. Durfee must have been smart enough, or crooked enough, to know that he shouldn't try to get papers on an offspring of hers using her name," Elizabeth said.

"Our ultimate plan for Safiyyah," Inga said, "was that she'd be our supreme broodmare after she retired from the show ring, the culmination of years of dedication to the Arabian horse. She possessed everything that dreams are made of. We did breed her mother in the years following and got six more foals from her. We could never try for another Safiyyah, of course, because the sire was in Egypt. You see, it could never be the same. There is never another to simply replace what you've lost."

"She went to the trainer twenty-nine years ago and she was three at the time. That makes her thirty-two then," Marc said. "Isn't that quite old for a horse?"

Knowing where the conversation had swerved, Inga said, "Arabians are a very long-lived breed. Yes, Safiyyah has some years, but her mother lived to the age of thirty-four. Some live even longer."

"She's had two bouts of colic. One was pretty bad," Rochelle said. She felt that Inga and Elizabeth should know that the elderly mare had special needs now. "And you already know about the founder."

"But you saved her," Inga said. "And you've taken care of her. That's what's most important."

"We don't know how to thank you enough," Elizabeth said.

"We've had a lot of fun with her, too," Rochelle said. "We've learned so much about horses, the hard way. One time she acted all scared, prancing and dancing, snorting and pawing. A bird's nest had fallen to the ground. She scared herself silly over that."

"That's a horse for you!" Inga said, laughing. "And if you showed her the nest, she realized that it wouldn't hurt her, then. But the next time a bird's nest falls to the ground she's going to react the same way all over again. It's all in how a horse is programmed. We can't change how we are wired." She scanned her attentive listeners. "She saw the bird's nest, not as you did, but as she should have, as she was created to see it."

She waited for her words to settle. "Elizabeth, dear, would you please put in the video of Scarlett at the regional show and the one of her playing with her mama."

With her audience held fast to the screen, baby Scarlett, almost black in color, romped on white-socked legs. Poor Leila whirled in circles to keep track of her. Scarlett leaped straight up with all four feet off the ground. She play kicked at her mother. And when she could invent nothing else, she bucked in place; a fierce rodeo bronco. She strained to reach nibbles of grass, slept in the afternoon sunshine, and cantered beside and ahead of her mother. A young girl skipped beside the filly and frolicked in the grass with her. A willowy blonde woman in short-shorts with endless legs swiveled her hips for the cameraman and made kissy faces at him. A traffic stopping beauty at fifty, Inga exuded sex appeal. And she hadn't lost her radiance at eighty-two. Inga hugged the girl, hugged the filly and hugged the mare. She ran with them up a knoll and over the crest.

"That's me and Grandma," Michelle said. "Grandpa was shooting."

"I didn't make it into the film," Elizabeth said. "I was sitting off to the side. I got dumped off a horse I'd been training and was on crutches. I broke my leg in two places."

Elizabeth fed a second video into the player. A dark, silvery-dappled gray horse exploded into the show ring, head up, nostrils flared, and tail cascading over her back. Three year old Scarlett, setting the horse show world on fire. The camera panned the audience: on their feet and screaming.

For two hours they watched the mare. Rochelle and Hanna and George and Marc, so captivated by the scenes, never looked away from the television. Inga, Elizabeth, and Michelle smiled, and watched *them*, not the screen.

"There's one more I'd like to show you," Elizabeth said. She switched the tape. The footage began with the dappled mare standing still. Then her white legs began to move and they launched her into a weightless trot as she sailed over the turf.

"That's her trot!" Hanna said. "What *is* that?"

"That's an extended trot. Each stride is long and suspended," Inga said. "All horses can do an extended trot. But no horse was ever born with . . . that trot. I've never seen it before her and I've never seen it since. She has the magnificent extension but also lofty action with those knees. There was nothing like her then and I've never seen it again. I must say, I am deeply impressed that you see it, too. Elizabeth, slow that down."

Safiyyah's trot had been such a gift that it filled an entire tape. Her front legs never seemed to touch the ground. That exquisite moment where each hoof hovered and appeared to stop in midflight, had been captured and preserved on film. They watched and they watched. They couldn't get enough of it; the white socks, the magnificent tail and mane, and the near airborne horse.

"I wish we could have known her then," Hanna said, wistfully.

"But then, you wouldn't have lived this miraculous story," Inga said. "As it is, you brought a miracle full circle. She was my dream, the most special, and you have brought her back to me. You have to grab the moments as they come and as they are. They don't repeat. You get once chance at each."

Michelle turned on the table lamp next to her. Daylight had begun to diminish and this offered a gentle reminder that the day neared its end.

"I hate to say this," George said, "it's getting late. I wish we could stay longer but I have a client to meet in the morning."

"You should spend some time with Safiyyah before you leave," Inga said.

Corky opened the door from the Ribbon Room into the barn hallway. Safiyyah whinnied. It stung Rochelle, painfully stung her.

Other horses in the barn whinnied, too. Six additional Arabian faces over the stall doors greeted them. Horses thrived on the love and respect in their home.

"I had Corky bring in a few of the horses that I thought you'd like to see," Inga said. "They are some of Safiyyah's half brothers and sisters and a few of her other relatives."

Like youngsters meeting horses for the first time at a county fair, Rochelle and Hanna breezed from stall to stall petting each horse and talking to it.

"I never knew that so many gorgeous horses existed . . . and you have them all in one place," Hanna said.

"They're beautiful," Rochelle said. "But not one of them is as beautiful as Scarlett."

"She is one of a kind," Inga said.

"I do have a question for you," Hanna said, "when your horses get old . . ."

"Come with me, dear," Inga said. "Michelle, push me to the back of the barn, please, dear."

Michelle grasped the wheelchair handles and guided her grandmother's chair down the bronze brick hall toward two large doors at the end. Corky rushed ahead and slid one of them open.

Rochelle counted ten stalls on each side of the barn. Two more hallways, one to the left opened into yet more stalls, and one to the right led to an Olympic-sized indoor riding arena. VanderZahn Arabians had been a magnificent operation in its day.

The doors opened up to a vast meadow, the one in the video with the knoll. Inga swept her hand out toward a series of pine trees of all different heights along the crest. She pointed to each tree and began calling out their names. "Sasha, Rain, Mac, Sammy, Angelique, Gloria, Becky, Bennie, . . . *Leila* . . ." She looked up at Hanna. "Do you see, dear? They are all here," she said, once again with a graceful gesture to the trees.

The pines would stand as testament on the horizon, honoring what was gone, and as a promise for all beneath them. More horses grazed in their shadows.

"How many horses do you have?" Rochelle asked.

"Not as many as we used to. We don't breed them as we did in the past, maybe just one or two foals a year. There are ten out there," Michelle said. "We've always had a waiting list for our horses. They're all over the world now."

"Every horse you see out there is, in some manner, related to your Safiyyah," Inga said.

Hanna's breathing skipped. Goose bumps sped over her skin.

Most of the horses were varying shades of gray. One bay and two chestnuts grazed with them.

"Awesome," Rochelle said. "Absolutely awesome."

Sadness tried to force its way into Hanna but she'd let nothing interfere with her confidence. Not today. If just one tear got loose she'd never be able to stop them and she'd embarrass herself if she broke down and wasn't able to stop.

Rochelle contemplated the stunning woman seated in front of her. Inga defined elegance. The perfectly coiffed hair, the diamond jewelry, of course, her slim and toned body. Rochelle hoped she'd age that well herself.

Michelle wheeled her grandmother back to the front of the barn. Everyone else strolled beside them, slowly. They didn't want to let go.

"You must spend some time with your horse before you leave," Inga said again, a ring of urgency, a ring of demand in her voice.

And everyone listens to her, Rochelle thought. *It doesn't get much classier than that.*

"George, Marc, let's head up to the house. Come along my girls," Inga said.

And then it was just the three of them again: Safiyyah, Hanna, and Rochelle, just like old times, one last time. Hanna pointed to the stall door. A tarnished brass plaque read: VZA Desert Wind, and in parenthesis below, "Scarlett." They never took her name sign down. The other plaques on the stall doors were shiny and polished. Scarlett's tarnished plaque spoke volumes. It spoke of grief, the ache of what could have been and should have been. It spoke of longing, it spoke of hope, and it spoke of the promise to never forget. To polish the brass would have tarnished the magnitude of her absence.

The pine shavings smelled clean and fresh, with a subtle turpentine aroma. The mare had a near Volkswagen-sized mound of hay in front of her and a bucket of fresh water hanging from a hook on the wall.

"Why didn't we think of a hook? Remember all those times she dumped her water over?" Rochelle said. She chuckled and then became somber. "Oh my. I don't know how I'm going to get through this."

"It's tough, Rochelle. But everything will be okay. You'll see."

"I thought you'd be the one falling apart . . . look at me."

Hanna kissed the horse on the muzzle. Rochelle hugged the mare around the neck and kissed her cheek. Rochelle stood on one side of the horse's body and Hanna stood on the other side.

"Remember when we used to pour coffee like this over her back?" Rochelle said. She sniffled.

"And now we find out that she's royalty."

"I don't ever want to forget anything about her," Rochelle said and she burst into tears. The force of the emotion crashed into Hanna and sent her own tightly-contained emotion pouring out of her, too. They reached across the mare's back and hugged each other. The mare stopped chewing. She turned her head first to the left and then to the right and bumped her muzzle against each woman's shoulder.

They let their arms fall to their sides as they stood facing her, lips trembling, teardrops finding their way down.

"You understand completely don't you little one?" Rochelle whispered. "You understand it all, don't you?"

"She knows," Hanna said. "She knows how much we love her. She knows how special she is to us."

They hugged her and palmed her beautiful face one last time. They lost themselves in those entrancing midnight eyes one last time. They hugged her again. Rochelle kissed her on her upper eyelid. Hanna kissed the horse's muzzle again.

Rochelle tipped her head, motioning, time to go. This was it. Rochelle stepped out into the hall. Hanna closed the door. The bedding rustled; quick and worried. The munching ceased. They knew that her head hung over the stall door watching them leave her.

Don't look back.

The horse nickered. In all their time with her, she had never nickered when they left her. She whinnied to them every morning and every night when they came into the barn to do chores, but never when they left. Rochelle knew this to be the last time she'd ever hear that sweet voice. It cut through her and hurt so badly she could almost feel her heart bleeding.

They hugged for a long time and cried and they wiped each other's tears away. Then, they face the door taking them out of the barn. They both looked down. Near the door, a brass bushel basket on the floor, filled with apples, seemed to almost jump out at them. They smiled at each other and stepped out of the barn arm in arm.

"You have two wonderful women as your wives," Inga said to George and Marc when she saw the women coming up from the barn. "I cannot begin to thank them enough. Be easy with them. This is not going to leave them any time soon."

Hanna and Rochelle stood before them, humbled, like spent soldiers reporting after arduous duty.

What now?

I have something I want you to have," Michelle said. She closed Hanna's fingers around it and held them tightly with her own hands.

"No," Hanna said. She knew instantly. "You mustn't . . ."

"It rightfully belongs to you. She's home now. She made it safely home."

Hanna clutched the bead in her fist. The journey for the little horse was over.

And I have a gift for you," Inga said to Rochelle. "This is her first blue ribbon . . . and this one is her last."

The ribbons had faded over the years. The blue had become a dusky hue. Six satin streamers fell from five-inch rosettes at the top of each ribbon. Gold fringe trimmed the edges.

"We have the story between the ribbons. You have the story that followed," Inga said.

"I will treasure these forever. Thank you," Rochelle said.

"We'll have to keep in touch," Elizabeth said. "I'll call you now and then and let you know how she's doing."

There had been definite times in Inga Anne Shultz Ellsworth VanderZahn's life when she drew upon that special measure of wisdom that she'd been given. This was one of those times. She read Rochelle through to her soul. The apprehension and the pain of what the future held, painted her face.

"Why don't we leave that up to Rochelle and Hanna? If they want to know how she's doing they should call *us*," Inga said. "Do not call them, Elizabeth. Understood?"

Elizabeth nodded. Understood.

"Now, if you'll excuse me, I'm going to the house," Inga said. "I need to lie down."

Hanna and Rochelle hugged her. George and Marc hugged her. And the stately woman guided her wheelchair on the brick walk leading to her home. The butler opened the door for her and the palace consumed her.

Ronald wheeled Inga into the library as she requested. He brought her jasmine tea, as he did every evening, and he left her alone. She would spend the twilight hours reading, as usual. She pulled the book wedged between Chaucer and Twain from the bookcase. *Gone with the Wind.* She opened it, ran her fingers over well-worn pages, and put it back in its place.

It had been a storybook life filled with all of her greatest pleasures. Photographs covered the library walls; many of Julius, of the two of them together, of Elizabeth, children on ponies, and countless photographs of the breathtaking Arabian horses. Vacations, holidays, when Michelle was first born, when she had a front tooth missing in grade school, and then in another, wearing a cap and gown for graduation. All of it held in frames and held in time.

There were no photographs of Bennett Ellsworth on the walls. There were no photographs of him at all. He had lived on only in Elizabeth; in the way she tilted her head when she smiled, in the clown faces she invented one day to soothe Michelle. Those were Bennie's pictures. Now, Inga had to strain her memory to see him in his uniform, laughing, and smoking Lucky Strikes with his GI buddies in Leipzig.

It hadn't happened at all like she'd envisioned; growing old with Bennie and believing his promise that he'd buy her a horse one day. She'd walked barefoot, through rugged mountains of emotions, during that time in her life. She'd chosen Bennie, to save her life and her soul from the ravages of war. She'd chosen Julius, to save her baby and herself from the ravages of poverty and despair.

She loved Bennie. She had loved him from that first night. She had never stopped loving him. He had stopped. Her love for him only grew and mellowed over the years, like it would have, had he been there.

She grew to love Julius, too. But it had taken time. Looking back, Bennie had always been her true love. She blamed Germany for destroying him but she blamed America for the final scene.

Time and again, back then, she had gone to the Army offices trying to make her attempts at English effective. A few of the men listened, but some of them snickered. She reasoned that it made sense for them to laugh at a German girl, but to laugh during any conversation regarding one of their own and the pain he carried? Unthinkable. Every time Bennie had an episode she would ask them to help him. Help never materialized. As a young woman, she believed that Americans could do anything. Frustrating as it had been, she grew to temper her unrealistic expectations and she'd come to realize that few resources existed at the time for Bennie. No one would have known how to help him soon enough.

And now, alone in her mansion, the memories kept her company. When the time came, she would go to Bennie and Julius.

She knew it would happen some night while she sat with her books, waiting for them to come for her. Bennie would offer his hand, just has he had done on a street corner in 1945, and she would go with him. Julius would be smiling.

She wheeled her chair over to the window overlooking her paradise. She smiled at the gathering of six, now saying their farewells. She let the curtain swing back into place.

"I don't know how we can ever thank you," Elizabeth said.

"Grandma has been such an active hell-on-horseback horsewoman all her life," Michelle said. "They both were. My grandfather passed away four years ago."

"As you can see," Elizabeth said, "my mom isn't well. She really wanted to have all of you in for a scrumptious feast but she gets so tired now. This is her second bout with cancer. It first hit her lungs. She smoked, Lucky Strikes, most of her life. Darn her. Now it's in her bones and they just found that it's spread to her pancreas. It had been her vision to build an empire here. And she did it. Mom and Dad did it. The bloodlines of these coveted desert-bred horses will live on . . . as long as the world has space for Arabian horses. They searched the world over for one special mare. Dad bought Leila for my mom as an anniversary present. She told him that he could have the mare. She wanted the baby she was carrying. Scarlett.

"Scarlett's disappearance was really hard on my mom. For years she blamed herself, that if she hadn't sent her to Jim we'd still have her. You can't imagine what it means to her to close this with such joy; bittersweet, but joy nonetheless."

"How did you come up with name of Scarlett?" Rochelle asked.

"Who knows?" Elizabeth said. "Mom just picks names that she likes or that mean something to her. For whatever reason, she came up with Scarlett and it stuck."

"I love her registered name," Rochelle said. "It's mystical and spiritual."

"My dad named her. He always used to say that the wind, the desert, and the sea all share the same soul, and that each carries promises and dreams in its waves," Elizabeth said. Her glance swept out to and along the far meadow. The wind blew the horses' manes and tails, swirling all around them.

"Your mother is wonderful," Rochelle said. "This whole day has been like stepping into another world. Thank you so much for spending the time with us."

"We have a long drive," Marc said. "I have to be in surgery in the early afternoon. I know George has appointments in the morning. We really do have to get home."

Hanna sat rigid and quiet in the car. She only caught snippets of the conversation: how classy Inga, Elizabeth and Michelle are, what a fantastic place they have and what a wonderful home for horses. *Blah, blah, blah.*

Rochelle joined in the conversation, too, and to the extent that she forgot about Hanna. Like a scruffy pair of old loafers, they'd become so comfortable with each other that they could just exist somewhere in the other's vicinity.

Hanna pitched herself into the deepest, darkest mental abyss she could locate. She listened to the tires of Marc's suburban clicking over the seams in the pavement beneath. That sound had always provided a boring, pleasant consistency. Yet, it didn't seem like she was in the vehicle at all. It was like she hovered above the scene watching it unfold.

"No!"

No one paid attention to her. They were too deep in their conversation.

The stars, like jewels, lit up a cloudless sky when Marc pulled into the Tauber's driveway. The men shook hands goodnight. Rochelle paused. She peered into Hanna's face before she gave her a squeeze.

"Nine o' . . . I'll call you tomorrow," Rochelle said, catching herself midsentence.

Hanna crossed her arms around her body as she watched Rochelle walk away. The night air and emotion chilled her.

"Are you coming in?" George asked. He waved to the Harris's one last time. Marc popped the horn a final goodbye.

"Not yet. I'm going to walk around in the yard for a bit. You go in. It's been a little much for me and I need to get settled."

The wind had picked up but carried only the sound of the dissonant swishing of spruce and ash. The same moonlight, one hundred and fifty miles to the north, also shone in her yard.

She opened the door to the shed. She didn't bother to turn on the light. Anger vexed and then possessed her. She rammed her fist into her pocket, latched onto it, and with as much force as she could muster, threw the blue bead into the darkness.

CHAPTER TWENTY-NINE

WHEN GEORGE CAME home from work the next day he surprised Hanna with a little box wrapped in green paper with a white bow on top.

He watched his wife. She stared at it. It was not a happy stare.

"Well?" he asked. Then he realized his mistake. "I'm sorry," he said. "It's too soon, isn't it?" She hugged him

With anguish in her heart, she set the box down gently in front of her. She looked at him. "No, it's pretty. I love it."

She lifted the gold chain out of the box and held it up so that it dangled full length. She knew its purpose.

"I thought you might want to wear the bead around your neck and I wanted you to have a new chain, a special chain for it," he said.

Her response hurt him. She knew it, though he'd covered it well. A lot of thought had gone into that gift. *She* wouldn't have come up with the idea to wear the bead around her neck. But George had. She didn't have to lay the chain against her chest to know. The bead would rest right on her heart.

The biggest fool ever.

She hugged him

With her chain, her box and its bow, she hustled to the shed. Once inside, she slammed the door and leaned against the first wall for support. She burst into tears so powerful they pulled her down the wall and onto the dirt floor.

"God, please . . . please, please find the bead. I'm sorry!"

She searched everywhere for that bead for two hours. It had held fast, moored to the horse's mane, a guardian for twenty-nine years, against all odds, against all weather, and against all evil. It took only one quick hand and one second to kill it and destroy its meaning.

She didn't find it. It was a frail, old woman, hunched over and lost, who walked back to the house. She'd have to tell George the truth. The bead was gone. But not until she'd searched again in the daylight. It had to be in there.

Soon, George would want to see how the bead looked on the chain around her neck. "I'm not ready to wear it just yet," she'd say, and that would work for maybe a week. Next she'd probably tell him that she lost it.

For four days Hanna returned to the shed to search. She didn't find it. She sniveled in her misery.

"So much for you, God!"

On that fourth day she shut herself in the shed. And at that point she didn't care if anyone heard her yelling.

"I hate you! Maybe you don't exist. If you do exist, you sure don't pay any attention to me! Why did you let that happen to her? Where were you?"

She punched herself hard on the thigh and kicked the wall of the shed. "I don't ask for much. I never ask you for anything, and this is what I get. Where were you!"

As soon as she'd finished her tirade, an immense cloud of doom descended. If there had been a whale nearby, she would have crawled into its belly. A closet would do, but there wasn't one of those in the shed either. She expected the shed to be struck by lightning, maybe by an earthquake, to end her evilness once and for all. She slid down the wall in her usual fashion onto the dirt and sobbed.

At the house, George told Rochelle, "I think she's in the shed."

"What are you doing in the dirt, girl?" Rochelle asked. "I brought you something." She deposited Ting Tang onto Hanna's outstretched legs. The kitty prowled back and forth, up and down her legs, purring, and rubbing against Hanna's chest. After the fluffy greeting, he dashed away, bubbling with cat glee. New spring moths lived in abundance here.

"We just learned this morning that Marc's allergic. You're going to have to keep him." Rochelle bent over for a better look. "What's wrong with you? You've been crying."

And what was that Rochelle saw hanging on the other wall? She walked two steps toward it. Melancholy met her at the halfway point and stopped her. Now, she understood. Now, she knew how Hanna had been able to remain so stoic and so composed through the ordeal of giving the mare back to Inga. Their bucket of brushes hung from a shiny brass hook. A new water pail sat on the floor beneath it, waiting to be mounted in its proper place.

Rochelle eased down onto the dirt floor beside Hanna, their arms touching. A forlorn breeze whistled through the rafters. Ting Tang zigged and zagged as he chased four moths that flitted just out of his reach.

It all made sense now. How could anyone not love Hanna Tauber? Such a bright, wacky woman, she seemed only to be impersonating an adult, most of the time. Quirky, edgy with sadness, and innocently funny, Rochelle never knew what to expect from her.

Rochelle cleared her throat. She spoke softly. "You thought they were going to give her to us."

Ting Tang caught the first moth and ate it. He brought the second one to Hanna and Rochelle. He tried to spit it out for them but it stuck to his tongue, so he ate that one, too, and went in search of the third and fourth.

"I really thought . . ." Hanna said. Her voice wavered. "I really thought they wouldn't want her. Who wants a horse that old?" Hanna drew her knees up to her chest, put her face tight against them, wrapped her arms around all of it, and cried.

"They did."

"But she was ours."

"No she wasn't. She was never ours. Girl, you are such a baby. Sometimes I just want to slap you. Other times, I want to hug you. You got to accept she was never ours. We loved her for a short while. They've loved her and missed her all these years. She belongs with them."

"I know, I know, I know," Hanna said. "It was foolish. But I believed it. I really clung to that hope. It's all I had. Even right up to the last minute when we were there I expected them to say that we should take her back home with us, even days later and every time the phone rang . . ."

"I'm so sorry," Rochelle said. "We'll get through this. I know it sounds hokey but we have to remember the good times. We had a lot of fun with this and we learned a lot, too. And we did a good thing. One of the best things I've ever done."

Hanna nodded. Yes.

"We have memories to last forever. Remember when we carried that first bag of feed?"

Hanna chuckled.

"And how many pounds of M&Ms do you suppose we ate?"

Hanna laughed out loud.

"Lots of good times. I'd do it all over again," Rochelle said.

"Me too."

They had a vault filled with memories. They laughed, they cried, and they laughed yet more as they sat in the dirt reminiscing. Ting Tang caught and ate the last two moths he'd been hunting. He curled up on Rochelle's lap and snoozed.

"Rochelle?"

"Yes."

"I have a question for you."

"What is it?"

In a weak, gravel-strewn voice, Hanna asked, "Where did you get your bike?"

Hanna went back to the shed the next day to sit on her dirt spot. She belonged in the dirt now. Ting Tang strutted over with another moth. She could always tell when he had a choice morsel in his mouth by the way he moved. Confident and cocky, he flipped his front paws out with each step, like a tiger back from a successful hunt.

"What have you got?"

The great hunter sat before her. He dropped his head and presented his prize to share with her. When she didn't jump at the opportunity, he batted the moth. It was a very dead moth. As much as Ting swatted, it never moved. He gave up and sat beside the trophy. He didn't want it. Hanna pitied moths he mangled but had no interest in eating. She stepped on those floundering moths and squished them dead since they'd never be able to fly again. She even stepped on the already dead ones that he didn't want, just to be sure they were truly deceased and out of their misery.

When she stepped on this moth, it resisted. She stepped harder thinking that she might have missed the moth and had stepped on a pebble. She ground her foot and wriggled it over the moth. She moved her foot. The moth left a deep indentation in the dirt. Near breathless with anticipation, she clawed into the hole and scooped out a smooth object. She flicked off the sand, still not fully daring to hope. The sunlight, streaming in from the cracks in the roof caught the gold flecks as it glistened and sparkled. "My bead! My bead!"

Hanna squeezed it so tight her hand ached. She kissed it. She grabbed Ting and held him. She kissed him and laughed through tears.

"I'm sorry," she whispered, again and again, "I'm sorry." She closed her eyes and lifted her face into the sun streaks falling onto her through the roof cracks. "Thank you! Thank you! Thank you!"

She danced. She danced in the shed in the dirt. She held her flopping, purring cat with his front legs against her and his hind legs dangling. She fiercely gripped her bead. She spun in circles. She laughed and she cried and she danced beneath the sun.

CHAPTER THIRTY

THEY EACH RETURNED to the comfort, and the expected, that their lives held. But the new days would never resemble previous days; the days before the horse. A horse that, without any knowledge or intent of her own, had changed lives, and filled craters of empty places.

And just as Inga foretold, Hanna and Rochelle didn't bounce back quickly. As a quilt comes together and nears completion, it could only happen one stitch at a time.

One night, as Marc held Rochelle cuddled in their big-enough-for-two recliner, he asked, "How are you doing with this?"

She shrugged. It hurt. She missed everything. She missed the routine, missed her morning and evening walks to the barn—trips that had real purpose. They still walked every morning but they went a different way. They never went past Safiyyah's Road, not since the day the trailer came to take her away. Rochelle couldn't shake the ache that had wedged in her heart. More than anything, she ached for the little white horse.

"What made her so special?" Marc asked.

Rochelle considered her words. She wanted to say it so that he'd understand. She sighed before she began.

"It wasn't just the horse. It was the whole experience. Who finds an abandoned horse worth millions?" she said, initially trying to force humor, nervous humor. But he listened, with no obvious emotion.

"She had no one, Marc. Think about all those times you drive by a field of horses or you see one being ridden down the road. Someone owns that horse. You *saw* it, people driving by *saw* it. No one, not one human on this planet knew she existed. It rips my heart in two to think that if we hadn't come along she would have died all alone. That beautiful creature, with that heritage, would have died without anyone ever knowing. Did she think that any day someone who had loved her in the past would come and take her home? Was she angry at people? Did she stay awake at night remembering the good days? The answer is, no. Horses don't think like we do. She was just an old, starved horse. She didn't know she'd been purchased for a million or a penny. She didn't see any difference in Durfee's rundown barn and Inga's castle. All that mattered on the day we found her was that she had water to drink and food to eat. That's all that matters to a horse. The moment they're in. Taught me a lot. And she was so happy to see us every morning. She'd whinny . . ."

Marc brushed a tear from Rochelle's cheek.

"A horse, so strong and fast, yet she can't do anything for herself," Rochelle said. "She can't get her own drink of water. She can't get her own hay down from the loft. She can't do anything on her own. Remember that television program that said that dogs are like perpetual puppies and that's why people love them so much? I think it's the same with horses. She was like a perpetual child to care for, that needs you, and who will never grow up into something wiser and different. She was a completely different being, yet our worlds meshed easily and without seam."

"Why don't you play your flute anymore?" George asked. Hanna had just poured them each a glass of orange juice.

She sat down and stared at him. "Do you know how long it's been since I've played?"

He blinked a few times, stumped. He hoped to pull out that one memory. He couldn't.

217

"It's been two years, George. Two years and I'll never pick it up again."

"What happened? What's changed?"

"I just found what was there all along. Me. You know the story. I told you I was given a flute when I was four. I don't remember *not* playing the flute. I cannot remember not playing the flute like I cannot remember not being alive. I didn't choose the flute. When I was little I thought everyone played the flute. When I got older, all I ever wanted to do with it was have fun. I just wanted to play jazz, pop, or kid music. I didn't want to get into all of that serious stuff. My parents wanted that. Everyone went nutso over this kid with a waterfall of hair and a flute and what they believed to be talent and they just had to take it and make it their own. I didn't want to go to recitals. I didn't want to go to college and major in music. I didn't want to play professionally. I didn't want to give lessons. I didn't want any of that crap. It was someone else's dream. Do you know what the most awful part is? I was average. That's it. Sure, when I was a little kid they proclaimed me a prodigy. But when I grew up and went to college, I was just average. All those years wasted and for nothing. I never wanted to play the stupid flute."

"So what *did* you want?"

"All I ever wanted, since the time I was a little girl, was to grow up, never go to college, marry a man just like the one I have and be a mom. That's it."

Hanna slid in her slippers to the sink, rinsed her sticky juice fingers, came back and sat down again. "There was nothing more. Not for me. There were no great dreams of becoming president or an astronaut. It was so simple and basic for me. My dream was to become a wife and a mom. Nothing more."

Hanna pulled a paper napkin out of its holder, smoothed it and refolded it. She crammed it back in with the other napkins, more crumpled than it had been.

"That one day, when I didn't play, felt so good, yet I thought cannons would blow holes through the walls if it became known that 'Little Hanna Glassman' had chosen not to play her blessed flute. I chose not to play and it felt awfully good. I didn't play the next day and then the next. I never went back. It's like I started to find my own brain then. I have my own thoughts and there are things I can do. I'm just not sure what . . . but something of my own choosing."

She tipped the glass to her lips and drained it. "I'll never play again. I think we should sell the flute. I'd rather have a . . . I'd rather have a . . . boat. Yes. Let's buy a boat."

George put his glass on the counter. He looked out the kitchen window noting that the birdfeeder needed to be filled. "You say it was a waste. Maybe it seems like a waste to you. But what about all of those people who heard you play over the years and were thrilled? What about the enjoyment people got out of hearing you play? What about me? It wasn't a waste. Don't think of it that way."

"How about matching canoes?"

Later that day, Evans Pharmacy called. George answered the phone. Hanna had gone to lunch with Rochelle.

"Mr. Tauber? Your wife brought in film to be developed a long time ago and she's never come to pick up the photos. Do you want them? They really should be picked up."

"Sure. I'll come get them today."

George didn't recall Hanna taking any pictures. In fact, he couldn't remember the last time she'd used her camera. Had it been that long, that he couldn't remember? Where had he been? No camera and no flute for years.

"There must be a mistake," George told Nola at the pharmacy when she plunked eleven packets of film down in front of him.

Nola pointed. "Isn't that her handwriting? She filled out the envelopes herself."

No mistake. Hanna had gone wild with her old 35mm camera.

"Eleven rolls of film." George kept saying it as he walked to his car. He turned on the ignition and opened the first packet. When the photos spilled out, he shut the car off. All of the Safiyyah days had been captured on film. The photographs flowed out in front of him: Hanna smiling with the horse, hugging the horse, laughing. Hanna kissing the horse on her muzzle, Hanna holding up a bottle of Pucker. *Pucker?*

An abandoned grocery cart wandered down the grade in front of him, smacked into a light pillar and tapped the Lexus. George didn't look up. He'd never seen his wife so happy. Never. He flipped through the photos: Hanna brushing the horse, holding the horse's front hoof, Hanna carrying a hay bale, sitting spread-eagle on the ground with a spilled bucket of water pooled around her.

"So that's where the muscles came from."

Hanna had taken pictures of Rochelle, too: Rochelle mixing something in a pail, Rochelle sitting on a blanket, Rochelle with an apple and a knife.

There were photos of the two of them, sitting side by side, grinning, like junior high school girls. They'd wrapped themselves securely in the missing Mexican blankets. They toasted paper cups to each other and to the camera. Christmas lights plastered the wall behind them.

"She finally figured out how to work the timer on the camera. They made their own fort, a clubhouse, in the barn," George said.

The horse graced all of the photographs in the next packet. She wore a red bow around her neck and a plaid coat of some type. Hanna had photographed the horse loose outside, in the sunshine, in the clouds, standing, moving, and eating an apple. The most compelling was a close up of just the horse's eye. The last photo in that bunch was another close up of the bead in Hanna's soapy hand. The impact of the image ... George coughed. *That must have been the day they found it, two crazy women with a hose.* He knew that one of them could be dangerous with a hose. He squinted and tried to discern what Hanna held while she scrubbed the mare's back. Good. Not a Brillo Pad, just the pink scrubby from the shower. He wondered what she'd done with it.

Hanna wore the top to the swimsuit she'd bought in California on their last vacation. *What, six years ago?* Sopping wet in the photo, her hair hung loose, like wet ribbons and water glistened on her arms and chest. A fountain of mascara swashed down her face. George chuckled again. "Who *is* that woman?"

The next day Marc picked George up at his office to go golfing.

"Look at these," George said. He flung one envelope of film onto the dashboard in Marc's direction.

Marc reached for it. "What's this you've got?"

The photos tumbled out onto his lap. He scrambled to scoop them up. He flipped through the first stack, slowing in the wake as he turned each three by five.

"I like this one of Rochelle," George said. "She's got nice . . . dimples."

"Yeah. She sure does."

Rochelle had been caught in the middle of a whooping shriek. Her T-shirt was soaked clean to the skin from the blast of icy cold water that Hanna had just delivered.

"Hey, give me that!" Marc said. "Don't you be looking at my wife's dimples like that." Marc ripped the photo away, laughing. He put the picture above the visor.

George peered down into the envelope to take out another collection of photos. *Should I remind him of the negative? Nah.*

"This one is priceless," George said. "I can't believe she finally figured out how to work the timer on the camera so that she could be in it, too. Look at those two. Soaked to the bone, arms around each other to fit in . . . I've never once seen Hanna smile like that, not in years anyway. The funniest part about it, check out that poor horse in the background. She looks like she's pouting and thoroughly pissed that they forgot about her. I didn't know a horse could show that much emotion."

"And she's purple," Marc said. "What the heck do you suppose they did to her? What is that stuff? The whole horse is purple."

"Maybe shampoo. The girls look like they're having a riot of fun, couldn't have been anything too bad. Only the horse looks pissed. A horse probably cares for baths about as much as a dog does."

George put the photos back into the envelope and into a side pocket on his briefcase. "I've been thinking. Maybe we should get them another horse."

"Man, I don't think there is another horse," Marc said. "I think it was *that* horse. I don't think we can replace it with just any old horse. It sounds like a good idea, in theory anyway."

"I suppose you're right." George watched the scenery rushing by as Marc drove to the golf course. It all blended into one solid canvas of colors. "I don't think I'll ever understand the nature of women."

"I'm not so sure we're supposed to understand everything," Marc said. "I think that's the rules of the game. They pulled a good one hiding that horse. But they did good, too."

"Hanna said Rochelle told her that you laughed about it, when they got arrested. You really think it's funny?"

"I laugh my ass off every time I think about it. I see a lot of humor in the whole thing," Marc said. One day, he'd tell George about that night. He walked into the police station and people called him Doctor Harris . . . and he hadn't been the one arrested. Someday, he'd tell him the whole story.

The weeks went by until they were more easily counted in months. Rochelle and Hanna still met every morning to walk. George and Marc played golf. The four of them got together at either home at least once a week for dinner and to play cards or a board game.

"We're getting old when we can sit here and play Scrabble for hours . . . and like it," Rochelle said.

Marc and George ventured over to the south shore one day and met Cappy, a black man in his nineties who owned a bait shop. He was the aged ruggedness of driftwood with a head of white hair the size of a bushel basket that he never cut. Cappy played his harmonica all day long. But he only played one tune, *Won't You Come Home Bill Bailey*. He promised Marc and George, "Fix you right up; bait and a boat or bait and a shanty, ten bucks. Come back and see me anytime. Come back just to chew with me."

Marquitta came home unexpectedly for her mom's fiftieth birthday in August. Hanna went to Rochelle's the morning that Marquitta came home and finally got to meet her. Marquitta carried her dad's athletic build and her mom's pretty face. She, too, wore red lipstick.

"They share that. They must have fun buying lipstick as a team," Hanna said under her breath. *What would we have shared?*

A little girl bounced down the stairs and into the kitchen. She couldn't resist the adult laughter. Marquitta brought the eight year old home with her. She was the daughter of Nathan Dorsey, Marquitta's colleague.

KeShandra's baby-skin cheeks appeared velvety soft. Her long dark hair was split and combed into sections and fashioned into five plaits, each with a pink barrette on the end. She wore pink pajamas and pink slippers with little elephants on them. Hanna wanted to pick her up and squeeze her.

"I'm going to make baked potatoes for us," the little girl said. She skipped away to another corner of the kitchen.

"He's a good man, Nate," Marquitta said. She glanced at KeShandra to make sure she was occupied and not listening. "Nathan Dorsey. He's our head biologist. His wife left him two years ago when she got tired of competing with dolphins. She said that he loved dolphins more than he loved her. She packed up and moved back to Burbank." Marquitta leaned forward and whispered. She tilted her head toward the child. "She just walked away from her, too. Can you believe that?"

Marquitta took another sip of coffee. "He does love dolphins just like I do. He set up a whole new training facility for them and a separate set of special tanks for orphans brought in from the sea. He's amazing. He's funny and he's so gentle with every one and every thing."

Hanna punched Rochelle in the thigh under the table. She winked at her.

"Momma, I have something to tell you."

Hanna punched Rochelle again. Harder.

"Nate is a little more than just a colleague."

Rochelle jumped up and squealed.

Marquitta, sweetly, coyly said, "He's asked me to marry him."

Rochelle yanked her daughter to her feet and hugged her so forcefully Hanna thought she would break her in two. She squished Marquitta's cheeks. "Oh honey, that's wonderful! I'm so happy for you!"

"We want to get married in Australia, okay Mom?" The words came out muffled because of the cheek squishing.

Rochelle, at first alarmed, hesitated, but she could think of no good reason why not. She released Marquitta's face. "Sure, if that's what will make you happy."

"And Hanna, you have to come, too. You will come, won't you?"

Hanna froze. Hesitated. Rochelle saw it all pass over Hanna's face as if on screen: the hopes and the dreams, the longing, the absence, and what would never be. Then Hanna nodded, slowly at first, and then with certainty. "Yes. Yes. I'll come. Nothing could keep me away."

In the middle of a group hug, the merriment came to a halt. A little voice, filled with Australia, piped, "Oh Lord, bless it, bless it, bless it." KeShandra had four baked potatoes lined up on the countertop steaming from their turns in the microwave. She brought the first one to Hanna.

"I asked the Lord to bless it for you. Keets said that you are only supposed to eat food that the Lord has blessed and has a 'K' on it to tell you that it's kosher. See? I cut a K in it with a knife. This one is okay. You *can* eat it," KeShandra said. A busy fledgling, she fluttered away. "I'll get the butter and the sour cream and the ketchup."

The women covered their mouths and fought back an explosion of laughter. Their bodies pulsed up and down, the seismic activity had to surface in some manner. The table rumbled from the boxed-in emotion.

Marquitta whispered, "I love her so much."

"And see? I made a K on my potato, too. But it's for KeShandra. Oops, I forgot our forks." She whisked to the counter.

"Keets?" Rochelle asked

"Nate calls me Keets," Marquitta said. "It started one day when we checked over a wounded orphan. He needed me quickly and said that Marquitta is too long to say when he needs me. Everyone calls me Keets now. *I* call me Keets," Marquitta said, laughing. "We have a lot of fun. I can't wait for you to meet everyone. Hey, 'Shandra, tell Momma and Hanna how many pets you have."

"I have seven cats, three dogs, a spider, my own dolphin, well, until Daddy turns her loose in the ocean, forty fish, two lizards, a snake, two gerbils, a peacock, a parrot, and a cockatoo."

"Almost sounds like that recitation should be a Christmas carol, doesn't it?" Marquitta said. "That reminds me. Do you know what she wants as a souvenir from this trip? All she has been talking about to take home with her from America is a frying pan. All she wants is an American frying pan."

Marquitta propped back in her chair. Her body language seemed to ask, what do you think of that? As if rehearsed, all heads swiveled to KeShandra. Rochelle pursed her lips. She nodded slowly in the affirmative. A frying pan. Hanna started to speak, changed her mind, and poured another cup of coffee from the carafe.

"Yes, we will get me that frying pan, the one with the little chicken on the handle that we saw in that magazine," KeShandra said.

"All she thinks about is cooking. She wants to be a chef," Marquitta said. "Tell them who you want to cook for."

"The queen."

No one snickered. Just a few minutes with the precocious child, it became obvious she'd be able to pull off anything she desired.

KeShandra came back to the table and climbed onto her chair. She raised both eyebrows and glanced from face to face with a look that appeared to ask, why aren't you eating?

And so, at nine-thirty in the morning, Rochelle and Marquitta, Hanna and KeShandra sat at Rochelle's kitchen table sipping on raspberry flavored coffee and eating baked potatoes.

Hanna got home late in the afternoon. "I'm going shopping with Rochelle and Marquitta and KeShandra now," she said. "We'll make it a full girls' day." She didn't take her over-sized paisley purse with her. She stuffed a wad of bills into the back pocket of her jeans. She waved at George. "I need shoes." The door closed with a loud rap and rattle.

Shopping? Shoes?

George rose to his feet. He scratched his chin. *No, this can't be.* Hanna had changed over the past months. Gone was the woman who put on lipstick to walk to the mailbox. Gone was the woman who cried mascara during sad movies. Gone was the woman who walked on her tiptoes so that her spiky heels wouldn't become mired in the lawn. And those spiky heels in every color only served as dust roosts in the closet now. She lived in track shoes and a pair of clunky old cowboy boots.

Of course, during the Safiyyah days, Hanna had been a mysterious creature because of the secret. But it was more. The musty, horsey smell, the slight fragrance of her own sweat and the nuance of whatever perfume she'd splashed on that morning, all blended together in a tantalizing, wild way. She wore no makeup at all, not even that sticky fruit flavored goo that stuck to his lips when he kissed her. She quit painting her fingernails, clipped them off, and she had more than one callous on the undersides of her knuckles. And she hadn't been on a shoe binge in a long, long while. He didn't want the old Hanna back. He wanted the old, new Hanna to stay.

Shoes can be dangerous. He drank a beer. He watched TV. He drank another beer. He waited. And all of that had been for naught.

She came home with one pair of sandals.

CHAPTER THIRTY-ONE

"YOU OKAY?" MARC asked in the middle of one September night when Rochelle sat up in bed.

"I can't sleep," Rochelle said. I think I'll go downstairs and read. I don't want to turn the light on and disturb you." Marc had already trailed off to sleep again.

Rochelle dug through the drawer near the phone in the kitchen and pulled out a note pad and a pen. She poured a glass of Diet Coke and sat at the table. She didn't want to read. She hadn't come down to the kitchen to crack open any book at all. Troubled thoughts and an uneasy sadness plagued her. Tonight there would be words. The words always came when emotions brewed strong, though she hadn't had words in a long time.

The first and only time that Rochelle wrote her words down on paper she'd been nine years old. Words came to her that first time about Mrs. Jarvis, who lived next door. Mrs. Jarvis described the rainbows that adorned the sky after a rain. Mrs. Jarvis had been born blind. Rochelle scribbled the lines of her first poem, all six of them, with a pencil stub. She went to school the next day and told Pauline, who sat in front of her, "I've got words! I've got words!" Pauline told all of the other kids to stay away from Rochelle. Whenever Rochelle tried to join them they screamed and ran from her. She chased after them and begged to know, "What did I do?" But the kids threatened, "Don't come near." They walked in large arcs to avoid coming in contact with her. Rochelle ripped up her poem and threw it in the trash. She vowed that she would never again tell anyone about her words.

Rochelle thought about how complete the damage had been to her little-kid psyche. She'd never fully connected at school and had very few friends there. She hung around with kids from church. Having words was a very bad thing and she dealt with the shame in the best way a nine year old could.

After graduation, Rochelle never went to a class reunion. But one year, Char Adamson located her and called her. "But you must be there. It's been twenty-five years."

So she went.

Within five minutes, Pauline waddled over to Rochelle, dribbling punch onto the floor as she balanced on gold sling back heels nearly squashed under her abundant poundage. She hugged Rochelle and motioned to two empty chairs against the back wall.

Rochelle listened as Pauline babbled on about her first and second husbands, both of whom had cheated on her. The third, and current husband, Stove (Rochelle couldn't bring herself to ask if that was a nickname or for real), couldn't make it to the reunion because he was loading logs onto a truck. Pauline pulled out forty-thousand photographs of her three husbands, nine daughters, eight grandchildren, twenty-six cats, eleven dogs, their old mobile home and their newer old mobile home, and one of Stove, glassy-eyed drinking beer with two guys sitting on logs. At least three dozen empty beer cans littered the ground at their feet.

"And how have *you* been?" Pauline asked. "Didn't we have fun in school?" Pauline cackled like a plump fryer. "Do you remember when I told all the kids to stay away from you? Oh, I can't believe I did that! Oh, the things we do when we're little! But I had never met anyone who . . . well . . . no one ever came up to me and announced that they had worms!"

"What?"

"You said you had worms. I thought I should warn all the other kids."

228

"I told you I had *words*, Pauline. Words, poetry, I was writing poetry."

For less than ten seconds Pauline halted the cackles. Then she started laughing so hard Rochelle couldn't tell if her honking gulps of air were those of laughter or of choking. Pauline waddled away into the crowd, still yowling, her spindly heels screaming from stress fractures.

Pauline had left a photograph of Stove on the chair that she'd filled. Pauline had married white, all three times. *Guess that's the best she could do.* Rochelle considered chasing after Pauline to give her the snapshot. *No.* She tossed the Polaroid back down onto the chair and walked through the mildew scented hall, with crepe paper streamers, red and white balloons, punch, and weird looking hors d'oeuvres made of warm ham rolled up in stale pita bread, and left.

Rochelle put her head in her hands and breathed deeply. The microwave clock made precise clicking sounds. She didn't know it made that much noise. 3:15. Emotion, like a shadow with no name, stole into the kitchen to sit with her.

One solitary red and pale green Gala sat in the middle of the table. It stared at her. It stared at her almost to the point she should ask, "What?" She stretched forward to touch the apple but she couldn't reach it. Her fingers only swirled as if trying to grasp wispy seaweed swaying just out of reach.

It would have been perfect for her.

She wanted to feel the apple's cool, firm weight once more. She wiped a tear away and stretched her arm out. Again, she couldn't reach the apple. It troubled her that she couldn't reach it. Her hand remained suspended and still. She closed her fingers and drew back. The apple sat there. It continued to stare at her, told her what she didn't want to hear. Rochelle picked up the pen and began to write . . .

Through the grassy meadow
I have been
Looking back, behind me,
Now it sleeps
Under silver stars
And beneath the Moon
Carry me away now
Far and beyond
To warm and shimmering sand
To desert sand
The sand in my dreams
The sand that gave me life
The wind, she whispers sweetly
Calling me, calling me, calling me home
She is singing now
The songs of places
I never knew
Lullaby songs, love me songs
Singing to my heart
Rise above
Rise above
Carry me away now
Far and beyond
Upon my wings
Beyond the desert Sun

She put the pen down. A teardrop fell on her wrist. She rubbed it into her skin. Another one fell and she pressed her forefinger into it.

"Baby?"

She felt his presence, felt his grip on her, though she hadn't heard him come down the stairs. She wiped her tears with a frayed tissue she'd found in her robe pocket. Marc clasped his arms around from behind, crossing them at her chest. He rocked her. He kissed the top of her head. Nothing, nothing, nothing in the world took the place of Marc's long, muscular arms fastened around her. One of his arms loosed and extended toward the table. He picked up the sheet of paper and read the poem. Rochelle did nothing to stop him.

He cleared his throat, the same way he cleared his throat when he told her of an impossible, yet successful surgery, how he'd cleared his throat when he first held Marquitta, how he'd cleared his throat when he lifted Marquitta up the first step to the bus on her first day of school. He moved to the side of Rochelle and pulled a chair over to join her. He knew the answer, knew her penmanship, but he asked, "Did you write this?"

"Yes."

"It's amazing. How long you been doing this?"

"Since I was a kid. They come to me in my head. But this is the first one I've ever written down. Do you like it?"

"Like it? It's amazing. You have to keep at it, Rochelle. I want to see more. How come you've never told me you write?"

"I don't actually write. This is a first. I've never told anyone because the words, the poems, just stay in my head."

"You absolutely amaze me, woman. I had no idea. I'm married to a poet." His surprise and joy showered Rochelle with subtle joy. It tempered the ache in her heart at three-fifteen in the morning.

Marc took her by the hand to guide her up the stairs. "I just want to hold you in my arms in the dark. Let's go up," he said. He reached for the light switch. She resisted and held back.

"Would you do me a favor?" she asked.

"Sure baby."

"There's an apple back there, sitting on the table. Could you . . . put it away for me?"

CHAPTER THIRTY-TWO

THE NEXT MORNING when the phone rang at eight, Hanna answered, "Hey, girl." Neither answered the phone with the traditional greeting anymore. They knew each other's ring.

"I'm heading over, bringing you something," Rochelle said.

Hanna didn't hear Rochelle pull into the driveway, didn't hear her zip through the backdoor and into the kitchen. Hanna swooped around the corner from the pantry, saw Rochelle standing by the dishwasher, jumped, and they burst into laughter. They didn't have to say what they were laughing about: Rochelle with a pitchfork—and Hanna armed with hay. No one else would have understood. "I'll throw this at you!" Hanna threatened with a sheet of paper toweling.

"Come outside," Rochelle said.

Rochelle's bike, parked on the cement walk, blocked the way. "It's yours. Marc bought me a new one, the *dark* green one I wanted. He surprised me with it this morning before he left. I wanted one with fatter tires, too. Not this kind. I've hated the color of this bike since I've had it. But I didn't want to hurt Marc's feelings so I never said anything until a few days ago."

"And I think it's the prettiest color. I've always loved this bike! Do you want me to pay you for it?"

"No, silly, it's a gift. I want you to have it."

Hanna's arms flew around Rochelle's neck. "Thank you so much! This is the best present ever."

Rochelle's *new* bike didn't come out of the Jaguar without a fight. A fifty pound bag of horse feed offered less resistance. But after they'd jerked and twisted for ten minutes, the bike's clean fat tires bounced on the cement at last.

"Let's go for a ride," Rochelle said.

They laughed and chatted about all kinds of stuff; fun stuff, serious stuff, girl stuff.

"Dunham's is having a meat sale tomorrow."

"Did you see the news last night?"

"I have to show you what I bought George for his birthday."

"Marquitta called last night."

They didn't pay attention to where they were going and they fell into an old habit. They noticed too late.

"We haven't come down this road . . . since," Hanna said, as they squeezed their handbrakes. But they pedaled on. They made the turn onto the two-track, just like old times. They stopped when their barn came into view.

The cabin had been torn down. Like eerie temple ruins, broken cement pillars of the foundation stood over left behind hunks of siding that came off during the destruction. A heavyweight bulldozer rested near the barn. The right side of the barn had already been pushed through and the dislocated wood poked up as giant Pickup-Sticks dumped out of their box.

The footpath to the barn hadn't grown over. "We wore this poor ground bald," Rochelle said, "permanently bald."

Inside, everything looked the same, except that there wasn't a horse in the barn. The structure had reclaimed its musty smell. An echo lived there now, that lonely sound that old buildings make when they weep. The spiders had come home in even greater number and had built grand fortresses with their new webs. No one must have told them about the bulldozer parked just outside the building, so close it touched the wood.

The sofa hadn't been moved. The blankets remained exactly as Hanna had smoothed them for the last time. They sat down once again, and faced the empty stall. A half-eaten pile of hay sat in its usual place, the water bucket beside it, so she could reach it. A film of dust covered what was left of the mostly evaporated water.

The door leading out to the paddock was sprung open and a breeze coaxed squeaks from its rusty hinges. They'd left it that way. No one had closed it when they walked her out to the trailer, there was no reason to.

The memory of her, so powerful, so real; she was right there with them again. She munched her hay, eyed them, and twitched her ears, listening to every word, listening to the music, coming over to nuzzle, to ask for an apple. She was there, again, lying in the straw in agony, unable to stand. She was there, clean and snowy white after her bath, floating above the turf, showing off that God-given trot.

Hanna ran the bead back and forth, back and forth along its chain, as she had grown accustomed to doing several times a day. Habit now. Habit forever.

"I'll never forget her. I can't think of any time that I've cried so much as I did during those days," Rochelle said. "But we laughed a lot, too."

"Remember when she screamed and scared us . . . all because she wanted an apple?"

"Remember when she rolled in the dirt and we gave the poor little thing *two* baths?"

"We'll probably go to hell for that one."

"Remember when she ate the book?"

"Remember when she first stood up?"

"For two women who'd never once been around a horse, I think we did okay," Rochelle said.

Hanna tugged something out of the wood behind her. She dangled several long white hairs in front of Rochelle. "Tail hairs."

"I'm wondering," Hanna said, "maybe we should call Inga and Elizabeth."

"No . . . we said we weren't going to do that, remember?"

"We didn't say that. *They* said they wouldn't call *us*. We didn't say anything about that."

Rochelle waited. She knew more would come.

"I suppose you're right. We'll leave it be."

Rochelle swallowed. She must not cry.

Hanna shook out and folded up the Mexican blankets. She draped one over her arm and offered the other to Rochelle. "Do you want your blanket?"

"I'd like that. Thanks." Rochelle pulled it to her chest with both arms as if to give it a hug. "It smells full of memories."

"How do memories smell?"

"They smell like grandmothers. And they smell like sweet horses."

"What a time we had with this," Hanna said. "It was the most amazing time of my life. And you know girl, it couldn't have happened with anyone but you. Sometimes it's hard to believe it really happened. But I guess all of this is the proof."

"How long did we do it?"

"Seven months," Hanna said. "Seven months and two weeks."

It was time for a final look, time for the final release, time to imprint. One last look, they scanned the empty barn that had been their second home not so long ago, when she lived in it. But it was no more.

At the end of the driveway Hanna got pulled to a stop, just as she'd been on that first day. In her heart, from her heart, in the wind; the little voice nickered once again, that one word, just as she'd heard it then.

Me.

Chapter Thirty-Three

"I want ice cream. Let's make a run into town," Rochelle said. So they cruised into Lake Luffit proper, as they did everyday, to get sundaes.

"What the heck is that big purple thing over there?" Hanna said. "And over there. And there."

Every street corner had a large pyramid-shaped purple thing positioned just under the street lamp. One man braced a ladder for another man on the top rung as he hung a purple decoration from a street light, as they had done for the length of the street.

"I'll pull over and check it out," Rochelle said.

She parked the Jaguar, still running, next to the curb. She picked up something at the purple pyramid and examined it. She came back to the car, got in, and sat motionless.

"Well? What is it?"

"Eggplants."

"Huh?"

"I'm telling you the truth. Each street lamp has a pile of eggplants stacked up beneath it. But they're fake. They're plastic. Plastic eggplants."

"Go to the library. Mildred will know what this is all about."

Into the Lake Luffit Library they marched. Hanna hadn't been inside the library since the day she'd had the colored conversation with Mildred.

"Have we hit the Twilight Zone or what?" Rochelle said, as their pace dwindled to cautionary steps. Every desk and table in the library had its own eggplants, three or four on each. But *they* were real. Purple banners hung from the library walls, purple decorations draped along the counter, and Mildred wore a purple ribbon in her hair. She held a purple pen with a tiny eggplant on top of it.

They startled Mildred. "Oh, I'm so glad you two came back!" she said. "I wondered how you've been. I read all about that poor little horse. That was such a wonderful thing you did, saving her like that. You're celebrities in town. But no one wants to intrude. We all thought that you're pretty private people since we don't see you that much."

"We'd do it all again," Hanna said. "But maybe we'd tweak a few things. Getting arrested isn't too swift."

"What's with all of the eggplants and the purple everywhere?" Rochelle asked.

"Oh, no. We mustn't use the word purple. The *correct* word is aubergine."

"Okay," Rochelle said.

"No one told you? I forget you are so new here and we just don't see you that much. This coming Saturday is the Eggplant Festival," Mildred said.

Rochelle repeated, monotone, "Eggplant festival."

"Oh, yes! It's quite exciting. We have a lot of fun every year."

"Who grows eggplants?" Rochelle asked.

"We all do," Mildred said, slowing her words down. "No . . . I can't really think of anyone who doesn't grow them."

"Do you market them?" Hanna asked.

"No. We just grow them for ourselves."

"What do you do with them?" Rochelle asked.

"We eat them. And we have the festival. You've never eaten eggplant? Have you ever . . . held . . . an eggplant?"

Hanna and Rochelle looked at each other, shook their heads and looked back at Mildred, still shaking their heads, no.

Mildred placed one of the aubergine fruits into each of their hands. She gave one to Hanna first and then one to Rochelle.

"This *is* neat!" Rochelle said.

Mildred sat back and winked. Told you so.

"It's . . . cold," Rochelle said, "and so smooth. The color is gorgeous!"

Hanna looked down at the stupid purple thing. Yeah it was cold. Yeah it was kind of pretty, cute maybe. Then she gawked at Rochelle, thinking, *my God, what's wrong with her? She's really getting into this.*

"Now knock on it, like you would knock on a door," Mildred said. She rocked forward to watch.

Rochelle knocked on the fruit with her knuckles. "Oh my gosh!"

"Isn't that a nice sound, a nice feel?" Mildred said.

"It sounds like a watermelon, like when you knock on a watermelon, like when you tap on a dolphin's head," Rochelle said.

Good Lord, Hanna thought.

"Plan to come to the festival. We really do have a lot of fun. It's all day Saturday and then they disappear for a whole year," Mildred said. "You can keep those. Help get you in the mood. Here, take two extras."

Hanna continued to stare at Rochelle as they walked out of the library. They nearly crashed into Erin Roderick.

"I see you have eggplants," Erin said, laughing out loud. "That's the spirit. Millie is the Eggplant Duchess. She really gets into this. Mayor Holbrook is the Eggplant Duke."

Hanna had had enough. "Where are you from?"

"Boston."

"So you're from a normal place. This is wacky. Nobody has an eggplant festival. This is like the secret eggplant society, like discovering that you live in a Mafia neighborhood. I had no idea these wacky people did this."

Still laughing, Erin said, "I used to think the same thing. But it really is fun. As I'm sure you've found out, there isn't a whole lot to do in Lake Luffit. There's the lake and . . . eggplants. There's a lake festival in the summer. You probably missed out on that. You'll have to come next year. The people here take their eggplants seriously. We all look forward to the festival. It brings everyone together for a lot of fun."

Erin had an eggplant pen, too, poking out of her uniform pocket.

"Some towns have a pumpkin toss," Erin said. "Some have cider festivals, corn festivals. Some throw tomatoes. There is a little town, Trufant, Michigan. They have a stump festival. No one knows where Trufant is, like no one knows where Lake Luffit is. Some towns have pumpkins, some have apples. We have eggplants."

"What do you do at this festival?" Rochelle asked.

"Everything eggplant. There are cooking contests. Chili with eggplant, lasagna, eggplant pizza, fried eggplant, eggplant soup and stew, eggplant pie, eggplant salsa, tacos with eggplant, it's quite the deal. You wear funny hats with eggplants. They sell key chains, pens, neckties, scarves, tote bags. There are games and contests for the prettiest color, the biggest, the littlest, the most perfect shape. And we roll them down a huge metal slide. The first eggplant to smash on the cement at the bottom wins. My eggplant won two years ago."

"What did you win?"

"Five hundred bucks! This is no little thing. All of the local businesses give out gift certificates for prizes. But the race is the biggy."

"Do you . . . eat them?" Hanna asked.

"Nooo. Tried it, hate it. They should not be eaten as far as I'm concerned. But most everyone loves them, in every way you can imagine. They smash nice."

Erin looked at her watch. "I've gotta go. You should plan on coming." She left them standing in front of the library.

"This is creepy," Hanna said when they got back in the car and headed home.

"What's creepy?"

"I feel unsettled here."

"Do you feel unsettled because of Lake Luffit or do you feel unsettled because of Hanna Tauber?"

"The town. The town is creepy."

"What's creepy about Lake Luffit? It's a secluded place that almost no one knows exists. It's beautiful. The people may be a little behind the times but they're pretty easy going. Think about it . . . we should be in jail right now. We broke into someone's barn, used up the hay and the straw, that's technically stealing, and we were kicked loose that same night because no one wanted to press charges, even though we broke the law. Go easy. Here, hold this eggplant. It's trying to roll around down by my feet and I have to work the pedals."

They had started out the day with no eggplants. They had a total of four of them in the car.

George sat at the kitchen counter reading the back of a small package. He took off his glasses. "Hey, sweetie. Mayor Holbrook just called. They want you and Rochelle to ride with them in the lead car in the parade this weekend."

Two eggplants staked squatter's rights next to the sink. That morning, eggplants didn't even exist. Now there were four in her kitchen. They apparently had a way of multiplying.

"I suppose you've heard," Hanna said when she called Rochelle for their evening chat, "that we're going to be in the parade."

"I know. Cool! We have to find something aubergine to wear," Rochelle said.

"George came home with a package of eggplant seeds today."

"So did Marc. He said he wants to make a huge garden next year. And I'm gonna help."

CHAPTER THIRTY-FOUR

"MARC'S COMING OVER to help George rake leaves," Rochelle said, two days later. "We're heading over. Let's go for a drive."

Rochelle came in the house to check out a new set of curtains Hanna bought that morning. They ate a skinny piece of cheesecake while George and Marc puttered in the yard.

"It's too nice to stay inside," Rochelle said. "Let's go."

"We'll be back in an hour or so," Hanna said to the men.

Rochelle pointed to the golf clubs. "Those don't look like rakes," she said to them. The guys met once a week to fire golf balls out into the large field behind the Tauber's house.

"Seems pointless to me and such a waste," Hanna told them during each practice session. Sometimes they went in search of the balls, if they could see them in the tall grass, but most of the time they just dug into a bag and got new ones.

"There must be five hundred dollars worth of golf balls out in that field," Hanna said, as she got in Rochelle's car.

They rode with the windows down. The air smelled of red and gold, the aroma of fall. Hope ran high that the oldies station would produce something Motown.

"Stop!" Hanna yelled. "Don't hit that rock!"

"I see it!" Rochelle said. She responded again with greater volume, hoping to quell Hanna's panic. "I see it!"

The Jag coasted closer to the large rock that occupied smack center of the lane that takes you straight into the west. Rochelle sloped toward the steering wheel. "That rock just moved."

Rochelle didn't park on the shoulder. She parked the car in the middle of the lane about two feet from the rock to prevent anyone else from hitting it.

"It's a turtle," she said.

They squatted down beside him, one on each side, to better view him.

"He's huge," Hanna said.

Rochelle snatched Hanna by the wrist. "Don't you dare try to pet him."

"I guess he is pretty nasty looking, stinks like the swamp," Hanna said. She pulled her hand back and waved it in front of her nose.

Rochelle looked up to the sky. *Why me?* "That is *not* what I meant," she said. "This is a snapping turtle. Look at his head. It's almost as big as your fist. I'm telling you, you don't want to mess with him. He could bite off a finger in one chomp. I've never seen a snapper this big. He's got to be ancient."

A most impressive creature, he spanned over a foot and a half in diameter, cavalier in manner. The sun glistened on the wet slime that had stuck to his body from the swamp just on the other side of the ditch from where he'd come. Swamp muck coated him and he'd dragged a good portion of it with him that now lay in a large glob drying on the pavement.

He'd clunked along across one lane and then stopped at the halfway point. Serene and confident, the old codger monopolized his spot on the centerline, taking up space, taking up time. He didn't rise up on his legs and hiss, as snapping turtles do. He didn't rotate like an army tank to attack. He'd finished with all of that nonsense. He didn't have to bite them. Yet, he was keenly aware of every move of the two creatures crouched near him. He was big, he was old, he was wise, and he didn't have to move for nobody.

Perhaps he enjoyed having a spectator, or two, to appreciate all that he'd become. He, with a nearly microscopic brain, held them captive in the middle of a road.

Black mud covered his back, cemented to his shell. The dirt grew plush, fine mossy-grass. The moss grew blue flowers, each blossom only as big as the head of a common nail.

He drew no deliberate attention to himself. All that mattered was to sit on that warm spot, and whether a car was approaching, did not.

As he sat in the sunshine, the moss dried. The flowers stood taller and the turtle's skin dried from shiny black to matte gray. He had one deformed hind foot, minus two toes. The remaining toes curled under from an old bout of gangrene, the result of being caught in a trap. The tip of his tail had been chewed off and it bent at a right angle in the middle. Scars from fights with other turtles, or other critters, animal or human, planning to eat him, dotted the top of his head. The wrinkled socket had sealed shut over his missing right eye. An aluminum ring from a beer can had settled into the sod on his back. The flowers sprung up inside the ring. No one, but nameless history, knew that it had been eighty-six years since he'd been hatched from one of six surviving eggs that the old female had laid in the sand near the swamp.

After he'd dried, his sole purpose for venturing out onto the road, the old fellow began to move. His claws scraped and scratched on the cement as they scored and pulled him forward, one step at a time. No hurry here. The underside of his shell thumped the pavement. No other cars came. But it wouldn't have mattered. No one would hit something of his size.

When he reached the gravel shoulder he moved quicker than expected of him. He lurched down into the ditch and torpedoed into the pond at the bottom. The water rippled out in waves at the point of his departure, wider and wider, until the pond became still.

Chaptr Thirty-Five

Rochelle stomped on the brakes. The tires skidded and ground into the gravel. The black and white patrol car sat, motor running, as Deputy Kompoltowitz talked with George and Marc in the Tauber's driveway.

"Just drive!" Hanna blurted. "Just keep driving. Drive to Mexico."

Rochelle mashed her foot down on the brake pedal again, threw the gear into park, and turned around in her seat to face Hanna. "What is wrong with you? I am in no way driving to Mexico. How do you come up with these things?"

Tauber and Harris exited the car.

With her head down and shoulders rounded, sheepish, they call it, Hanna avoided CK's face. "We didn't do it," she said.

"Normally, I'd find that hard to believe. Except this time you aren't in trouble."

Hanna hadn't meant it as a joke.

"We have a horse that needs a home," CK said. "Erin Roderick and us seized it. Actually, the owners relinquished their horses willingly. If you want the horse, Erin's got it on a trailer right now. I can radio her and she'll bring it right over."

"What happens if we don't take it?" Rochelle asked.

"There were seven horses. Erin found homes for six. This is the only one left. There's no place to take it. All of the foster homes and rescue places in every county near us are full. There's an auction tonight in Ashton and I'm thinking if you don't want the horse, Erin won't have any choice but to keep it on the trailer and haul it over there."

Just then the county animal control truck, towing a stock trailer, pulled into the driveway. Regina, carrying Josh and also towing a trailer, came in right behind Erin.

Erin popped out of her truck. "I just decided to take the chance and bring her over here. You did a great job with the Durfee horse and I know that you'll be able to bring this one back to health, too. You know Josh already. Father Dan said he'd be over here soon."

Erin knew that to cinch this deal she'd have to act quickly and brazenly. She knew that if they got one look at the horse they wouldn't be able to turn her away.

Josh left Regina and opened the back door of Erin's trailer. He had taken two of the horses himself to his place. He would work with them, get them back in shape, train them, and hopefully sell them for a bit of a profit, finding good homes for them to boot. But the horses weren't the only reason that he'd become involved in this particular seizure. The biggest reason happened to be Erin Roderick. He'd heard about the knockout animal control officer. All of the guys talked about her. All of the guys drooled when they talked about her. And they were right. She was bucking-bull-stopping gorgeous, beyond a ten, type of looks. She made men nervous. They said and did stupid things around her. But for Josh, more than looks lassoed him. She held his interest for other reasons; the manner in which she'd controlled the situation professionally and how she hadn't made the owners of the neglected horses feel like moose dung. She had been firm but decent with them. He watched how she moved around skittish horses, how she'd reassured the young gelding and calmed him so that he walked quietly beside her and into Josh's trailer. Erin had that rare mix of winning attributes: looks, personality, and self-confidence. Josh envisioned that brown uniform falling to her feet.

None of the other guys, though all had tried, had met success in their pursuit of Erin Roderick. Josh knew why, and he wasn't about to make the same mistake. After they'd all morphed into fools, stepped on their tongues and ground them into the dirt with their boots, they'd backed away, exhausted, and out of ideas. They'd rushed her and come on too strong. As always, Josh knew what to do. He wouldn't repeat their mistakes. He'd just be available to help her haul horses if need be. She'd be at the horse auction in Ashton that night. So would he. They'd sit together. He'd buy her a pop. This wasn't just a matter of getting into Erin's pants, which he knew he could do, he really liked her. He wanted to know her. But at the moment, Josh's attention reverted to the horse.

Erin allowed the horse to turn around in the trailer and walk out rather than forcing it to back the full length and have to step blindly backward to reach for the ground. The horse stumbled out and awaited inspection from the circle of people gathered around.

Heavy lids shut out the world. A halter, far too small for her, and left on far too long, had gouged oozing sores into her head. Erin had peeled the halter off, taking hide with it. It had been there for years; all the while the filly grew into a horse. It had sliced and stuck into her flesh. Erin put salve on the wounds and fitted her with a soft cotton-rope halter.

Rochelle sighed with relief when she saw the horse the horse's feet. Though its hooves were long, they weren't deformed. They weren't foundered. And Josh would fix them.

The mare's head hung to her knees. She didn't have to speak to convey her shame.

George frowned, a forged-in-iron frown. The most pitiful sight he'd ever seen stood on display in front of him. The ribs and hip bones protruded like an angular chunk of modern art, like jagged metal pieces. Bald areas outlining a saddle skinned the horse's back. There wasn't enough meat on the horse to keep the saddle from rubbing her raw. *They actually tried to ride her in that condition?*

Dr. Marcus Harris, the oncologist, the doctor who had seen so much, stood gaping. This, caught him off guard, caught him out of his element, and was almost too much. *Who could do this to any living thing?*

"Is she . . . is she going to live?" George asked.

"She's in rough shape," Erin said. "I'm not going to lie to you. But Dr. Huffstead didn't put her down. That means she has a chance. It's not going to be easy. You know that. You know there are ups and downs with rescues. But I think it's worth the effort."

"She's dehydrated. She needs water," Marc said. He ran into the Tauber's house. He returned with a bathroom waste basket filled with sloshing water, the closest thing to a bucket he could find. She drank it empty.

George hauled out the hose from the side of the house. He filled the basket again.

"What is it with these people and not giving their horses water?" Hanna said.

"I don't know," Erin said. "Makes no sense. Laziness. Indifference. Both."

"Tell us what we need to do to house her," George said.

"She needs a barn, at least a roof over her head."

"We have that big shed," George said. He pointed to the old building, taken for granted for the most part, until that day. "It doesn't look like much but it's sturdy and clean. I can move some stuff around in there. I think it would work. What do you think, Hanna?"

"She'll do fine in there. We can set it up nice for her."

"Gonna need some fence," Josh said. "I'd be happy to help you guys put it up. Today. Need to get at least a corral fence up, make a bigger pasture for her later."

"What do you know about her?" Rochelle asked.

"The people have had her since she was a yearling," Erin said. "She's only five. That's young. She's in her prime. They said she's well broke. If you want her, she's yours to keep. No one will ever take her from you."

"What do you call that type, that color of horse?" George asked. The mare looked like a huge Dalmatian dog (a white body dotted with black spots). Her mane, tail, and ears were black.

"She's an Appaloosa. That's the breed. The color pattern is leopard." Erin said.

"Ghost Wind," Josh said.

"What did you say?" Rochelle said.

"Ghost Wind Appaloosa. Leopard. But her markings mean a lot more. See these black triangle markings on each leg just above the hoof?" He bent down to point to a front hoof, and then to the other three legs.

"Symmetrical. One on each leg front and back. Symmetrical black shading on each knee, hock, one on each side of her chest, at her flanks, both ears are black. Markings make her a Ghost Wind. Where I come from, Nez Perce have a legend about the Ghost Wind horses. They're the spirit horses of the Plains."

"What's her name?" Hanna asked.

"She doesn't have registration papers," Erin said. "They said that they called her Looking Glass Sue."

"*Allalimya Takanin*," Josh whispered. No one but the wind heard him.

A battered John Deere tractor towing a wagon load of hay sputtered into the driveway. It hacked a few times and stalled beside CK's patrol car.

"Father's here," Erin said.

"Did your father move here from Boston to be near you?" Hanna asked.

"Oh, no, he's not *my* father. He's the retired priest from St. Michael's. I brought him a Beagle puppy two years ago . . . he invited me in for lemonade and we spent the afternoon talking about all sorts of stuff going on in my life that I needed to talk about. Nice guy. He's on that tractor all day now. He brought Cagey with him."

Cagey traveled with Father Dan riding as a princess in a polka-dot print dog bed bolted to the tractor frame. Father Dan stepped backward off the tractor, cautioning with a finger. "Stay," he said. The Beagle cocked her head and obediently curled down on her bed. As Father Dan walked away from the tractor, the dog hopped down in search of a cat to chase.

He wore a John Deere cap, a red bandana tied around his eighty-eight year old neck, coveralls, and waterlogged, then dried out, stinky boots.

Didn't know a priest could do this, Hanna thought.

"You're going to need hay for the horse," Father Dan said. "It's first cutting, so it's good horse hay. This is last year's hay but it's still good, full of nutrients. I had fifty bales left so I brought you the fifty. Where do you want it? My neighbors, Susie and Chuck, will be over in a bit to stack it. Just tell me where."

"Thank you," George said. "What do we owe you?"

"You don't owe me anything. I want to help you." He pulled a stalk of timothy out from a bale, stuck it between his lips and chewed on it. He spat on the ground. "Many years ago my dad and I used to cut that field of yours out there. You still got hay out there, enough to feed her. I'll cut it for you next year if you'd like," he said.

George and Marc's eyebrows cocked. They nodded at each other. Forget about the hay: golf balls. We'll get them back.

Hanna glared at them. She shook her head. *All they think about are their balls.*

Erin and Josh wrote out a list of things they'd need to build a fence and fix up a stall in the shed for the horse. Father Dan unhooked the tractor from the hay wagon. Cagey, in just under the wire, watched from her perch.

"I'm pretty good with a hammer," George said.

Interesting, Hanna thought. She'd never once seen a hammer in George's hands. But if it got a fence and a stall built, she'd be more than happy to go along with it.

They all headed into town. Marc and George took the Jag. Josh followed them in Regina. "You'll need a truck to haul stuff," he said.

"I'll drive the tractor into town in case you need it," Father Dan said.

They made a processional exit. The Jag zipped out of the driveway, Josh and Regina, Erin and the stock trailer, CK's cruiser, and the John Deere straggled behind. The Beagle onboard wagged her tail, her yapping drowned out by the Deere. Hanna laughed. *How many Lake Luffiters does it take to change a light bulb?*

Rochelle stood with the horse in the grass next to the driveway. She kept her back to Hanna. Her right arm slung over the mare's withers, left hand holding the lead rope, thumb hooked on the hip pocket of her jeans; she stood riveted to the scene before her—Marc drove the Jag.

Ting Tang rubbed his body back and forth against Hanna's leg. She must not forget his supreme importance. She subconsciously lifted the blue bead and touched it to her lips.

She looked down at her feet; her good old, reliable feet. They had carried her securely and safely all this distance, carried her to this day: left, right, left, right. She was no fool. How strange life can be, how it fishtailed down, bobbed up, jerked down, swirled up, and fought to stay afloat.

Those who meant the most in her life now had just been before her. George, a good man her man, Josh, Erin, even CK, and a tractor driving, spitting priest; all of them, good people. But at the end, only one remained. The one worth more than anything Hanna had ever known: the one with the red lipstick and the witty words, the one who-makes-faces-behind-your-back, the one with whom she shared.

Seagulls and spiders and horses—Hanna knew them now.

Her home, proud of its bricks and smart white trim, had a mint-green bike stashed on the walk. This pleased her. The shed would soon have a fence around it, for an Appaloosa, not an exotic Arabian, but a spotted horse named Sue. On Saturday, she would ride in an eggplant parade.

The Sun sent its rays, spilling over her warm and tingling, an effervescent tide. She raised her right hand and waved. Her shadow waved. She raised her left hand and it, too, waved. *Did she wave back at me or did she wave in front of her?* She'd contemplate that when she did chores that night. Right hands, left hands, apples and umbrellas, she knew them now.

She was not sure what all clustered behind her. It would be a long and sometimes haunting road to hook all of it together into some semblance of order. This she knew. She could leave it back there. Perhaps she'd never find all of the pieces that fit into the gaps anyway. But the choice was hers alone. She thought about many things; how the quest for answers you don't even know how to phrase can bog you down like swamp muck, if you let it. Maybe the best you can do, is believe that you have blue flowers on your back. Though you can't see them, someone else might see them for you.

"You have to grab the moments as they come and as they are. They don't repeat. You get one chance at each." She remembered Inga's words.

She could do this. She could grab them. She would let her heart speak when it stormed against her, begging for voice. She would look forward. She would live forward, as her shadow waved.

She closed her eyes. She pressed the bead to her lips. Home, safely home. The wind blew into her face, filled her; held her in place, without having to breathe. Suspended. Close to her soul. She heard the seagull cry. She felt the fire lick her skin. The scent of smoke made its entrance, billowing around her. And the drums thundered in to seize her, volleying with the beats of her heart. Different drums, blood song drums, drum songs that live in the trees, in the leaves, and in spirit horses of the Plains.

THE LOST CHAPTER

IN A PICKUP truck, on a dusty road, many miles south and east of a small town with a puzzle piece-shaped lake, a young girl said, "Gramps, I think this is the place."

"Calm down now Heather, calm down. We'll get there."

Clifford Eubanks studied his sixteen year old granddaughter in earnest. He likened her to one of those hot air balloons that need cement blocks or sandbags to hold it down onto the Earth. Anything concerning horses nearly caused her to fly up and away. It pleased him to do this for her.

Clifford's daughter, Amanda, had called him asking him to take Heather because she couldn't handle her anymore. Heather had been arrested for shoplifting and for possession of alcohol.

"She's running with the wrong crowd, Dad. If anyone can get her straight, you can."

"Send her down. I'll see what I can do," Clifford said. Two days later, Heather arrived at his farm in South Carolina dragging a duffle bag behind her.

Today, they'd driven forty miles to get to Jim Garland's farm. Jim was a horse dealer from way back. Clifford had known him for, in the neighborhood of, four decades. Clifford called Jim a month ago to tell him that he wanted to buy his granddaughter a horse for her sixteenth birthday. And Jim told him that he'd have a bunch of new arrivals in from the north in a few weeks. "I'll call you when," he said.

"There's one in particular you gotta see," Jim said last night on the phone.

The GMC pickup barely came to a stop. Heather bolted out of the door and sailed right past Jim on her way to a small field that held about a dozen horses.

"Which one is it?" Heather asked when her grandpa and Jim joined her at the fence.

"That fiery chestnut over there, the one with the four white socks, in the corner with the pinto," Jim said.

"Where did you say you got her?" Clifford asked.

"I bought this whole herd at a sale. Another dealer trucked them down here from Virginia. They all came from a kids' riding camp even farther north, so I was told. But nobody really knows for sure where each came from. The camp had them five or six years. They're all well broke, been ridden at this camp for years, day in and day out."

"Where did she come from originally, where did the camp get her?" Clifford asked.

"They don't remember. She's been on their string of stable horses for a number of years. They buy up twenty-five horses a year at auctions and send them back through after a few years. Said they've bought and sold hundreds of horses and they don't keep track of where they come from. Said they think they got her where it's cold, where there's snow, from an auction in the north."

Heather squealed and said, "An Arabian! Do you think she's a purebred?"

"Her head sure makes her look like a purebred. But the dealer who brought her to the sale seemed to think she might be half Quarter Horse. I guess you can see it. The muscling she's got tells me she's got Quarter Horse in her. I'll tell you what, this is the finest bred horse I've *ever* seen," Jim said.

The petite mare left her pasture buddies and walked with purpose over to the fence.

"And she has the most beautiful face I've ever seen on a horse in my life. You just don't see that. Look at her huge eyes and those little pointy, tipped-in ears. This mare was no accident," Jim said.

"How old is she?"

"Well, Cliff, the auctioneer said she's smooth-mouthed, so I'd say she's 'bout fourteen. You got a lot of great years ahead with her. She's sound and she's safe. I rode her the other day. She's flawless on the trails. If you get her trained right and you take her in 4-H there won't be anything that can touch her. You'll win everything with her."

"What's her name?" Heather asked.

"Frosty."

"Oh no! How could *anyone* give such a beautiful horse a horrible name like that? It doesn't even match her color."

"With hundreds of horses like they go through at a camp for kids I'm sure they have to keep the names simple and easy to remember," Clifford said.

"You've gotta see this mare move," Jim said. "Never seen anything like it. In all my days, I've never seen a horse trot like this. Makes me think she's got royal breeding behind her. She probably had, or could have had, papers at one time. I've never seen a horse like this go through an auction."

Jim had planned on making the mare cavort around the pasture and he'd set an old coffee can on the ground next to a fence post. He'd dumped a few rocks in it so that it would rattle when he shook it at the horses.

"It don't frighten them," he said. "Just causes them to take interest and strut their stuff."

Jim shook the can and the rocks pinged against the metal. The red mare's head flew up. She arched her neck, her tail plumed up and over her back and she held it straight up, like a flag in the wind. She snorted and burst into a trot that carried the mare over the ground, seemingly without ever touching it. Her slim front legs, each with a perfect white sock, thrust forward, reaching out. Each leg remained suspended in flight at the end of its full extension before the other leg effortlessly replaced it in midair.

"She's magical," Heather whispered. "She's like . . . *watching* music."

Heather could no longer hold herself back. She climbed over the fence and went out into the field to be close to the mare. Her fists clenched with excitement, with anticipation, palms sweating; she couldn't wait to get her hands on that horse. The mare trotted, floated in circles around Heather, flaring her nostrils, filling her lungs, tasting the salt of the Atlantic, so near, its scent swept over her.

With her back to the easterly, her grandpa, and to Jim, Heather stood entranced at the scene before her. She spoke softly, to no one but the mare.

"I name you . . . Summer Symphony . . . Daughter of the Wind."

CPSIA information can be obtained
at www.ICGtesting.com
Printed in the USA
JSHW042219310321
13131JS00001B/13